W9-BPL-476

Advance praise for Pintip Dunn's
DATING MAKES PERFECT

"Sweet, spunky, witty, and wise—I fell in love with Winnie and her sisters. Pintip has a rare knack for blending action and adventure into a contemporary rom-com that keeps the pages turning."
—**Abigail Hing Wen, *New York Times* bestselling author of *Loveboat, Taipei***

"A witty, culturally immersive romance… A masterful story about family obligations, first crushes, and second chances."
—**Nisha Sharma, award-winning author of *My So-Called Bollywood Life***

"This book made my Thai-American heart soar. Every detail—from the mouth-watering foods to Winnie's tight-knit but strict Thai family—serves to tell a story that is authentic, layered, and rings so true."
—**Christina Soontornvat, author of *A Wish in the Dark***

"Fun, heartfelt, and full of warmth…the ideal feel-good book for the summer. Do yourself a favor and read this book right away."
—**Jodi Meadows, *New York Times* bestselling author of the Fallen Isles trilogy**

"A smart, funny, and endearing portrayal of budding romance, the power of sisterly love, and the pressure to be the perfect daughter."
—**Farrah Rochon, *USA Today* bestselling author of *The Boyfriend Project***

"Looking for all the feels? Look no further than Winnie and Mat. This one will keep you up all night reading."
—**Kate Brauning, author of *How We Fall***

"A delicious rom-com concoction that immerses readers in a Thai teen drama they'll adore. Add a pinch of sister envy, the cute guy you love to hate, immigrant parent dynamics, a few kaffir lime leaves, and you'll get a dish that'll keep you entertained until the last page."

—Lydia Kang, award-winning author of *Toxic*

"Bubbling over with charisma and charm, *Dating Makes Perfect* is a swoontasm of adorable characters, sparkling wit, and captivating Thai culture. You will totally want to date this book!"

—Darcy Woods, award-winning author of *Summer of Supernovas*

"Reading *Dating Makes Perfect* brought back a whole lot of childhood memories growing up Thai American. I wish I'd had this fun story (that even brought a few tears) to give me hope in my teen years when I was definitely not allowed to date until college."

—Piper J. Drake, author of the bestselling True Heroes series

"An absolute feast for readers. The characters are deliciously complex, the family dynamics are rich and intense, and the tension between the main character, Winnie, and her enemy, Mat, is drool-worthy. This book will completely quench your hunger for a believable enemies-to-lovers rom-com!"

—Becky Wallace, author of *Stealing Home*

"So. Much. Fun! Pintip Dunn's rom-com is an authentic, hilarious, and irresistible love letter to Thai culture—not to mention desserts. Foodies, be warned—don't read this on an empty stomach!"

—Vanessa Barneveld, award-winning author of *The Abduction*

Dating
=MAKES=
Perfect

Dating

≍ MAKES ≍

Perfect

NEW YORK TIMES
BESTSELLING
AUTHOR

PINTIP
DUNN

This book is a work of fiction. Names, characters, places, and incidents are the product of the author's imagination or are used fictitiously. Any resemblance to actual events, locales, or persons, living or dead, is coincidental.

Copyright © 2020 by Pintip Dunn. All rights reserved, including the right to reproduce, distribute, or transmit in any form or by any means. For information regarding subsidiary rights, please contact the Publisher.

Preview of *Adorkable* Copyright © 2020 by Cookie O'Gorman

Entangled Publishing, LLC
10940 S Parker Road
Suite 327
Parker, CO 80134
rights@entangledpublishing.com

Entangled Teen is an imprint of Entangled Publishing, LLC.

Visit our website at www.entangledpublishing.com.

Edited by Liz Pelletier, Lydia Sharp
Cover Illustrated by Bree Archer
Cover images by
Evgeniya Gaydarova/Gettyimages
Look Studio/Shutterstock
Interior design by Toni Kerr

ISBN 978-1-68281-497-0
Ebook ISBN 978-1-68281-498-7

Manufactured in the United States of America

First Edition August 2020

10 9 8 7 6 5 4 3 2

entangled teen
an imprint of Entangled Publishing LLC

To my beautiful A-ma, who loved fiercely and without hesitation. I hope you and my dear mama are together once again.

Prologue

The Tech sisters don't date in high school.

Not because we're not asked. My older sister Aranee holds the record for five invites for a single dance, while my other sister, Bunnisa, follows closely behind with four. The discrepancy has nothing to do with their appearance. They look exactly the same, being twins and all. Shiny, ruler-straight black hair gliding sleekly over their shoulders; expressive, nearly black eyes that Bunny spruces up with fake lashes and a piece of Scotch tape to create a double eyelid. If Ari has the edge, it's only because she's warmer—while Bunny's icy perfection can be intimidating (notwithstanding the cutesy family nickname).

And me? Orrawin, the youngest sister, the baby of the family, the one who's always struggling—but never really able—to catch up? True to form, I lag way, way behind with a single invite for homecoming in the ninth grade. I wasn't even asked the other years, but I like to think—to hope, to pretend—that it's just because word of the Tech sisters' dating prohibition had gotten around.

It's also not because we're not interested. Ari famously got caught in digital art studio creating photos of her future children with crush and classmate Adam Scheffer. I would've died on the spot—or at least burst into tears and spent the rest of the year hiding in the girls' bathroom, where the stink of cheap perfume mixed with used feminine products would've killed me anyway. But Ari, being Ari, just smiled sheepishly and wrinkled her nose, and Adam fell headlong into love, if he wasn't already halfway there.

Not that it did either of them any good.

And it's not even because no one can pronounce our ridiculously long, Thai last name—Techavachara. There've been valiant attempts, that's for sure. My favorite was Josh Neven's "chicken cacciatore" in the sixth grade. Thank pra Buddha cho our family friend Mat Songsomboon shortened our last name to its current moniker. It stuck, and even our mom goes by "Dr. Tech" with her pediatric patients.

Which was maybe the last good thing Mat Songsomboon ever did.

But no. The Tech girls don't date in high school for one reason and one reason alone: because we aren't allowed.

"I don't think so," Papa said when Bunny wanted to go to the movies with a group of girl and guy friends.

"Mai dai det caut," Mama said when Ari asked to invite the partner of her history project over to study, which loosely translates to "absolutely, positively not."

"What will people say?" they asked in unison when the twins pointed out that the candidates for homecoming queen are typically escorted down the football field. My sisters ended up accompanying each other—and thank the mother hen and her six chicks reincarnated as stars that neither of them won. Just imagine if Ari or Bunny were kissed on the cheek by the homecoming king, in front of—gasp!—our entire small suburban town. Mama probably would've had heart failure—which her cardiologist husband could've diagnosed but not treated, since he would have been keeled over himself.

And so the Tech girls do not date—and have *never* dated—in high school.

Until now…

Chapter One

"How come you're not engaged yet?" Mama asks my sisters three months before my high school graduation.

"You did *not* just ask us that." Bunny's hands freeze over the egg roll she's wrapping, her eyes flashing dangerously. Or maybe they just look dangerous because of the cat-eye she's applied on top of the lashes and Scotch tape. If I tried to pull off the same effect, I'd give myself a black eye—literally and figuratively.

Ari groans, even as her fingers continue to move. Already, she's amassed a pile of precisely wrapped skins larger than mine and Bunny's combined. "Seriously? We've been in college for how long? Two seconds?"

"It's not like flipping a switch," Bunny adds. "We can't go from not dating to married in four seconds flat."

"Six months." Mama whisks away the large metal bowl, now empty of the ground beef, vermicelli noodle, and shredded cabbage mixture, and plunks a new one in its place. "Six months ago, Papa and I gave you permission to start dating. Given how much you girls grumbled and complained about *not* having relationships in high school, I think it's perfectly reasonable to ask if you have any serious prospects."

"That's not what you said, though." I grin impishly. "You said, and I quote, 'How come you're not engaged—'"

"Hush, Winnie," Mama says automatically. At least once in every family discussion, someone breaks out with these words. Normally, it makes me straighten to my full five five—two inches taller than my sisters, thank you very much—as if they have to pay attention to me if I'm in their line of sight.

But today, I'm just happy to wrap egg rolls while my mom and sisters bicker.

Because *they're* here, Ari and Bunny. Home for spring break. No doubt they're Mama's favorites. Ari is premed, while Bunny is prelaw. Together, they're a Thai parent's dearest fantasy come to life, which is why Mama's hosting a fifty-person farewell party for the final night before they have to go back to college.

I'll never be able to compete, so I don't even try. Anything I could hope to do, they've already done and done better.

But I don't mind. Because Ari and Bunny are *my* favorites, too. We're like three sides of an isosceles triangle. I'll never match their lengths or their angles, but they'd be hard-pressed to exist without me shoring them up. I think.

Ari stands and begins to sort through our egg rolls, setting aside the ones that have been wrapped too sloppily (me) or have too much filling (me again but also Bunny). Either infraction will make the egg rolls break apart in the frying oil or create unattractive air bubbles in the skin. Behind Ari's back, Bunny shakes her head bossily, crossing her eyes and sticking out her tongue.

I giggle. Man, I'll miss them when they leave me tomorrow. *So* much.

"I want to introduce you girls to some people tonight," Mama continues.

Bunny puts her tongue back in her mouth. "People, Mother?" My super-sophisticated sister never calls her "Mama" like the rest of us. "You mean boys?"

"Well, yes."

The twins exchange a look. While I'm fluent enough in their silent-speak to get the gist, they have entire conversations with their glances. Whole debates, complete with opening statement, evidence, and rebuttal.

Ari sits and begins wrapping again. "I don't know who else we could possibly meet," she says. "Pretty sure we've come across every Thai family in the greater Chicago area."

"Ah, but some of them, you've only said hello to. Take Jack, for example. Auntie Took's son. Very nice young man." She directs a nod at Bunny. Jack is an acquaintance of ours but not actually a relative. In Thai culture, all my parents' friends are considered "aunties" and "uncles." "He's a lawyer, you know. You two should have plenty to talk about."

"He's positively ancient!" Bunny says, horrified.

Mama grimaces. "Nonsense. He's only thirty."

"Like I said, ancient," Bunny mutters. Ari kicks her under the table, and Bunny kicks her back. Their movements are like a well-orchestrated symphony. I'm so used to the vibrations, I can narrate exactly what's happening, even if I can't see through the wood.

Not wanting to be left out, I kick them both. In return, I get two swift kicks to either ankle.

"Owww!" I yelp.

"What is going on here?" Mama demands.

"Something!" we chorus together. It's a response that Ari came up with a decade ago, when Papa said we were clearly doing more than *nothing*, especially with those mischievous looks in our eyes.

Mama's face softens. "You three," she says fondly. "It's lovely to have you girls back, even if it's just for a week. We've all missed you terribly. Especially Winnie. She's been moping around the house like someone took the last bite of her sankaya."

I frown. Fine. Maybe I *do* pout—a tiny bit—when we run out of my favorite pumpkin custard, but Mama's definitely exaggerating on both counts.

My sisters shoot me twin glances of concern. I shake my head and wink, as if to say that Mama's just being Mama, and they relax once more.

Mama barrels forward. "What are you wearing tonight?"

"Faux leather pants and a sleeveless top," Bunny says at the same time that Ari responds, "My rose lace dress."

I know Mama's not asking *me*, so I keep my head down and continue wrapping.

"What about you, Winnie?" Ari asks loyally. "I think you should wear your black corduroy skirt. You have the legs for it."

"Oh, nobody cares what Winnie wears," Mama says breezily.

"Mother!" Bunny's tone holds the only note of warning that Mama ever heeds. "That's so rude."

"Oh, Winnie knows what I mean." Mama ruffles my hair, apparently forgetting that her hand is covered with bits of noodles and cabbage.

"Hmm..." She tilts her head, examining the concoction that she's just deposited on my head. "You might want to wash your hair before the party tonight," she stage-whispers.

I roll my eyes. "Thanks, Mama."

"As I was saying," she continues in a louder voice. "I love all my daughters equally. Winnie knows this. But Winnie's not meeting the man she's going to marry tonight. You two are!"

She waves her hand with a flourish, and the twins exchange another look. The glance is shorter this time—it's got to be. I mean, they've already held an entire debate with their eyes. What else is left to be said?

Ari squares her shoulders. "Actually, Mama, we regret to inform you…we've come to a decision."

Bunny nods vigorously. "It wasn't easy. We thought long and hard, but after dissecting all the options, this is the only possible conclusion."

I snort. Pretty sure they decided two minutes ago, during their eye debate, since we just found out about Mama's sudden desire to see them engaged.

But I have more pressing concerns. Whatever the twins say, I'd bet my entire collection of costumed rubber duckies that it won't make Mama happy. And if Mama's not happy, somehow, someway, it will be bad for me. It always is.

"We've decided…" Bunny begins.

Ari picks up seamlessly. "…that we're not going to marry…"

"…for *ten* years."

"Maybe even twenty."

"Probably *thirty*."

The words come out fast and furious, overlapping like the red-wrapped firecrackers that people set off during Chinese New Year.

"We need *lots* of dating practice, after all," Ari explains.

"Because, you see, we can't possibly settle down until we know what's out there," Bunny chimes in.

"And we gain the skills necessary to make a relationship successful in today's world."

They exchange another look. I know what's coming. The trump card. The bomb that's going to blow Mama's mind. The fate that's worse than death for many Thai-American parents.

"You don't want us to get a divorce, do you?" they conclude in unison.

Mama slides into a chair, boneless. She looks from one twin to the other, blinking rapidly. Who can blame her? My sisters are top-of-the-class smart, but even I am impressed by the logic and construction of this argument. Nothing short of a tour de force.

Ari and Bunny turn back to their wrapping, identical smiles on their lips.

Mama continues to sit and stare. Her mouth is slightly parted, her eyes dazed, as though she's just glimpsed the many heads of the Great Naga itself. Seconds pass. And then minutes. The only sound is the *plop*, *squish*, and *crinkle* of the egg-roll skins.

"You're absolutely right," Mama says after Bunny and I have each rolled another three pieces. Ari, the show-off, has finished five. "I've been going about this all wrong, haven't I?"

Her voice is a strange combination of stunned and determined. We don't respond—we don't dare. My sisters, because they don't want to push their luck. Me, because I'm desperate to keep Mama's attention off me.

Too. Damn. Late.

Mama's gaze snaps up. "You. Winnie," she barks. "I want to hold a grandchild before I die." Never mind that she's in her mid-fifties and in perfect health. "Which means you can't dillydally until college. You have to start dating *now* so that you can get your practice beforehand."

Wait. *What?*

I jostle the blended raw egg that we're using to seal the rolls, spilling the yellow liquid onto the table. Out of all the words she could've uttered, that was the last statement I expected. Other than giving me permission to get a body piercing. Or a tattoo. Or, you know, a hole in the head, which in her view is just as unfathomable.

"That's not fair!" Bunny shoots out of her seat, knocking into the table. The platter of egg rolls tilts precariously, and Ari grasps the plate before it crashes to the floor.

"Really, Mama?" Ari whines. "I begged you to let Adam come over for dinner. To take me to the *library*, of all places. And you refused every time. Why does Winnie get to have all the fun?"

Mama frowns. "Oh, this isn't going to be *fun*. Winnie's going to be *practicing*, not actually dating. You girls managed to score 1550 on your SATs with the adequate prep, and that's exactly what Winnie will do. Only she'll be scoring the perfect husband instead."

My pulse races. I've never dreamed that dating in high school was possible. I don't care *why* Mama lets me date. The end result will be the same. I'll be able to go to prom. Experience my first kiss. Maybe even have a boyfriend.

Is my entire life about to change?

Mama turns to me. "I'll decide when, where, and how each date occurs," she announces, dashing my hopes. Shoulda known such a concession would come with strings attached.

"Also with whom. *Especially* with whom." Her eyes glitter. "And I have just the right boy to be your first candidate."

Oh no. Don't say it. Please don't say it. She wouldn't torture me like that. She couldn't.

But then she goes ahead and does it anyway. "Mat Songsomboon," she says, a pleased tilt to her voice.

My heart falls like it's been kicked down by a Muay Thai fighter.

Mat Songsomboon is the son of my parents' longtime friends…

…and he also happens to be my sworn enemy.

Chapter Two

I look down the sight of my Zombie Sidestrike Blaster Nerf gun. When I fix on my target, I pull the trigger. Viciously.

Pop!

A foam bullet flies out of the gun and hits Mat Songsomboon right in the middle of his big, annoying nose.

Well. It's not his real nose, unfortunately, because it's not the real Mat. Instead, my prey is a pencil sketch of his firm jaw and sleepy eyes, of the black hair that constantly falls over his forehead and of his distinctive nose—long and thin on top, flaring out at the nostrils.

Just like a guava, I think as I let loose another bullet. This one rips the paper by his cheek. Good. A few more direct hits, and the sketch can join the other mutilated faces in my wastebasket. All of the same person.

Have to say, my aim has improved significantly since my friendship with Mat dissolved into hate. Practice, as they say, makes perfect.

I reload my Sidestrike. Maybe I'd feel guilty about the

guava comparison if he weren't so damn arrogant. Besides, he's got enough girls—and a few guys—fawning over him. Pencil-sketch Mat can take it.

I bring the sight to my eye again just as the door opens and Bunny pokes her head inside. My finger startles on the trigger, and a bullet hits her in the shoulder. Oops.

"Ouch." My sister steps fully into the room, rubbing the red mark that's sprouted on her skin. "The guests are here. Mama sent me to check on you." She scans the pajama bottoms and tank top I threw on after my shower. "But I can see you're *very* busy doing *very* important things."

"I can't get dressed until I rip this picture to shreds." The excuse doesn't make any sense, and we both know it. I'm not a fan of parties, and I hate attention of any sort. But I'll go downstairs eventually. I'm too much of a good Thai daughter to skip out entirely, especially when that's the only thing I have going for me. As perfect as they are, Ari and Bunny aren't always so good at listening to our parents. Who can blame me for seizing that role? Still, every minute I linger in my room is a minute I don't have to spend making small talk.

Bunny flops onto my bed, her hair billowing out like black silk. "Are you and Mat still mortal enemies?"

"Yep," I say darkly. "I bet he's got a voodoo doll or ten of me in his closet. Remember the massive migraine I had last night? Pretty sure that was Mat. When I tripped over the threshold of our front door and sent the groceries flying? Also Mat."

Bunny props herself on her elbows, her lips quirking. "What about the cold front last week? Are you going to blame that on Mat, too?"

"I can try."

She shakes her head. "I don't get it. You two used to

be so close. What happened?"

"No idea," I say with a straight face. "I guess we just grew apart."

I'm lying, of course. I know exactly when and where our friendship evaporated. On a blustery Monday morning during the eighth grade. In the school cafeteria. With the painfully empty seat next to mine.

Back then, Mat and I always sat together so that we could trade lunches. I loved the homemade meals his mom packed him—my favorite was bah mee moo dang, or wavy egg noodles and roast red pork—and he preferred the unique concoctions I assembled. That day, my family was out of bread. And cheddar cheese. And roast beef. So I made a bagel sandwich out of packets of mustard and mayo, stacking Doritos and sweet pickles inside.

I was dying to see what Mat thought of my latest culinary creation.

Except…he didn't sit with me that day. Or the next. Or the next.

What I did then was petty to the extreme. But I was mad and jealous and a little—okay, a lot—hurt. Mat had been crushing on Denise Riley since the beginning of the year, and I kinda, sorta let it slip that he carried around her yearbook photo in his binder. And then I possibly, accidentally, definitely knocked into that same folder, sending the picture sliding across the floor for the entire cafeteria to see.

Mat's face turned deathly pale…and so did our friendship.

My actions crossed a line. I know that. To this day, it's still the meanest thing I've ever done. I'll go to my grave still ashamed of my betrayal. I wanted to apologize; I would've loved nothing more than to get down on my knees and beg for his forgiveness.

But he never gave me the chance. He ignored my calls and blocked me on social media. When I approached, he would turn and walk rapidly in the other direction. After a while, I stopped trying.

He finally spoke to me after a few months, making a cutting remark about my appearance. I retaliated, he responded in kind…and now, here we are, four years later. Enemies who ignore each other at school, only to bicker at Thai community events. It's just as lovely as it sounds.

Once in a blood moon, I wonder what would've happened if I had locked away my pettiness. Would we be friends now? Or would we have drifted apart naturally as we grew older and developed different interests?

Doesn't matter, really. Because I *did* humiliate Mat. So I have to deal with the consequences. Not just for the rest of this year but also for the next four. Lucky me, my enemy will be attending the same college as I will next year. Simply perfect.

Bunny rises from the bed in one fluid motion and peers at the sketch on my door. "This is really good, Winnie. You've got an amazing eye for detail. Or maybe…" She slides a glance at me. "You've been paying more attention to Mat than you thought."

"Gross." I shudder. "More likely, I'm just talented," I say lightly, even though I feel pretty much the opposite. My art will never be more than a *frivolous hobby*. My parents' words, not mine. They have a future doctor and lawyer in Ari and Bunny. All they need to round out the perfect trifecta is a future professor. In any academic area, really, but preferably economics.

So a year from now, I guess I'll be studying economics at Northwestern University. And not art.

I hand Bunny the Sidestrike. "Best out of three? Whoever gets closest to his guava nose wins."

She smiles, taking the Nerf gun. When we were kids, I would always pick target practice when it was my turn to choose an activity. Probably because it was the only game in which I could ever beat my sisters.

"What should I do?" I ask as she brings the gun to her eyes. "I don't want to practice *anything* with that jerk, no matter what Mama says."

Defying Mama is pretty much unthinkable, but there's got to be a work-around. I just haven't come up with one yet.

"Oh, come on, Winnie. You've got the best parts of senior year left. Prom. Senior Skip Day. Appease Mama now, and you won't have to suffer the way Ari and I did, by ourselves and dateless." She shoots, and the bullet goes wide, nicking the frame of the door.

Making a face, she hands me the gun.

I line up the sight. *Boom.* Direct hit on Mat's left eyebrow. "The less we see of his features, the better he looks, don't you agree?"

"I really don't think you're appreciating the significance of this," my sister says. "I mean, you may not have a crush now, but what about later? Just sayin', dances are a lot more fun if you go with someone. You could have study dates! Attend parties at the lake! The possibilities are endless. All you have to do is play along, and before you know it, you could have the high school life we always coveted."

I fire off a succession of shots. Ear, cheek, upper lip. Boom, boom, boom.

Behold the champion of the Nerf Gun Battle. I am unbeatable!

Bunny puts her hand on the rifle, pushing it down.

"Listen. You could be the first Tech girl to date in high school. An experience Ari and I never had."

This stops me. Not once in my life have I ever walked on territory that my sisters haven't already trampled.

"I'll convince Mama to choose someone else," I say. "There're plenty of guys I could practice dating with. Every last one of them nicer, cuter, and more pleasant than Mat."

Bunny beams. "That's the spirit! And if you need any more motivation, he's waiting right down these stairs."

"What do you mean?" I ask.

She grabs my black corduroy skirt off the floor and throws it at me. "Get dressed. And I'll show you."

Chapter Three

*A*ri is hardly ever wrong. It's one of the most annoying things about her.

But tonight, she is wrong.

Because we *haven't* met every Thai person in the greater Chicago metropolitan area. And the proof is standing right there, munching on an egg roll and talking to Ari.

Holy wow, he looks good. He's about our age—maybe five six, preppy clothes, angelic smile. And judging from his melty brown eyes, worthy of the heroes in every Thai soap opera, he's about to break every teenage heart from here to the temple.

Bunny and I creep along the wall, using the kaffir lime potted plants as cover. My sister bends at the waist, attempting to blend with the figure-eight green leaves. I do her one better and drop to my hands and knees.

"His name's Taran, and his family just moved to Chicago," Bunny murmurs above me. "We think he's a senior in high school, but Ari's confirming."

I crawl forward. Interesting. What are the chances I

can get Mama to replace Mat with this guy?

"What the phuk tong are you doing?" a voice says above me.

I freeze. I haven't heard his voice in a month, since the last party I attended with my parents, but I'd recognize it anywhere. Probably because it makes a regular appearance in my nightmares.

I look up, and sure enough, it's Mat, a ridiculous smirk on his ridiculous face. Even worse, Bunny is nowhere to be seen. What did he do? Send her scrambling for cover by his mere presence?

I rise stiffly to my feet. Ari insists that Mat's profile is uncommonly attractive. All I know is that my feelings toward him are uncommonly violent.

"Seriously? Phuk tong?" I roll my eyes. "Phuk tong" is the Thai word for pumpkin, and it's pronounced—you guessed it—uncomfortably like the f-word. "You sound like you're in the second grade."

Out of the corner of my eye, I notice Ari and Mr. Short & Handsome retreat to the kitchen. Leaving me with Mr. Tall & Pukey.

"You *look* like you're in the second grade," he returns blandly. "Your tights are torn."

I cross my arms. *Do not glance down. Do not give him the satisfaction.*

"I must've ripped them during the travel here," I say breezily, my standard excuse for torn pantyhose.

"We're at *your* house," he says incredulously. "You tore them while walking down the stairs? More like, from crawling on the floor."

What if he has a point? I'll never admit it. "Surely you've got better things to do than stare at my legs."

"Um." He coughs into his hand. "At the risk of pointing

out the obvious…that fault line is probably visible from the moon."

I can't resist any longer. I look down. Chib-peng, he's right. The rip starts mid-thigh, winds around my knee, and then explodes in a starburst pattern.

"It's the new look," I say. "Kinda like fishnets. The holier, the better."

"Sure it is." His expression is knowing, superior. I wish I could punch him in the stomach. Maybe then he wouldn't be able to eat the five or six egg rolls he's piled high on a plate.

As if reading my mind, he dunks an egg roll into the pool of sweet chili sauce and shoves it into his mouth. He then grins at me with his mouth closed, the egg roll bunching out his cheeks.

My anger builds. Just think, I could've wrapped that appetizer with my very hands. (Okay, so probably not, since the egg roll's too neatly sealed to be one of mine. But still.) I did *not* spend precious minutes this afternoon preparing food to feed the likes of Mat Songsomboon.

"You're one to criticize my wardrobe," I say, gesturing at his boring khaki pants and button-down shirt. He wears the exact same thing at every party. So predictable. "Where did you get dressed, in the dark?"

He smirks, the light in his eyes settling into a warm and familiar arrogance. "Been dreaming about me… undressed…in the dark? Let me help out your imagination." He lowers his voice seductively. "I wear boxers."

My cheeks burn. I would never, in a million years, have imagined him in his underwear. Now that picture will be imprinted in my mind forever.

"Ugh," I groan, grabbing my temples. "Get me some bleach, quick, so I can scrub away that image."

His lips quirk. "You're so dramatic, Winnie."

"Yeah? Well, you're…you're…" I falter, grappling for an appropriate comeback. I'm not like Mr. Perfect here, who always knows exactly what to say and when to say it.

At least he doesn't seem to have heard about Mama's scheme.

"I've left you speechless," he murmurs, way too pleased with himself.

"You've left me nauseated," I shoot back. It's not the most original insult, but at least I can string a sentence together again.

"You should channel all that passion into something useful, like getting out from your sisters' shadows." He shakes his head. "I almost feel sorry for you. It can't be easy to get the new guy's attention when he's met your sisters first."

I flush. "Who says I want his attention?"

He looks pointedly at my legs, scanning them from ankle to thigh. "Were you—or were you not—crawling on the floor in an attempt to spy on him?"

Damn Mat for being so observant. It's one of the top one hundred most infuriating things about him. Believe me. I keep a list.

"I was picking kaffir lime leaves," I say haughtily. "Mama needs them for the green curry."

The lie is so pathetic, he doesn't even bother to acknowledge it.

"I suppose it's not your fault," he says musingly. "Ari and Bunny are so smart, so talented, that it would be hard for anyone to stand out next to them. Take this egg roll, for example. It's obvious that Ari's back home." He takes a huge bite, chewing with his mouth open, even though his table manners are normally impeccable. I should know.

Before his mother moved back to Thailand to take care of his sick grandmother, she schooled us both on proper etiquette. That was back in the days when we used to shape sticky rice into grenade balls—and launch them at each other.

"I've missed your sister's cooking," Mat continues.

If he's trying to rile me, he's picked the wrong tactic. First, I'll be the first to admit that my culinary skills are questionable. I'm a way better taste tester than cook. More importantly, I will never be insulted by a compliment to my sisters. The competition among us has never amounted to a grain of rice. Their wins are mine and vice versa.

I plaster on my best smile, coconut-milk sweet. "Don't worry, Mat. I'm always here to prepare an *extra-special* dish, just for you. The way I did with that chili sauce."

He drops his gaze to the egg roll drenched in red sauce, just a few inches from his mouth. I stifle a laugh. The sauce is perfectly safe, a traditional mix of simple syrup, vinegar, and crushed chilies. But *he* doesn't know that.

"The bathroom is right around the corner," I singsong. "In case you need to find it in a hurry."

Mat puts down his plate on the window ledge and steps menacingly in my direction. I gulp. Every fiber in my body screams at me to back away. To run. But I can't. I will never admit defeat to Mat.

I stand my ground as he continues to approach. We haven't been this close in months, maybe even years. I can feel the brush of his khaki pants against my knees, torn tights and all.

"You forget, Orrawin," he says silkily, using my formal first name. Reminding me that we're not friends—will never be friends. "I know this house like I know the fifty-nine letters of the Thai alphabet. I know the location of every bathroom. Every bedroom." He drops his voice. "I know exactly where you sleep at night."

I shiver. He doesn't mean the implied threat. In all these years, he's never physically hurt me. And yet, my pulse races all the same.

He reaches out and tucks a lock of my hair behind my ear. I almost scream. The gesture is mocking, an empty facsimile of what the real action should be. It's like he's telling me what I've always feared. I'll never experience real dating in high school. Never have a romantic memory other than what I observe vicariously. Never have a person touch me, with interest in their eyes and feeling in their heart.

And if Mama has her way, and I have to fake date Mat? Well, I'll have no hope of turning my dreams into reality before I graduate.

"Sweet dreams tonight," he whispers. His voice is low, rough. "If you need any more inspiration—you know where to find me."

Sweeping up his plate, he takes off. I stare after him, emotions jumbled, knees weak. Baffled as usual over our interaction. There's always so much animosity between us, so much hate. Sometimes, I wish we could just peel away those complex layers and be what we used to be: friends.

Yeah, right. I'll be friends with Mat Songsomboon when thunder manages to catch the lightning across the sky.

Chapter Four

I hate him. I hate his annoyingly straight eyebrows that waggle on his forehead like worms. I hate his arrogance. His suave manner, his easy confidence. I hate how he can drop that bombshell of a line on me, without blushing or even flinching.

I stomp into the kitchen. The new guy is gone, but Bunny and Ari lounge by the marble island, their bodies casting shadows on the stainless-steel refrigerator. Pots of green curry, five-spice pork stew, and tom yum goong sit on the induction cooktop, with dirty plates and empty glasses stacked to the side. But my sisters aren't cleaning—not yet. That will happen later, after the guests leave. Bunny will put on her latest playlist, and Ari will bump me with her hip, and the three of us will laugh (loudly) and sing (badly) and wash dishes (slowly) until the wee hours of the night. I miss cleaning with my sisters almost as much as I miss having their presence at these parties.

My elbow catches on a plastic cup of wine, and the burgundy liquid spills all over my white blouse. "Look what he did to me," I moan.

"Who?" Bunny grabs a sponge and begin to mop up the spill on the tile.

"The guy Mama's selected to help me be marriageable, that's who," I snap. "Freaking Mat Songsomboon."

Ari blinks. "He's not even here. Are you seriously suggesting it's his fault you spilled wine on yourself?"

"Oh, Winnie blames him for everything," Bunny chimes in from the floor. Her shoulders vibrate as though she's trying not to laugh. "Sleeping past her alarm clock. The yogurt going bad when it's been left on the counter. Even climate change."

My lips twitch. "Well, overpopulation *does* contribute to global warming. If Mat had never been born, that's one less person using fossil fuels."

Ari grins so widely that I can count her teeth. "You know? I'm beginning to think that Mama picked the right practice boyfriend for Winnie."

"Don't be gross. I just ate." I lift the soaked shirt away from my skin. "Help me get this stain out before someone sees."

Someone, of course, is code name for the new guy, Taran. Luckily, my sisters don't make me say his name out loud.

Ari picks up the edge of my shirt, squinting at the red blemish. "Don't worry. Taran's making his rounds. He won't be back in the kitchen for a while."

Bunny wets a paper towel under the faucet and scrubs at the stain. "We were right. Taran *is* a senior, and he starts at Lakewood High next week. His family just moved here from a small town in Kansas. He's a total math geek, is kind to his mother, and looooves our egg rolls!"

In unison, the three of us snicker. These qualities make up the holy trinity of a perfect mate from Mama's perspective. Still, when a boy looks like Taran, even I have to admit it's not a bad foundation.

"Will you stop?" Ari grabs her twin's hands. "The paper towel's disintegrating. You're making the stain worse."

"What do *you* suggest?" Bunny retorts.

"I could go upstairs and change," I venture.

Ari snorts. "Yeah, right. Do you know how long it would take you—or even us—to make it through that crowd of our parents' fifty closest friends? By the time we finish paying our respects and satisfying their curiosity, the party will be over."

They both study me.

"We could cut it out," Bunny suggests. "You would look cute in a midriff shirt. Plus, it would match the holes in your tights."

"Not you, too." I groan. "Have you been talking to Mat?"

She raises a brow. "Um, I didn't have to talk to *anyone*. Those runs are practically assaulting my eyes."

Right. Maybe I should rethink wearing tights ever again.

Ari snaps her fingers. "White vinegar! If you pour white vinegar over wine stains, it neutralizes the red and purple pigments."

"How would *you* know?" I ask.

"You sound just like Mama." She winks. "Let's just say we've been learning more than just the core curriculum at college."

Bunny is already opening the pantry door. "There's only one problem," she says, surveying the contents. "We used the last of the white vinegar to make the prik nam som."

Ari picks up a jar of jalapeños marinating in vinegar from a tray of traditional Thai condiments—and sniffs it.

"Oh no." I back away. "I'm not pouring *that* on my shirt. It has jalapeños in it."

"So you'll feel a little spicy." Bunny grabs ahold of my shirt tail. "We could all use more heat in our lives."

"You don't want to sacrifice that shirt, do you?" Ari wields a cooking brush like a weapon. "It was one of my favorites, and I just gifted it to you this week."

I look from Ari's bright eyes to Bunny's playful smirk and sigh. I've never been able to resist my sisters, ever. "Just be quick about it," I mutter.

They get to work.

*B*unny pours a spoonful of jalapeño vinegar onto my shirt. A few drops splatter onto my skin, and I clench my jaw. Maybe I should've taken off my shirt first. Possibly, we could've found a more private location than this kitchen. Best of all would've been if I hadn't jostled the wine to begin with.

"Hold still." Ari dabs on the vinegar with the cooking brush, her eyes laser-focused.

I exhale slowly. Clearly, it's not Mat's fault that I spilled the wine. Sure, my annoyance at him made me flail more than usual. But the truth is, my limbs have been clumsy ever since I was a kid. The only times in grade school that I *wasn't* picked last in gym class was when Mat was a team captain.

Like a true friend, he chose me first every time. Even if it meant we wound up losing. Even if our teammates grumbled and shot him dirty looks.

"Ignore them," he would say, nudging my shoulder. "I've

got enough skillz for us both. Which means, as a team, we're unbeatable."

Okay, so maybe the guy was arrogant even when he was ten. But I didn't mind. In fact, I used to think he was sweet.

"One...more...should do it," Bunny mutters.

More liquid splashes on me, just as the kitchen door swings open and Mat steps inside. He takes in the situation—my sisters crowded around me, my shirt yanked up and around my stomach—and a wide smile spreads across his face. Jerk.

Even worse, someone's behind him. A person who's a few inches shorter, but with broad shoulders and preppy clothes. Aw, chib-peng. It can't be... Of course it is...

Crap, crap, crap.

Taran. The new boy I want to impress. The one I'm meeting for the first time looking like I got into a food fight with a toddler.

"Oh, sorry." His face flushes. I'm not sure what he thinks he's interrupting, but it's clear the Tech girls are up to *something*. "We'll just leave you—"

He starts to walk out of the kitchen, but Mat grabs his arm, stopping him.

"Taran, have you met Orrawin?" Mat practically purrs. On a teenage boy, the dulcet, catlike tone should sound absurd. But he somehow manages to pull it off, which makes me want to punch him all over again. "The youngest Tech sister." He gestures grandly. "Not as polished as Ari and Bunny. Nowhere near as pretty. But as you can see, she's got her own *charm*."

"I spilled wine on my shirt," I mumble to the floor. Might as well address the elephant in the kitchen. "We ran out of white vinegar, so I had to, um, get creative."

Oy tai. Right about now would be the perfect time for

the gods to conjure up a conch shell for me to hide inside.

Someone snorts. And then chuckles. And then straight-up laughs. Gathering my courage, I glance up. Taran's looking at me *not* like I'm a total weirdo but like I might actually be fun.

"I've had to do that, too," he says warmly. "My brother once put gum in my hair, and we ran out of peanut butter, so I used the satay sauce."

My mouth drops. There are guys like this in the world? Really? I sneak a glance at Bunny and Ari, and they nod, as though telling me to go with it.

"That's brilliant," I say. "There's got to be other uses for peanut sauce beyond a vehicle for falang to label any meal as Thai."

His eyes light up. That's the great thing about talking to other Thai Americans. I don't have to explain that "falang" means "foreigner." "Exactly. They add peanut sauce to a regular old turkey club, and all of a sudden, it's a Thai sandwich. What will they come up with next? Thai mac-n-cheese?"

I giggle. "Thai clam chowder."

"Thai meatloaf."

I gesture ruefully at my shirt. "Thai Cabernet."

We grin at each other. Ari and Bunny beam like proud parents, and Mat snorts, as though disgusted by the entire conversation.

Someone from the other room calls Taran's name. The high-pitched voice sounds too old to be his girlfriend, so here's hoping it's his mother.

"I have to go," he says reluctantly. His smile acknowledges all of us, but his eyes remain on *me*. Pretty sure no boy has singled me out when my sisters were around, ever. "You're a senior at Lakewood High, right?

I'm starting there tomorrow."

Bunny stomps on my foot—literally crushes my toes under her sexy black stiletto—and Ari jabs me with her billiard stick of an elbow. Subtle, these two are not.

"Uh, I could show you around," I say before my sisters can attack me again. "Give you a tour of the gym. Introduce you to our cafeteria, with its fine dining options such as nachos. With fake cheese sauce. From a squirt can."

Taran laughs again, and the sound travels along my spine in a delicious tingle. I could get used to this sensation. "I'd love a tour."

"Great," I squeak. Clearing my throat, I try to sound older than five. "I can meet you by the flagpole tomorrow morning. Around eight?"

He looks straight into my eyes. "I'm counting down the seconds."

He leaves. My sisters leave. And I'd melt into a puddle right next to the soggy paper towels if it weren't for the one person who remains. The kink in my gold chain, the bubble in my egg-roll skin, the absolute bane of my existence. Freaking Mat Songsomboon.

He plops on a chair at the small kitchen table and plunks his jaw onto his overly large palm. He faces my direction, his eyes glazed. I can't tell if he actually sees me or not.

Ignoring him, I cross to the sink and dunk the bottom of my shirt under the faucet to wash off the vinegar. The stain has faded, but half my blouse is now a sopping mess, and I smell distinctly like Eau de Vinegar. Lovely.

I peek at Mat. His eyelids are at half-mast, and he looks like he might fall asleep. This, for some reason, infuriates me. Am I really that boring?

"Will you stop it?" I snap.

He blinks, stretching his arms back so that his biceps flex. He's doing it on purpose. He's got to be. There's no way I'd notice those rock-hard muscles if he weren't shoving them in my face.

"I'm renowned around here for my near-psychic genius," he says lazily, "but you're going to have to be more specific."

"Stop sitting there," I say. "Breathing."

His lips quirk. "You do know I can't actually make myself stop breathing, even if I wanted to?"

"You don't have to do it so loudly," I complain. "I can hear you sucking in air and then puffing it back out. And it's just—"

"Distracting?" he supplies, wagging his eyebrows.

"*Irritating,*" I correct.

He leans back against the chair, lacing his fingers behind his head. My eyes drift to his biceps—again. Gah. What is wrong with me? It's like the image of him wearing boxers has short-circuited my brain.

"You've been thinking a lot about my breathing patterns," he remarks.

"Only because I'd like to change them," I mutter.

"Oh, really?" His black eyes turn even blacker. "Exactly how would you like to change my breathing, Winnie? Would you like to...speed it up?"

For one ridiculous second, an image of us, intertwined, flashes through my mind. What the hell? Has my brain gone on strike?

I quash the image with a vengeance. "Don't call me that. That's a nickname only my family and friends use. You belong in neither category." I stalk to the chair where he's sitting, so close that my tights-covered toes (no holes *there*, thank goodness) almost touch his socked feet. "The only way I'd change your breathing is to make it end. Forever."

32

Dating ⇒MAKES⇐ Perfect

"Why? For introducing you to the new guy?" He smirks. "For your information, I was trying to *help* you. He was never going to notice you. I made sure you stood out."

His words slam into me, forcing me back a step. "I could've done that myself."

"How? You're not bad-looking. Some might even say"—his eyes flicker down my body—"somewhat attractive. But no one will see it, the way you cower behind your sisters."

He gets to his feet, making me retreat another step. It's like we're partners in a strange dance. No, not a dance, and *never* partners.

Heat gathers behind my eyes. But I will not let him see me cry. I'd drink the entire jar of jalapeño vinegar first.

"I don't cower." I lift my chin. "And you're a jerk."

"You don't cower around *me*," he corrects. "And I'm only telling the truth."

"You're still a jerk."

He lifts his shoulders in acquiescence. "A jerk your mama wants you to date."

I freeze. Chib-peng. She told him already? I thought I had a few hours at least. Enough time to talk Mama out of her choice. To replace him with…anyone, really. It doesn't even have to be Taran, so long as it's not Mat.

To give myself time to think, I move to the stove and begin transferring food into plastic containers. "Wow. That was fast, even for Mama," I finally say.

"I know," he says. "Remember the time we cut your hair, because you wanted bangs like mine? Your mom found out before we could even get the broom to sweep up the evidence."

Do I ever. Mat and I weren't allowed to play together for a week. At the time, it felt like an eternity. Now, a seven-day reprieve of his company would be nothing short of a blessing.

"Let me guess," I say. "You turned Mama down before she could even finish her request."

Instead of nodding, he just shrugs.

I stare. "You've got to be kidding."

"I had no choice." He approaches the stove and gets to work on the tom yum koong. "You should've heard her. 'Mat, you have to help her,'" he says in a surprisingly good imitation of Mama. "'You wouldn't want her to go to college without any relationship skills, would you? She'll end up alone, with nothing but a bunch of cats for company. And she's allergic to cats!'"

I sigh, taking the empty pot from him and placing it in the sink. "It's true. Cats make me sneeze like I've inhaled a pepper grinder."

"I know." He's laughing, showing off the straight, white teeth that are the result of three years' orthodontic work.

But I will not be distracted. "Why are you really doing this? If we have to date, you'll suffer, too."

He sobers abruptly. "I've been begging Dad to let me backpack through Asia after graduation. I've got the trip all mapped out. I'll start in Thailand, but I also want to go to Vietnam. Indonesia. Singapore. Hong Kong. He's always refused…until now."

My jaw drops. "Are you saying—?"

"Yep." He grins as though he's eaten an entire plate of sticky rice and mango. "For every day I fake-date you, he's granting me another day for my trip." He lowers his face so that it's inches from mine. "Better get used to these devastating good looks, Winnie. My itinerary is three months long, and I intend to take every. Single. Day."

Chapter Five

Three months.

How am I supposed to survive three months fake-dating the most obnoxious boy in the entire world?

I begged Mama. Pleaded with her. I even recruited my sisters to the cause, with their quick thinking and their sweet mouths (what Mama likes to call falang who tell you what you want to hear).

But Mama stood firm. Her youngest daughter *will* practice dating in high school, and the candidate/boyfriend/victim *will* be Mat Songsomboon.

There's no crossing Mama when she's made up her mind. Even Papa's hard-pressed to sway her, though he has yet to weigh in on the situation. Ultimately, I acquiesced because I want to maintain my role as the good Thai daughter.

"Remind me again why I agreed to do this," I say the next morning, for maybe the fiftieth time.

After cleaning up, my sisters and I stayed up the entire night, reenacting our childhood by snuggling on my bed with a couple of old-school flashlights—and Bunny's smartphone. She's so attached to that thing that she can't even nostalgia properly.

"Freedom," Bunny answers me now as we hover in the foyer, grasping for those final seconds before they have to leave for college.

"Study dates where your socked feet brush each other's under the table," Ari elaborates.

"Getting a corsage from a prom date who isn't your sister."

"A kiss or two on the darkened front porch." Ari takes my hand. "For that chance, you can do anything for three months. Even date gorgeous but infuriating Mat Songsomboon."

I gag—and it's not entirely pretend. I can feel our breakfast congee climbing my throat.

Papa calls from the driveway that the Honda Odyssey is packed and ready to go.

Oh no. *No.* My sisters can't leave yet. It feels like they've been home for nine seconds, not nine days. They cannot travel three hundred miles away, relegating me to the last Tech sister standing.

The *only* Tech sister left.

The loneliest modifier in the English language.

We reach for one another at the same time, in a three-way embrace of long limbs and silky skin. Bunny's chin jabs into my shoulder; Ari's hair is in my mouth. But I just hug them even more tightly.

"We'll miss you, Win-win," Ari murmurs.

I squeeze my eyes shut. She hasn't called me that since we were kids. Wrapped up in those two syllables are all the laughter, angst, and tears of my seventeen years.

My sisters were twenty months old when I was born,

and they spent so much time holding me on a pillow in their laps, singing me "Rock-a-bye Baby" in their lisping voices, feeding me milk bottles warmed in cups of hot water, that when I said my first word—"Ma-ma"—I was looking right at Ari. Or maybe it was Bunny. Mama could never remember which, so she alternates between the two each time she tells the story.

Maybe that's where our closeness comes from. I'm not sure. All I know is that saying goodbye to them feels like yanking out a small but important organ. Not the useless appendix, but maybe a thyroid?

Slowly, we pull apart, and Ari and Bunny tuck me in between them. We move forward, arms linked, and turn at an angle so that we can fit through the front door.

By the minivan, Mama is stashing Ziploc bags of sticky rice and homemade beef jerky onto the center console. I don't see Papa, so he must've stepped into the garage.

Mama looks up, her cheeks softening at the sight of us. "I hate to break this up, but the day's not getting any earlier. And Wash U's at least a five-hour drive."

We shuffle to the edge of the car, and the twins fold in on me like an accordion.

"Promise you'll call," Ari says, scrunching up her eyes. Even narrowed, they twinkle more than her statement necklace under the sun.

"Text," Bunny demands.

"FaceTime. I'm going to miss these chubby cheeks." Ari grasps my face, squeezing gently.

"Initiate emoji wars," Bunny says. "Smiling poop wins."

"Are you *sure* you're okay?" Ari scans me so carefully, she might as well be searching for enlarged pores.

"I'm fine," I say and hope they believe me. "Mama's exaggerating, as usual, about me being lonely without you two."

"So you have friends?" Ari presses.

"And you don't eat lunch by yourself?"

"And you don't mope around the house every Friday night?"

I push them toward the car. "Get out of here. I had plenty of friends while you were around. Why would I suddenly lose them when you leave?"

The twins exchange a look, but Mama's already gotten into the driver's seat and turned on the ignition, so they just peck me on either cheek and hop into the car.

"Miss you already!" Bunny yells through the rolled-down passenger window.

"Miss you more," I say as the Odyssey backs out of our driveway and speeds away. "I will always miss you more."

*S*econds or minutes later, I'm still in the driveway. Still staring at: a patch of dirt in our otherwise thriving lawn, whose grass Ari ripped up during one of her driving lessons. An overturned scooter in front of our neighbor's house, complete with pink and blue tassels. The empty street, which used to hold a Honda Odyssey carrying the two best sisters in the world—and now doesn't.

"Ari!"

Papa's voice intrudes into my reverie, but if he's looking for my sister, then he's too late.

"Bunny!"

Yep, she's gone, too. Hasn't he learned after nineteen years that you can't find one twin without the other?

"Sophie!"

My eyes widen. Okay, now this is officially strange, since our beloved miniature schnauzer passed a year ago.

"Winnie. That's right." Papa strolls out of the garage, shaking his head. "One of these days, I'll be able to keep you girls straight."

I gape. "Did you just call the *dog's* name before mine?"

"I'm not actually confusing you." He jingles a set of keys to the Prius. Since Mama's driving the twins to college, he's taking me to school today. "I read this article. I'm only used to saying the twins' names because they were home this week. And I was remembering how Sophie used to bark and bark whenever a car pulled out of the driveway."

I sigh. "Of course you read an article about it." Although Papa is a cardiologist by profession, he prides himself on knowing a little bit about everything. The most densely populated island in the world (Santa Cruz del Islote); the relative speed of sound through solids, liquids, and gases (fastest to slowest, in that order); even how to dye his own hair ruthlessly black, like most of the men of the older generation in Thailand.

"You missed the twins, by the way," I say.

"Oh, I said goodbye to them this morning," he says as we both settle into the Prius. "I gave them each a jar of under-eye cream. To keep the wrinkles away."

I let go of the seat belt, and it snaps across my body. "You gave them wrinkle cream? As a farewell gift?"

"I certainly did." He backs out of the driveway. "Goodness knows, I don't really understand all this beauty nonsense, but I heard some of your mother's friends raving about it, so I picked up a few jars in Chiang Mai last summer. The formula's all-natural. Made from a combination of twenty herbs."

"Papa! You can't give your teenage daughters *wrinkle* cream! That's so rude."

His eyebrows scrunch together, as though he's genuinely confused. "Why not? I thought they would appreciate it. Aren't you girls always watching those YouTube videos about skin care? It's so hard for me to figure out what to give you as gifts, and Ari's always putting on some sort of cream or another."

"But *not* wrinkle cream," I say between gritted teeth. "That implies that they have wrinkles, which is just insulting." I fumble with the seat belt again and finally click it in place.

"It is?" He turns, surveying me innocently. "Would you like some, too? I have a couple of extra jars. Maybe your skin would benefit from an early start."

I sigh. "Thanks, Papa." He means well, even if he can be a little clueless sometimes.

"Speaking of early starts..." He flips the turn signal. "No kissing."

Huh? I struggle to recalibrate the conversation. Does he think I'm about to plant one on the leather seats...or is he talking about romantic entanglements?

"No hugging."

Gotcha. Entanglements it is. This must be about Mama's newfound change of heart, which Papa and I have yet to discuss. "No worries." I shudder. "I have no interest in hugging overly tall boys with overly large egos."

Sweet, funny boys with angelic features, on the other hand? Different story. But Papa doesn't know I'm giving Taran a tour before school. And he's not about to find out.

Papa ignores me. "No touching, either."

"Seriously, Papa? If I'm going to practice date someone, there might be occasions when touching is appropriate. A handshake at the beginning of the evening, for example."

"You can wear gloves," he says firmly.

I snort. "Should I get the ones that go up to my elbows?" As he actually seems to consider this, I shake my head. "If you're this worked up over me spending time with a boy I don't even like, what are you going to do when I go on a real date?"

"I don't know," he groans. His hands shake, and his skin is the color of wax paper.

Uh-oh. How did I miss this? Papa and Mama are always so in sync. From the time we were kids, it was a nonstarter to go to one parent if the other had already said no. I had no idea he wasn't on board with her new scheme.

"Dating Mat wasn't *my* idea," I say slowly. "I'd rather stick a smoldering incense stick into my eye. But Mama insisted. If you don't agree…" I lick my lips, not sure which outcome I prefer. If I date Mat, I'd be the good girl following my parents' wishes. But in order to do so, I'd have to put up with the boy who told his father that I was dying to see photos of the tea leaves he took on his trip to Shanghai. All one thousand of them.

"If you don't agree with Mama," I try again, "why don't you just tell her?"

He pulls into the lot in front of my high school. It's early enough that there's only a handful of cars parked in front of the red brick building and smudged stone pillars. "I can't."

"Why not?"

He sighs. "I shouldn't be telling you this." He turns off the ignition, along with the air conditioner, and the interior of the car is suddenly too quiet. "Mama never wanted to restrict you girls from dating in high school. She only enforced the rule as a concession to me."

My jaw drops. What is he saying? The only Mama I've ever known turns inside out like a hand puppet. And since wearing clothing inside out is a signal to the spirits that a person has passed, she would *not* be happy.

"I don't understand."

"Mama didn't marry me until she was in her mid-thirties," he says. "That might not be a big deal here in America, but in Thailand, she was considered positively ancient. Let's just say her family gave her a hard time."

I believe it. My relatives are boisterous, loving…and very, very direct. If they considered Mama to be on the shelf, then they would've reminded her, day and night.

"She didn't want you girls to suffer the same criticism. And so she was inclined to let you date in your teens. But I insisted. She agreed to try things my way." His fingers toy with the raised, stitched seam of the steering wheel. "But then it backfired."

He looks up, his eyes quiet and thoughtful behind his glasses. It's what I love most about Papa. He may be socially clueless and fixated on his articles. But he is a good person, with a thoroughly kind heart.

"Now, it's only fair for me to try out *her* way." He lifts a hand and cups my chin. "Indulge her, will you, Winnie? All she wants is for her daughters to be happy. Because that's the only way she'll find peace for herself."

I nod slowly. Mama never talks about the past, before she had children. You'd think she sprang into being the moment the twins were born. She's always made her priorities clear: a mother first. A doctor second. A wife somewhere below that.

Her own needs, her own wants and desires? Nonexistent. After all she's given me, the least I can do is go along with this scheme.

"Fine. She didn't really give me a choice in the matter, but okay. I'll do it. I'll date Mat."

Relief and panic simultaneously war over his face. "Good," he says unconvincingly. He reaches past me and opens the passenger door. "Because your first date is after school today. We've arranged for Mat to drive you home."

Chapter Six

I hurry across the neatly clipped school lawn, my mind racing. The sun is bright and booming, unseasonably warm for this late up north. But I'm too distraught to even appreciate my skirt, printed with cat heads across a burgundy fabric, unreasonably cute given my recent winter wear.

I have a date with Mat. After school. That's less than seven hours from now. I thought I had *way* more time to prepare for a forced entrapment with him. Such as a week. Or a month. Maybe even never.

In a car, no less. What were my parents thinking? They must not have heard the rumors about Mat and Delilah Martin at homecoming. She lost her hoop earring, and he climbed in the back seat to help her search for it—for an hour.

Clearly, Mama was drawing inspiration from *To All the Boys I've Loved Before*, which we watched together recently. I know how her mind works. Noah Centineo drove Lana Condor to school and back. Ergo, all teen dates should begin with one party schlepping around the other. Of course, in the movie, Lana was a bad driver. *I* don't drive only because I don't have access to a car.

Still, how bad can the date be? It's only a twenty-minute ride from here to my house. Add in the pleasantries—or ugly-tries, as the case may be—and the whole thing will be over in less time than an episode of *Never Have I Ever*.

For now, I have more pressing matters. Such as: giving the most intriguing boy at Lakewood High a tour without tripping over my brown suede lace-up boots.

When I arrive at the flagpole, however, no one's there. I sit on the stone retaining wall, which surrounds a bed of mulch and shrubbery, and carefully arrange myself in a pose. Ankles, crossed. Face, tilted toward the sun. Attitude, oh-so-casual.

Except…it's colder than I expected. The wind bites into my bare calves, and I have to press my palms into the stone to keep from hugging myself.

I hold the pose for ten more seconds and then grapple for my phone. With any luck, my best friend Kavya Pai—as close to me as a sister, if I didn't actually have sisters—is just now fluffing her pillow, as her snooze alarm blares for the fifth time. Last night, I told her all about my upcoming tour—dare I say date?—and she's obligated to provide some much-needed emotional support. It's in the best-friend contract.

Me: I'm at the flagpole, looking all sorts of cute, and he's not here

Kavya: Don't tell me you're wearing the cat skirt *again*. It's the third time this week

Me: News flash. I wear it among *different* people, so nobody knows I'm recycling

Kavya: Except for me. I know. But you do look adorable this morning. What did you do to your hair? Hello, good hair day!

Me: Awwwww...thank you

Beaming, I send her a dozen kiss emojis before I remember that she can't actually *see* me. Damn it. Can't fault Kavya for not being a good cheerleader, anyway.

Me: Ari let me use her special jasmine shampoo

Kavya: Nice. Hope you stole it

Me: NO. Sisters (and friends) don't steal from each other... even if they're obsessed with my ruby lipstick with the gold glitter gloss

Kavya: *cackle* You mean, *my* ruby lipstick?

Me: Whatevs. Take it. Take all my worldly possessions. Just be here to pick up the crumbling pieces of my body because he is totally. Standing. Me. Up.

Kavya: Now you're offering up body parts? Relax. As much as I'd like a Winnie ear or a Winnie finger, it's only 7:55

Me: Oh. You're right. I'm early. Does that make me desperate? Should I leave? Hide?!

Kavya: Deep breaths, hon. Repeat after me. I am A-OK

Me: I am A-OK

Kavya: A-OK

Me: Does that sound like a steak sauce? *presses hand to stomach* I'm hungry again

Kavya: Of course you are. I mean, it's been what? A whole hour since breakfast?

A shadow falls over me. Finally. Panicked, I shove the cell phone into my purse, in case he's got mad skills at reading upside down. My heart battering against my chest, I look up.

But it's not Taran. Instead, it's another Thai guy, a whole lot taller, but in some people's eyes—the ones who should probably get their visions checked—just as cute.

I scowl. "What are you doing here?"

Mat arches an eyebrow. He tried to teach me that trick once. For hours, we sat in front of my mirror, as the ten-year-old Winnie tried—and failed—to make her left brow rise in that smug, questioning way.

When I admitted defeat, Mat consoled me by praising my tongue-rolling skills. He even went so far as to pretend that he couldn't roll *his* tongue, a lie that I totally caught him in six months later. Still, it was nice of him to try and make me feel better.

Too bad he hasn't shown the same consideration since.

"I go to school here," he says. "Last I checked, you don't own this particular patch of lawn."

I resume my basking-in-the-sun pose. "We don't talk at school," I say loftily. "It's one of our rules."

He blinks. "I wasn't aware we had rules."

"Oh, yes. They govern our every word and action. I'd be lost without them."

Up goes that eyebrow again. I hope it gets stuck there, the way body parts always seemed to in the moral tales my parents used to tell us when we were kids. If you hit your elders in one life, you'll have overly large hands in the next. If you speak ill of a person, you'll be reincarnated with a pinhole mouth. Surely there's got to be a karmic consequence to arrogance.

"Where are these so-called rules written?" he asks. "Let me guess. In your diary, where you pour your heart out every night, rhapsodizing about yours truly."

He's kinda right—and also entirely wrong. Once, a couple of years ago, I jotted down the rules in my journal, next to a drawing of Mat with the devil's horns and a forked tail.

But I've never, ever waxed poetic about him. Unless you count "dirty, rotten rat bastard" as lyrical.

"I don't need to write the rules down," I say. "They're imprinted on my brain."

"This I've got to hear." He plops down next to me. Not touching, but entirely too close for comfort. Mere inches separate our hips, and I can feel the heat rising from his body.

I scoot away a full foot. I hate to admit that his proximity affects me, but I can't think straight when he's that near.

"One, do not speak at school." I tick the rules off on my fingers. "Two, if we pass in the hallway, look the other way. Three, interact at Thai events only when necessary. Last but not least, never, ever forget that we hate each other's guts."

He doesn't respond. A couple of girls from art class walk by, peering at us curiously. Either they've heard about our intense dislike for each other…or they think he's hot. Which, *ew*. But you never know how hours locked up with paint fumes can alter your perspective.

I shift on the wall, scraping the skin at the back of my thighs. Minus one for the cutest skirt on the planet. I cross and recross my ankles, and the suede boots whisper through the blades of grass.

And he's *still* lost in his reverie.

"You've given this a lot of thought," he says after a minute or ten. He lifts his face, and our eyes lock. For the briefest moment, I flash through incarnations of those deep black eyes. Glinting mischievously as we crawled under the table at our parents' dinner parties. Wide with horror when Mama caught us sneaking an R-rated movie. Blinking furiously at his mother's empty place mat after she left for Thailand.

"But you're wrong," he continues. "I don't hate you. I never have."

My heart raps against my chest. He doesn't? But that

can't be right. He's *implied* as much on countless occasions, even if he's never come right out and said it.

He smiles. "I only loathe you."

Of course. I knew that's what he meant.

I bare my teeth. "Well, I loathe you, too. With the heat of a thousand suns, over the span of a thousand lives."

I catch movement out of the corner of my eye. Taran. Great. He picks *now* to finally show up?

Too late I realize my mouth is still arranged in a snarl. Deliberately, I close my lips for a beat before attempting to talk. "Taran. Hey. How are you?"

In the space of one night, I've forgotten how attractive he is. His jeans are freshly pressed, the top button of his shirt artfully undone. His face is a model of symmetry— even if those full lips seem a little frozen.

"Is everything okay?" the best-looking transfer student in the history of Lakewood High asks.

Huh? Why would everything—? Oh. Gotcha. Mat and I are turned toward each other, our knees almost touching. His eyes are wild; we're both breathing hard. I suppose, from the outside, the scene looks rather intense.

"Of course. What could be wrong?" The laugh that comes out of my mouth is as fake as the pad se-ew at Thai chain restaurants.

"We're good, man." Mat gives me a distinctly withering look and gets to his feet, his pants leg brushing against my knee. I jerk away, but that slight touch lingers like a burn. "Just having a few words with my best girl." His voice drips with sarcasm.

I wince. This is so embarrassing. Now Taran will know that the first guy he bonded with finds me disgusting.

But Taran's eyes widen, and he takes a step back. "Hey, sorry. I didn't mean to cause any problems."

Wait—what? He can't possibly think that Mat was serious?

"No." I shake my head so vigorously, it might screw right off. "You've got this all wrong. Mat and I—we're not together." My voice rises. "We've never *been* together. We never will be. Not unless I were dead. And if I were, and he was *still* into me, which, let's be honest, is a distinct possibility…then, *gross*."

I'm babbling. This is what happens when I'm nervous. And upset. And hungry. Unfortunately, I'm all three at the moment.

I whip around, giving Mat my best glare (which, admittedly, is probably less effective because we also practiced this look for hours in front of the mirror).

"Tell him," I spit out. "Tell him how little we mean to each other."

An expression I can't read crosses Mat's face. We look at each other for a few confusing seconds, and then he turns to Taran. "Oh, she means less than nothing to me," he says stiffly.

I asked him to say the words. Hell, I practically demanded it. And yet, his statement makes me feel less than the worms crawling beneath our feet.

"But that wasn't always the case." He lowers his voice. "Once upon a time, we were close. Very close." He rubs his neck. "I probably shouldn't be admitting this, but what the hell? We're all friends here, right?" His gaze moves from Taran to me—and stays there. "Winnie and I are so close that we've even seen each other naked."

Chapter Seven

Time seems to stop. The wind ceases blowing; the flag above us freezes mid-wave. Did he actually say we had seen each other naked? Oy tai, he did.

Heat rushes to my face, and my heart roars back to life, pounding and twisting. I won't look at Taran—I can't! And even if I did, I probably couldn't see past the red film blurring my vision.

Mat's smug, annoying face comes into focus. He leans over, so close that his hot breath caresses my skin. "Gotcha," he says very, very softly.

Two syllables, one word, but it splits my head right open. So *this* is why he broke one of our rules. This is why he deigned to approach me at school. He only wanted to torture me.

As if I needed any more proof that Mat Songsomboon is a demon in disguise.

He straightens, and I swear his skin has taken on a burnt-sienna tint. If I looked in his mouth, his tongue would be forked. If I sliced open his stomach, his bowels would definitely be fire.

"Well, I'd better let you two get to your tour," he says mockingly. "Have fun."

He saunters away, and Taran and I both watch him leave. At least, I assume Taran's staring after Mat, because we're certainly not facing each other. The new boy's not laughing at one of the half dozen witticisms I'd prepared last night. (Although, come to think of it, maybe a crack about how he's not in Kansas anymore isn't particularly witty?)

I take a deep breath and turn to him. His hands are shoved in his pockets, and he's looking everywhere but at me: the fluffy cloud formations; the school crest carved into the stone facade; Maria Ruiz's shapely legs underneath her super-short skirt. Not that I can fault him for the last. Everyone checks out Maria's supermodel limbs—even me.

"Listen." Mustering up my courage, I put my hand on his arm. My stomach doesn't churn wildly, and my nerves aren't even slightly frazzled. But that's a good thing. That means our relationship is *normal*. Not plagued by rampant confusion and fluctuating emotions, unlike some other relationships I know.

"I'm really sorry about Mat," I continue. "He's an old friend." Well. He's probably more accurately described as a preta, which is a spirit cursed by karma and returned to the world of the living, with an unquenchable hunger for human waste. But potato, potahto. "We've known each other since we were kids, and he was referring to the fact that our moms used to give us baths together when we were little. Not—" I flush as an image of a naked seventeen-year-old Mat, with water dripping down his taut brown skin, flashes through my mind.

"Not any time more recent," I finish. "He was trying

to embarrass me—what can I say?" I shrug helplessly. "It worked."

Finally, Taran looks at me. I fully expect him to scan me dismissively under raised brows. That's what Mat would do. Instead, he covers my hand, which is still resting on his forearm, and squeezes. Startled, I realize that I've been touching him for way too many seconds—when Papa would have had a heart attack over just *one*—and snatch my hand away.

His lips curve, and the breath gets caught in my chest. Holy wow. That smile is more potent than a weapon.

"No worries," he says. "I'm the youngest of three brothers, and I'm pretty sure they live to torment me."

I blink. "You are?"

"Oh yeah. One of my brothers is a senior in college. The other's a sophomore." He leans forward. "You probably know how it feels to be the forever recipient of hand-me-downs. Not just clothes but also advice, parties, rules."

"Mrs. Granger, my math teacher, still refers to me as 'Ari or Bunny,'" I confess. "Sometimes, she gets confused and calls me 'Arunny.'"

His eyes crinkle. "Up until we moved, my parents assumed I would attend KU. They never even asked what I wanted. Because that's where my brothers go. And that's where they're succeeding."

I'm grinning now. I don't often meet someone who understands me so thoroughly. "I've never had a new formal dress, ever. Why should I, when I have not one but *two* sisters' prom dresses to choose from?"

"You! What about me?" he asks. "I've never had a new baseball mitt."

"School supplies," I counter.

"Underwear," he says, and this stops us both.

"Ewww." I wrinkle my nose. "Are you kidding?"

"Dear God, I *hope* so. My parents always presented them to me as new, but you never know. Maybe they just recycled the plastic wrap."

We catch each other's eyes and burst out laughing. The students weaving around us turn to stare, and I realize that the crowd has doubled in the last few minutes.

"Should we start the tour?" I ask, and the words actually sound natural. "Wait until you see our cafeteria. You haven't lived until you've tried our school's rather unfortunate version of deep-dish pizza. They serve it in an extra-tall container, as if that will somehow trick us into thinking that the toppings are more than paper-thin."

He laughs. *Again.* Maybe this tour can be salvaged after all. No thanks to Mat.

Cheered, I lead him into the building, chattering about the size of the student body (1,200) and the teachers to avoid (Mr. Mercer, who doles out paragraphs like candy—handwritten, no less). But now that my thoughts have conjured up Mat, I can't seem to exorcise him.

We've seen each other naked, he said. *Naked. Naked. Naked.*

"And here are the locker rooms. Where you get—" *Naked*, my mind screams. "Changed," I finish. My cheeks, my neck, even my ears blush.

The tour goes downhill from there. My attention keeps wandering, and as a result, I may have missed a couple of Taran's questions. I definitely walked past the aforementioned cafeteria altogether.

By the time the first bell rings, I've managed to cover only one of the three sprawling floors.

"Oh no. I'm sorry we didn't get to everything," I blurt. "You'll have to figure out the rest on your own."

"Not a problem." He gestures at a sign featuring the unisex symbol. "Let me guess. Using my vast powers of deduction, I'm going to say this is the bathroom. Am I right?"

It's impossible not to smile back. "Why, Taran. You've been holding out on me. Guess you didn't need my dubious tour-guide skills after all."

"Maybe." He reaches out a hand and tucks a strand of hair behind my ear. "But I sure enjoyed the stories. In fact, I'd love to hear more. Rain check?"

My mouth parts. I lift my hand, brushing the ends of my hair. And here I thought no boy would ever perform that gesture sincerely. Guess I haven't ruined everything with Taran.

"Yes!" I practically shout.

I would be embarrassed, but Taran's grin widens, as though he finds me incredibly amusing.

Not gonna lie. I skip all the way to first period.

Now I just have to figure out how to get even with Mat, and my first day back without my sisters might not be a total disaster.

Chapter Eight

*L*ater that afternoon, I fasten construction-paper eyelashes over the headlights of a Jeep Wrangler, fighting back a giggle.

"Quick!" Kavya says from the roof of the car, where's she attaching a jaunty pink bow. She tosses back her brownish-black hair, her eyes glowing in the sun. My best friend is Konkani, which is a group of people from the southwest coast of India. The group is so small, she tells me, that even other Indians haven't heard of them. As a result of her Persian ancestry, her eyes are the pale yellow of golden topaz. I've never seen anything like them, and they're just as gorgeous as the rest of her. "Only five minutes left until the end of last period. Almost…there…"

We finish up and stand back to admire our handiwork. Mat's sturdy and rugged Jeep has now been transformed into a cutesy work of art, complete with ruby-red lips, curling lashes, and trailing ribbons. I even painted polka dots on the back windows, because, you know, *polka dots*.

I rub my hands together. "He's going to die when he sees this."

"You killed two birds with a single pair of pouting lips, anyway," Kavya says. "Now that's inspired."

She's telling me. I've been struggling to settle on a medium for my art project, which is to depict a series of five emotions. I'm not sure why I was having such a hard time. Maybe because this is the last art project of my senior year. Who knows when I'll have the opportunity to explore my art again in such an intense, concentrated way?

I'll be expected to be serious in college. Focused on my economics courses. Not distracted by "frivolous" pursuits.

When I saw Mat on the list of students willing to volunteer their time to the art department for community service hours, I leaped at the opportunity.

Mat, being Mat, probably thought he would be offering up his good looks for students to paint. Serves him right that it's his car—instead of him—that's functioning as the model.

The first expression I picked for the Jeep is coquettish. No doubt you can buy the flirty lashes and hair bow in any car costume kit. But I'm also planning on exploring more subtle and complicated states of mind—another reason I couldn't pick a medium.

Truth is, I've been feeling too much lately. And I don't want to confess them to anyone, much less display them for the entire school to see. The thought of showcasing the emotions on canvas or in clay had me balking, hard.

But expressing my feelings through a car is unexpected. Playful. It creates both a distance and a shield, giving me space to explore these very real emotions in a safe way.

And if I get to embarrass Mat while I'm acing my art project? All the better.

Kavya slings an arm around me, and I rest my head on her shoulder. She's so leggy that she makes me feel petite, even though I'm used to being taller than Mama and my sisters. "Thanks for helping me out," I say.

"It *is* the last day to declare a medium. I was beginning to worry." She snickers. "Of course, it doesn't hurt that I'll have front-row seats to Mat's reaction. We could sell tickets to this event. In fact, we probably should."

I grin. It's no secret that Mat considers the Jeep to be his baby. She has a gender, probably even a nickname. He vacuums her carpets once a month. Washes her exterior weekly. Even when it rains. *Especially* when it rains.

Most pets aren't this tidy. Except for cats, maybe, since they self-clean.

"What. Is. This?" a voice growls.

It *sounds* like Mat. It uses one-syllable words consistent with his primitive manners. But the voice is also two octaves lower than normal and more ferocious than anything I've ever heard.

I whirl around, and it's Mat all right. His scowl is so deep that he'll soon be in need of Papa's wrinkle cream.

Kavya giggles nervously. "Whoa," she murmurs. "Is he always this hot when he's mad?"

I would sigh—if I weren't too busy keeping a straight face. Is it the height thing? What else could explain my best friend's bizarre attraction to Mat?

"Winnie," he says slowly. Deliberately. "Can you please explain why my car is wearing your lipstick?"

Not sure how he has the first idea what shade of lipstick I wear, but okay.

"Meet my new art project," I say brightly, using the acting skills I developed playing a bird during our middle school play. It's harder than you'd think to squawk properly.

"Your. What?" He's back to biting out each word as he walks slowly around the car, getting the full impact of my artistic vision.

"You were on the list of volunteers to help students with their final project. Mrs. Woods was thrilled when I told her my idea of depicting five human emotions via a vehicle." My throat vibrates with the need to laugh. "I don't have a car, as you know. So I thought I would use yours."

He stops by the rear windows, as though he's particularly flummoxed by the polka dots. Yay, polka dots! They haven't let me down yet.

"You thought?" he echoes.

"Um, yeah." For the first time, doubt creeps in. I'd wanted to annoy him, but I didn't actually intend for him to get upset. "If you don't like it, I'll clean her right up," I babble as the guilt sinks in. Why, oh why is it so hard to deviate from being good, even with my mortal enemy? "Better than new. You'll never be able to tell she once had a pair of luscious ruby lips."

"It's fine, Winnie." He shakes his head, his lips pressed together. If I didn't know better, I'd think he was trying not to laugh.

But I do know better. Forget funny. He doesn't have a mildly amused bone in his body.

"I suppose I deserve it," he says, jingling the keys in his pocket. "The naked comment was over the line. I'm sorry."

Wait—what? Kavya and I exchange confused glances. Since when does the guy who's always right admit that he was wrong? Not in the last four years, that's for sure.

He takes the keys from his pocket. "Let's go. Kavya, do you need a ride, too?"

"Who, me?" she squeaks. She always gets the squeegee-on-glass effect when she talks to Mat. "Uh, no thanks. I've got my own car."

I elbow her in the side. She's supposed to save me, not abandon me. Either our silent communication skills aren't as developed as my sisters' or she just wants to live vicariously through my date.

Rubbing her side, she grins wickedly. "Have fun, you two. Please do something I wouldn't do. And take lots of notes, so I can hear all about it."

I shake my head. "You're such a gossip."

"One of the reasons you love me."

I soften. "You're right. I do love you."

We hug, and then she scampers away.

Swallowing hard, I turn to the Jeep as though I'm facing the gallows. A particularly well-dressed gallows, with a pink bow and polka dots, but a structure for execution nonetheless.

Mat honks the horn and then sticks his head out the open driver's side window. "Let's go. The sooner we get this date started, the sooner it can be over."

What every girl wants to hear before every first date, never.

When I finally get inside the car, Mat pulls out a composition notebook and a rolled-up measuring tape from his messenger bag. "How long should I leave on the decorations?" he asks. "Poor Mataline's not used to this fuss."

I snort. He calls his car Mataline? Why am I not surprised? The guy's so egotistical that he used to dream about having a hundred wives, with a hundred kids, all of whom would live in a hundred-story house, with a wife and a kid on each floor.

"Don't touch a thing," I say. "I'll change out the accessories every few days, until I've depicted all five emotions."

I wait for his protests, for his exasperation. I may not want to hurt him, but that doesn't mean I'm not looking for the teensiest, tiniest sign that I've gotten to him.

But—nothing. Nada. Suun. He opens up the notebook and starts scribbling inside.

"Whatcha doing?" I ask casually, even as I sit on my fingers to prevent from ripping the notebook out of his hands. Because, you know, I'm not ten.

"Oh, here." He eagerly shows me the notebook, which probably hasn't happened since we *were* ten.

I scan the categories written across the top of the page: Location. Topics of Conversation. Duration. Distance in Inches. Overall Grade.

My forehead wrinkles. What on earth?

Mat snickers, sounding like his old self, which is both comforting and disturbing. "Winnie, Winnie, Winnie," he singsongs, taking back the notebook. "I had no idea your parents trusted you so little."

I grit my teeth. "Spit it out, Songsomboon."

"As you wish, Chicken Cacciatore." He stretches the measuring tape between us and makes a notation on the page. "So the whole point of this dating thing is to improve your relationship skills. Your parents don't want you going to college as hopeless as you are now. But how are they going to evaluate your abilities when they're not here? That's where I come in. All-around dreamboat, fake boyfriend…and spy."

I blink as the categories float through my mind. I think I'm going to faint. Or vomit. Or both.

That's why he didn't care that I dressed up his car like Hello Kitty. He had bigger *cat*fish to fry.

"I'm sorry. Are you saying that you're recording the distance that separates us? With a measuring tape?" This has Papa's fingerprints all over it. "And holy guacamole. Don't tell me that you're *grading* me."

He grins. "Yep. Your parents asked me to keep a record of our dates. They even picked the categories. Kiss-up procedures commence…" He squints at his cell phone. "Right about now."

"You wish. I'd rather kiss anything other than your—" I clamp my mouth shut, not wanting to finish the sentence.

"You can say it," he says encouragingly. "Pretty sure you've been admiring it."

"Whatever, dude." Leaning over, I bang my forehead against the glove compartment. "I know I'm the baby of the family. I know they barely trust me to wipe my own bottom. But really? How could they do this? Do they think so little of me that they'd take *anyone's* word over mine? Even a person who would happily throw me overboard to make room for his pop?"

"For the record…" He turns on the ignition. "I would never throw you overboard to make room for my pop."

I settle back against the leather seat. "Really?"

"Sure. I mean, I gave up pop a year ago. A Perrier, on the other hand? I'd have to think about that one. But if it were an ice-cold green tea? You'd be in the water before you could grab a life preserver."

I roll my eyes. Mat tosses the notebook on my lap and backs out of the parking lot. We don't speak. The radio blares the afternoon news. Only when the car beeps at me to put on my seat belt—and I obey—does Mat turn down the volume.

"In all seriousness, I don't think it's you," he says quietly. "It's just the way parents are."

I frown. "They would never treat Ari or Bunny this way."

"Maybe not, but your sisters probably had to endure situations you didn't. My dad's always saying, since I'm his oldest and only, that I get to suffer his mistakes without benefiting from the wisdom that comes with multiple children. Poor guy doesn't even have my mother around to help him out."

"Yeah." I'm quiet for a minute, thinking it can't be easy with just the two of them, father and son. Does Mat miss his mom? Or have they both just accepted their new life? "I still wouldn't call my parents' actions wise."

"People don't always get it right the first time. And this situation? Definitely a first," he says wryly.

I peek at him. The sun's on its descent, dappling his face with shadows. I have the strangest sensation that he's not the boy I've hated all these years. It's almost as though he were someone new and yet familiar…

"You actually sound reasonable." I shake my head. "I'm going to do something I never dreamed possible—"

"Kiss me?" He smirks.

And the sensation evaporates.

"What? *No*."

"You're right. What am I saying?" He signals the turn for my street. "My kisses probably figure in your dreams on a nightly basis."

I gag. "Excuse me. I just threw up in my mouth—a lot. I was going to say *thank you*, you world-class, insensitive, thoughtless, arrogant—"

"Go on," he urges. "You can curse, you know. I won't tattle on you in the notebook. I triple-bear dare you. Say it!"

"Donkey," I say primly. "You're a donkey."

He smiles. "It's not a bad word. Especially when you define it like that."

He pulls into my driveway and turns off the car. His

eyes sweep over my face, and he leans forward ever so slightly.

My breath catches. What is he doing? He wouldn't *kiss* me, like he threatened. Would he? No way. But he's so close…

He leans even farther—and then plucks the notebook right off my lap.

Right. That's what he was going for. The notebook.

"So what are we going to write in this thing?" He peers at me over the cardboard cover. "Pretty sure you don't want your parents knowing we discussed them."

My mouth opens, then closes. I can't believe he's willing to cover for me. Even more surprised the gesture even occurred to him.

"How about our hopes, our dreams?" he asks when I don't respond. "Parents love that serious career stuff. Are you going to major in art at Northwestern? I'm going there, too, you know. So you'll have four more years of my magnetic personality."

"Ugh, don't remind me," I say, avoiding the question.

"I'll be premed. But you were always different from the rest of us. I remember how impressed I was when you told me you wanted to be an artist in the fourth grade." He shakes his head. "At that age, I never dreamed such a career choice was possible. Still can't, if I'm being honest."

"People change," I say stiffly. "They grow up. I'll probably major in economics."

He blinks. "That doesn't sound like you."

"Well, you don't actually know me, do you?" I bite out. "You don't have the first clue who I've become, so don't pretend like you do."

I want to take back the words as soon as I say them. I wish I could rewind the conversation. But it's too late. As

I watch, he packs away his open, friendly expression. All that's left are tight lips and granite cheeks. His aloof face. The one that he seems to reserve especially for me. The one that forms a wall so impenetrable, I haven't been able to break through in the last four years.

"You're right. I don't know you." I can hear the full stop in his words. In our conversation.

He moves the pen across the page. "We talked about school. My Jeep. The new boy. That's more or less true." He glances up, his eyes opaque. "Your sisters might advise you not to bring up another guy when you're with me. But otherwise, you were average." The pen slashes into the paper so violently that it rips. "B-minus."

I bristle. "B-minus? I think I deserve at least a B-plus, since I brought the decorations—"

"This date has been thirty minutes long," he interrupts. "You can go now." His tone clearly implies that he can't tolerate one more moment of my company. I could say the same thing.

"I hope I don't see you later," I snarl as I hop out of the car.

He raises his eyebrows. "Have a terrible day."

"Bad-bye," I say childishly. I can't help it. Being with him brings out the toddler in me. "Because you don't deserve a goodbye."

His lower lip trembles, as though he might laugh. At me or with me. I don't wait to see which.

Instead, I slam the car door and run inside my house.

Chapter Nine

I lean back against the heavy oak door, breathing hard. My heart's racing a mile a minute, and my brain's doing its best to catch up.

I haven't been this flustered after an interaction with Mat since…well, ever, really. But we also haven't actually *talked* for four years. Sniped? For sure. Snarked? Most definitely. But the actual content of our conversations wouldn't fill an earbud. I've never even asked how he's adjusted to life without his mom.

Our fake-dating changes all that. Instead of insulting each other and walking away, we'll now be forced to spend long entire minutes together. What will we even discuss? I can't imagine. Like it or not, we'll have to dip below the surface. In that process, we might accidentally get to know each other—as the people we are today, not the kids we used to be.

Weird.

I'm not naive enough to think that he's the same guy who dove in front of me during a particularly creepy scene of *The Ring*, as though he might be able to protect me from what was on the screen. At the same time, I don't know *whom* to expect, either.

And that, maybe, is what's freaking me out most of all.

Puffing out a breath, I take off my shoes and lay them in the shelves that my parents had custom-built for the front hall.

Underneath my boots, my socks don't match—one is yellow patterned with bright green pickles, while the other is orange and purple striped. But that's okay, 'cause there's no one here to see them. Papa's still at work. No doubt Mama's on her way home from St. Louis, after dropping the twins off at college.

It's just me here. Alone. Like I have been most nights for the last seven months.

I scan our great room, with the deep green leather sofas and the nearly black mahogany end tables. A chandelier hangs from the two-story ceiling, sleek sheets of wood arranged in rippling layers. The room is modern. Immaculate. There's not an empty cup to be seen.

It's as though last night's party never happened. As though Mat and I didn't bicker over egg rolls. As though my sisters never came home for a visit.

For all the evidence left behind, the whole night could've been a figment of my imagination. Ridiculous, I know. And yet, I shudder, feeling lonelier than ever.

Desperate, I grab my phone and video call my sisters. Ari, specifically, because she's first in my contact list.

She picks up in approximately two seconds, and a close-up of her face appears on my screen. I can see the pores on her otherwise perfect nose.

"Winnie!" she screeches. Conversation buzzes behind her, but her face blocks every inch of the background. "I've been counting the seconds until you called. Tell me.

How was the tour? Your ride home with Mat? Was Taran just scrumptious? How many times did Mat's delicious eyebrow go up? Tell me everything, and don't you dare skimp on the details."

My lips twitch. Calling my sisters was the right move. I can always depend on them to make me feel better. "Oh, Ari, he was the worst. First, he told Taran that we had seen each other naked—"

Ari's face suddenly falls away, as though the phone's been knocked out of her hand. I see a blur of movement, and then the screen focuses on streams of pink ribbons. Plastic silver crowns. Bowls of candy gummies that are shaped like…penises? What?

Muffled laughter rings through the phone.

"Two hours, people," an authoritative voice says. "Our bride-to-be arrives in two hours."

"A little help with the streamers, please," a second voice calls.

"Stop eating the penises!" another voice shrieks. "We won't have any left!"

A moment later, Bunny picks up the phone. Even through the screen, I can tell it's her. Her eyes are slightly narrower than Ari's, her cheekbones a little higher. But it's the dramatic black eyeliner that gives her away.

"Sorry 'bout that," she says. "Ari was summoned, even though she was talking to our favorite younger sister. There was a pecker emergency."

I blink. "A what? Where are you?"

"Oh, one of our sorority sisters is getting married after graduation, and we're throwing a bachelorette party for her." Bunny lowers her voice conspiratorially. "Pin the Pecker on Peter was *my* brilliant contribution. Here, take a look."

She flips the phone around so that I can see a row of

girls wearing cute athletic wear—sports bras and leggings and cropped tops. They're lined up in front of a life-size cutout of a naked man, and they're each holding a piece of cardboard that *might* be shaped like a penis.

I squint. The cutout is a handsome blond with blue eyes. And his nether regions are suspiciously blank.

"Is that a Ken doll?" I ask.

"Yes!" The phone flips back to Bunny. Her wide smile takes up half the screen. "Aliyah drew the line at actually using her fiancé for the cutout. And Ken is oddly appropriate, since he never had a pecker. But now, she's freaking out because she says the penises are too small." She shrugs. "I wouldn't know. But we gotta keep the bride happy, so Ari's been drafted to draw bigger penises."

My face flushes hot, then cold. I'm looking into my sister's laughing eyes, but in the bottom corner of the cell phone screen, there's a tiny image of my own face. Even shrunken down, I can see the red splotches on my skin.

"Now, what were you saying?" Bunny demands. "You were going to tell us about your date."

"Oh," I say awkwardly. "It was nothing."

All of a sudden, my desire to confide in my sisters has dwindled to the negative integers. I'm scandalized because Mat said we had seen each other naked…while my sisters are preoccupied with penises. Gummy ones, cardboard ones. Penises that may or may not be an accurate representation of the real ones. I don't think I've even *thought* the word in the last six months. That's how sheltered I am.

How young, how inexperienced.

Once again, my sisters have raced ahead to their next adventure. And this time, I'm not sure I want to catch up.

"Really, it's not important, Bunny," I say. "Go back to your friends."

"It *is* important," she insists, her eyes striking and mysterious with her taped eyelids. She's so glamorous. Age has nothing to do with it. I wouldn't be as sophisticated as her if I lived to be 110. "Anything that has to do with you is important to me."

"I don't want to interrupt —"

"You're not interrupting."

"I just…" I squeeze my eyes shut. I felt so happy when my sisters were home. Like life was returning to the way it was *supposed* to be. Like I was complete.

Little did I know that the visit home was just a break for the twins. A reprieve before they returned to their real passions, their real friends. Their real lives, of which I'm no longer a part.

"The date didn't happen," I blurt. I don't usually lie — to anyone, least of all my sisters. But if this untruth helps me get through this moment, I won't regret it. "Mat had car trouble. So his Jeep is in the shop. The date's postponed to next week."

"Ah. Too bad," Bunny says. "I was hoping you could report on whether Mat's lips are as pillowy soft as they look."

I snort. "Clearly, planning this bachelorette party is turning your brain to mush. Because I'm never going to be able to answer that question."

"Never say never." She sweeps up a red gummy and bites off its head. "What about the tour with the new guy? Was he just as cute today?"

"Didn't happen, either." This time, I don't even falter. I suppose, once you start fibbing, each additional lie becomes easier to tell. "He overslept."

"Oh, I'm sorry, Winnie," she says. "I know you were really excited to spend more time with him."

"Guess I'll just have to be excited about your pecker project," I say cheerfully.

I keep up the optimistic act through the next several minutes, during which Bunny is asked to weigh in on not just one but *two* potential sizes of cardboard penises. My sister, the Pecker Inspector. Who knew?

I'm so convincing that I wonder if I've overlooked my true calling. Forget being a professor of economics. Maybe my actual future lies in politics.

Finally, I get off the phone.

Only then do I let the tears drop from my eyes.

Chapter Ten

That night, I dream.

It begins as many dreams do, with the events of my day jumbled together as though they were in a blender. One moment, I'm attaching penis gummies all over Mat's Jeep. He takes one off the windshield, his eyebrow artfully raised, and pops it into his mouth. The next moment, Taran picks up the ruler that Papa so thoughtfully provided. Instead of measuring the distance between us, however, he breaks the ruler in half and pulls me against his chest.

Here, the dream melts into one of those weird states where I *know* I'm dreaming but the scene is so vivid, so delicious, that I don't want to be. And I'm just confused enough to convince myself that it's sufficiently real, if only for the moment.

I'm walking through a lush forest, hand in hand with Taran. Dazzling flowers bloom in the bushes, and the scents of pine and moist earth engulf me. The sun slants though gaps in the living canopy, warming my skin. The leaves dance with the barest of breezes. Everything feels perfect.

He holds my hand just right. Not too hard and not too soft. Our fingers intertwine like pieces of a jigsaw puzzle.

Presently, we stop by a set of large boulders and descend into a shallow pond. The water laps at my bare waist. I'm wearing a tiny red bikini—one that I've never seen, much less owned. A waterfall thunders next to us, and stray drops flick onto my skin. The water is cool and refreshing. I'm so heated that I'm surprised the drops don't evaporate upon contact.

Taran's hand is on the move. His fingers leave mine, and he skims them over the back of my hand, onto my wrist. My skin sizzles where he touches, but I can't tell if it's from excitement or anxiety. The waterfall continues to pound next to us, but I don't notice. I don't care. The whole of my being is focused on his hand, on those long and elegant fingers—and how I'm supposed to react to them.

He walks his fingers up my arm, all the way to my shoulder, where he pauses.

"I've wanted this for so long. You have no idea." His voice sounds different. Lower, raspier somehow.

He moves his hand again, gliding it across my collarbone, tilting up my chin. Anticipation swirls in my stomach. This is it. My first kiss. The one I've been waiting for since I saw Adam Scheffer plant one on Ari in a darkened alcove next to the art room. But am I ready for it? And do I want my first time to be with Taran? As cute as he is, I barely know the guy.

Still, I lift my own chin, telling myself to go for it. I need to have my first kiss sometime.

But I'm confused. What does he mean, he's been waiting so long? We only met two days ago. He couldn't have wanted me for longer than forty-eight hours.

A pair of lips comes into view. Soft-looking, pillow lips. And I'm even more puzzled. Because Taran isn't that tall. And dream or no dream, shouldn't I be locking eyes with him right about now?

The answer dawns on me the moment my gaze clashes with a pair of eyes so dark that they're almost black. Lashes so long, they evoke cries of inequity. An expression so arrogant that it can belong to only one person.

Mat Songsomboon.

My mouth drops in horror. Oh, holy hell. I'm having a kiss dream about Mat?

No. Freaking. Way.

He continues to lean closer. And closer still.

Gasping, I jerk awake just as those famed pillow lips touch mine.

Chapter Eleven

Several days later, I stir a perfectly soft-boiled egg into my bowl of hot congee, the steam buffeting my face. I haven't quite recovered from my dream-turned-nightmare of kissing Mat. How could my subconscious betray me like that?

It's Bunny's fault. It has to be. She was talking about his pillowy lips, and my mind twisted that into something that *I* would find attractive.

Damn Bunny. Damn subconscious. Damn Mat for being way better-looking than his personality deserves.

Okay, I'll own up to it. Much to my chagrin, even after I woke, I imagined—for a few fleeting seconds—how it might feel to kiss those lips. So sue me. He's…passable, okay? That's not a terrible thing to admit. Just because I can recognize an objective fact doesn't mean that I'm attracted to him. Doesn't mean I *like* him as a human being.

"You're going shopping today," Mama announces, sprinkling sliced ginger and scallions into my jok (what we call congee). "I'm giving you my credit card. You can charge whatever you want."

I rub my eyes, as much from the steam dislodging my contacts as from her words. Mama, giving me free rein of her credit card? I must be dreaming.

"The Songkran holiday is next week," she continues, "and I hear the Tongdees are hosting a party for all the young people that evening."

"Yes," I say, trying to keep a straight face. "They feel badly about yanking Taran out of school his senior year. So they thought a party might ease his transition."

She smiles, which proves that she doesn't have the first idea that I've been obsessing over the new boy. In spite of our promising beginning, however, I haven't crossed paths with Taran all week.

"I thought you might want something new to wear," Mama says.

Now I know I'm *definitely* dreaming. The Songkran festival marks the beginning of the Thai New Year on April thirteenth, and the holiday is celebrated with water. Pouring water, splashing water, spraying water—all symbols of washing away the previous year's negativity. It's a blast. When we were younger, Mama would set up an inflatable swimming pool in the backyard and arm all the kids with water guns. The twins would commandeer the hose, but Mat and I held our own. Back to back, a water gun in each hand, we would spin in a slow circle, soaking every last person who stepped into our range.

As much fun as the holiday is, however, we don't usually give or receive presents. Plus, I can count on two hands the number of new dresses I've gotten in my lifetime.

I shove a spoonful of jok into my mouth—and then pant as it burns my tongue. Mama made my favorite breakfast. She didn't even use the packet. Instead, she ground up grains of rice in the food processor and fashioned meatballs out of minced pork. Add a soft-boiled egg, and I'm in food ecstasy.

And yet, I can tell that something's up with Mama. I mean, I would love a new outfit for Taran's party. (Something sleek and elegant, maybe in a deep jewel tone?) But the offer doesn't make any sense. Is Mama feeling nostalgic? Gripped with premature empty-nest syndrome? Or maybe—

"Mat's picking you up in thirty minutes. You're going shopping for your second date."

Ugh. I should have known.

I let my spoon clatter to the table. "Seriously, Mama?"

I've barely seen my nemesis all week, much less talked to him. Our only communication was when I traded out the curly lashes on his Jeep for dollar-sign headlights and lots of gold bling, transforming his baby from flirty coquette to greedy monster. The decor—and the thought of his reaction—made me giggle.

I know my intention was to explore deeper, more vulnerable emotions. But after our last interaction, I couldn't open myself up like that. Not to him or the rest of the world.

So, greed it is. That should put Mat in his place.

But instead of slinking into the parking lot after first bell or finding an isolated spot in the overflow area, Mat rolled into school as confident as ever. He smiled and waved when the decorated Jeep drew honks and catcalls, as though the whole car costume was *his* inspired idea. I'd be impressed at his ability to make the best of any situation if he weren't so aggravating.

I take another huge bite, even though the jok is still hot. "I don't know how to tell you this," I say around a mouthful of runny egg yolk. "But people don't go shopping on second dates. That's just — " My mind scrambles for an appropriate word. Weird? Embarrassing? So uncool that it makes me cringe? I settle on: "Awkward."

"Nonsense." Mama waves a hand, dismissing my concerns like dust motes in the air. "That's what they did in *Pretty Women*."

I groan. Shoulda known. Not only is it *Pretty Woman*, singular, but more importantly, this means that the car ride wasn't a fluke. Mama was deliberately referencing *To All the Boys I've Loved Before*. She never dated in this country, after all. She came to the United States in her thirties, with a medical license and a fiancé. It figures that she would draw her dating knowledge from American rom-coms — especially ones that didn't even release in this century.

"First of all, I don't need any man — or, excuse me, *boy* — to take me shopping. And second, Richard Gere's not even with Julia Roberts when she goes on her first shopping spree." And yes. I have seen it. The movie might be old, and it's definitely cheesy, but that doesn't mean it's not a classic. "I'll be spending *your* money, not Mat's. And finally, can't forget that I'm not a prostitute. So the scenarios aren't at all similar. They only have one thing in common. Clothes."

Mama beams. "Good enough for me."

I sigh. Of course it is. Why do I get the feeling that this date is going to be a big mistake? As Julia Roberts says, not just big. *Huge.*

Chapter Twelve

I frown at my reflection in the mirror. I'm wearing, without a doubt, the most hideous sweater I've ever seen. A garish yellow that hurts my eyes, it's covered with big, droopy bows, including two that are unfortunately— um, strategically?—placed. The rest is a woven disaster of apples and picnic baskets and checkered tablecloths.

How is this thing even on sale? It looks like my five-year-old niece designed it. I'd bet half of what I own (which, to be fair, isn't much) that Mat pulled it out of the ugly sweater bin—except there's nothing Christmassy about it. Are there ugly sweaters for every holiday now? Thanksgiving and Valentine's and, I don't know, May Day? What holiday could half-eaten sandwiches and a row of ants represent?

"Come out, come out, wherever you are," Mat singsongs outside the heavy navy curtain of the dressing room. "You have to show me what you're wearing. That's part of the deal."

I suppress a groan. This is awful. I don't think Mama

could've designed a worse date if she tried. Whose idea of fun was it for Mat to pick out clothes—and for me to model them?

Not mine.

And not—wait—maybe—oh, yeah, *definitely*—his.

His strategy, so far, has been to pick the most ridiculous clothes in this out-of-the-way store, clothes that I would neither buy nor wear if I lived until the next century. This yellow monstrosity is just the first sweater. I look balefully at the pile of clothes that I have yet to try on. Kill me now.

"Are you coming out?" Mat asks. "Otherwise, I'll be forced to go in. And I really don't think either of us wants that to happen, since we're no longer toddlers. I may never recover. Won't finish my senior year. Won't tour Asia as planned. Won't attend college—"

"Okay, okay," I grumble, pushing past the curtain. "Do you ever stop talking? Seriously. Must every last thought exit your mouth?"

Mat breaks into a grin as soon as he sees me, his eyes dancing. "You look like Big Bird gorged on a dumpster and threw up."

"Lovely." I keep my eyes trained on his chin so I don't have to see my reflection in the mirror behind him. "Are we done now? I've got, oh, about a million more sweaters to try on."

"Not yet. I need to savor the view." He stalks around me, scrutinizing every loop of yarn, every dangling ribbon. "I like the pattern." He snickers.

My cheeks flame. I cross my arms over my chest, even though he hasn't so much as glanced in that direction. Either he's a gentleman—or the sight of my body disgusts him. I'd bet the rest of what I own that it's the second.

"I think Taran will appreciate this sweater, don't you?" he asks.

"Who said anything about Taran?"

"You did," he says. "We're looking for something for you to wear to his party. And you told Kavya you'd take a bucket of water over your head if you could have five more minutes of his company."

I stare. I did say that—almost word for word. It happened one morning at school, when I was inviting Kavya to the Songkran festival.

"What, are you eavesdropping on me now?" I ask.

He snorts. "Hardly. I was going to thank you for Mataline's new look—but then I remembered there was somewhere else I had to be."

That's right. I vaguely recall the sensation of a person behind me. When I turned, however, I only caught Mat's overly tall frame disappearing around the corner.

He was going to thank me? Mockingly or sincerely? My head throbs with all the things I don't understand about this guy.

"This is torture," I blurt before realizing that what I'm saying is way too vulnerable. I need to add that to my set of rules: Never admit to your enemy that he is getting to you. *Ever.*

"You're telling me," he says, to my surprise.

"What do you mean? I'd think you'd be having the time of your life, making me model these awful clothes. Make Winnie look ridiculous. Isn't that on your bucket list? Your every wish come true?"

He looks at me for so long that I don't think he's going to answer. "Nobody wants to spend the afternoon picking out clothes for some other guy to enjoy," he says finally. "End of story."

My brow creases. Huh? But Mat's not interested in me. Not for real. Not beyond what we're playacting for our parents. So why should he care what Taran enjoys—or doesn't even notice, as the case may be?

I start to ask, but Mat sighs and gestures to the dressing room. "Go on, Winnie. You still have half the store to model. It's going to be a long afternoon."

The atmosphere shifts during our exchange. Mat no longer laughs at me. He doesn't seem to derive any joy from my comical appearance. Instead, we are almost subdued as I try on the rest of the clothes—if there can be anything subdued about a bright-purple dress, complete with the fire-breathing snout of a dragon.

To my surprise, Mat has actually selected a couple of decent options in my pile of absurdity. One dress, in particular, is an emerald silk. It has a V-neck that is deep enough to make me feel striking but not so low that it would give my parents heart failure. The fabric skims my curves softly and swishes around my thighs to end a few inches above my knees.

After I put it on, I blink at the mirror for a few confused seconds. I look...pretty. Ethereal, even. That's not an adjective I've ever applied to myself. When you have sisters like mine, you get used to being okay—even thrilled—with moderately cute. But how I look now is in a completely different league.

This dress is everything I've ever wanted. So much more than I've even dreamed.

"How are you doing in there?" Mat calls, his voice husky.

There's nothing playful about his tone now. I've been quiet for so long that he's probably just making sure I haven't passed out.

I bite my lip. I don't want to show him. Mama gave him the power to approve my purchases, and the second he sees me coveting this dress, he'll veto it so quickly that I'll get whiplash. I'll end up wearing the yellow sweater with the floppy bows to the Tongdees' party, and Taran will never take me seriously again.

Which might be the only reason that Papa agreed to this plan in the first place. Mama has paired me up with a guy who would never be interested in me...but who just happens to scare off every other prospect. Even I have to admit, it's a brilliant way to guarantee that I'll be single and distraction-free for the rest of high school.

"Winnie?" Mat calls again.

"Coming!"

With one last look in the mirror and a resigned recognition that this dress will never be mine, I square my shoulders and walk out of the dressing room.

I stop in the middle of the hallway, where the overhead light shines straight down, and squeeze my eyes shut. I wait for his vehement denial, his snort of disbelief, that I, for even a moment, would believe he would let me buy anything so flattering.

But the seconds tick by. And he doesn't speak. All I can hear is the whir of the overhead fan, the muffled conversation of the mother and daughter next door, and the coy giggles of the salesperson as she flirts with one of the customers.

Chib-peng, maybe Mat's not even standing here anymore. Maybe he took off the second I closed my eyes, so that he can make an even bigger fool of me.

I wrench open my eyes. He's here, all right. A sheen of sweat coats his upper lip, and he's staring at my legs.

"Mat?" I ask because there's a very real chance that he's having a stroke.

He shakes himself. "The dress is…" He trails off, and my mind immediately fills in the blanks. Hideous? Pathetic? Desperate?

"Passable," he finishes. His eyes have become opaque and unreadable. "It's the only thing that makes you look halfway decent. Might as well get it."

My temper flares. Not least because I used the same word to describe him. "Careful, Mat. You might accidentally say something nice about me."

My hands are shaking; my chest is tight. That's when I realize I'm not just angry. I'm…hurt. Silly but true. A small part of me, one that I'm only now understanding, wanted him to compliment me. For once in the last four years.

He lowers his eyes to the bristly brown carpet. "Trust me, you don't want to know what I'm actually thinking."

I lift my chin. "Oh yeah? Try me. There's not a damn thing you could say that would hurt me any more than you already have."

"Hurt you?" He glances at me and then quickly shifts his gaze to the storage boxes stacked in the corner. "Why do you always assume the worst? I don't know what's made you change, but the twelve-year-old Winnie never would've acted this way. She wouldn't have stayed like a mouse in her sisters' shadows, content to be second—no, *third*—best. She had so much confidence; she cut her own path. It didn't matter what anyone else thought. And I was more than happy to follow in her wake. What ever happened to her?"

"She lost her best friend!" I shout. "The boy who was supposed to have her back, for always, dropped her like last season's trends. Did you ever think of that?"

His eyes turn flinty. "Try again. Because the Winnie I knew wouldn't have let *anybody* hold her back. Not even her best friend."

I clench my jaw, hard. But I can't unhear what he just said. The details won't unstick from my brain, which means I'll be thinking about his words, this conversation, later tonight when I'm in bed but can't sleep. And many more nights after that.

"You're wrong," I manage. I can barely hear myself over the blood that's roaring in my ears. "I was never that confident. Never that strong."

I stumble backward, although I'm not sure if it's to get away from him or the truth. Past the navy curtain. Back into the dressing room. Where I can hide away once more.

Except this time, he follows me.

"What did you want me to say?" he asks, advancing. I back into the flimsy wall, across from the full-length mirror. Not because he's crowding me but because I'm crowding myself. "You want me to say that you're stunning? That I wish I could take a photo, so that I can look at you all day? That the material is soft and touchable—and as skimpy as it is, it still covers way too much?" His eyes are black and furious and mesmerizing. I couldn't look away if I tried. "Yeah, I could've said all that. No doubt, that's what Taran's going to be thinking. But I didn't, because I have too much respect for you. Even after everything we've been through."

"You're lying," I croak.

He raises an eyebrow. "Actually, that's the most truthful I've been all day. Which part do you think I'm lying about? Taran having those thoughts? Or me wishing I could take a photo?"

"You d-don't actually want that," I stammer. "You don't

like me. Which means, you're not attracted to me."

"Two separate things," he corrects. "I'm a heterosexual guy. And you're a beautiful girl, standing within arm's length of me, wearing a dress that could easily fit into my pocket. I can loathe you all I want. I'm still going to have a reaction."

My thoughts race. I don't understand why he's telling me these things. Where is he going with this? What angle can he possibly have?

He takes a step closer to me. "You think too much. Really, Winnie, it's not all that complicated. Not everyone has an ulterior motive. Sometimes, a compliment is just a compliment."

When I don't respond, he sighs. "Here. I'll prove it to you." He picks up my palm and places it directly on his chest, where the only thing that separates my hand from his flesh is the thin cotton of his T-shirt.

Underneath my hand, his heart drums steadily—no, the beats aren't at all steady. They're frantic. Erratic. Skittering off in every direction.

What does it mean? Is he so good of an actor that he has control over his heart rate? Or is he genuinely and sincerely feeling...something?

I don't know. I don't know!

I lift my eyes, and I lose track of my thoughts. Because his lips are right there in front of me. Perfectly shaped. Pillow soft.

The air around us is hot, humid. We could've teleported to a swamp, with all the steam rising around us.

"What, exactly, are you proving?" I whisper. Somehow, my other hand has joined the first one on his chest, and he makes a growly sound in his throat.

This close, his eyes have lost all shade and shadow, so

they're just black. Deep-space black. Bottomless-pit black.

He takes a shaky breath. "I'm proving that one thing has nothing to do with the other. For example, you could kiss me right now. And I'd let you. In fact, I'd kiss you back. But that wouldn't change my feelings toward you. I'd still loathe you just as much as I did before."

I narrow my eyes. Because I don't believe him. I could never kiss my sworn enemy. Even if his chest is warm and solid under my fingertips. Even if his lips are soft and inviting—and inches from my own.

"I'm going to call your bluff," I warn.

"I dare you," he says in a strangled voice.

I trail my fingers up his neck, and he sucks in a breath. He settles his hands hesitantly over my hips, on top of the thin silk, and wow. He's on to something. This silk does cover way too much.

I move forward, backing him up until he's against the chair in the corner, the one that's covered with ugly sweaters and cringe-worthy dresses. If this were a rom-com, I'd make him sit and straddle him right about now. But it's not. And no matter what he says, I'm not that brave.

Our breaths come out uneven and jerky. Me, because I don't know how far I can push this. And him…well, I'm not entirely sure why.

"May I…may I kiss you?" I ask, because I really do want his permission. But also because I'm stalling.

He nods helplessly. His mouth parts. I lean closer. A couple more inches. Closer still. Only a few centimeters separate us now.

My brain scrambles. Am I really going to do this? In the name of what? I'm no longer sure what I'm trying to prove. All I know is that I want to kiss him. This guy. My sworn enemy. My former best friend.

"How's it going back here?" A cheery voice drifts through the navy curtain. Argh! The salesperson.

I spring away from Mat as though he were a hot stove. And in a way, he is. Because heat courses through my body. My palms burn where they were pressed against his shirt. My lips tingle, although the only thing *they've* touched is the air he's breathing.

"Doing great," I babble to the salesperson. "I found the perfect dress. Let me take it off, and then I'll be out to pay."

I'm looking right at Mat when I say these words. So I feel his breath hitch; I see his eyes flicker. I don't wait to see what other reaction he might have.

Instead, I push him out of the dressing room before I act as foolishly as I did in my kiss dream.

Chapter Thirteen

I almost kissed Mat. I almost kissed Mat. I almost kissed Mat.

The words run in a loop through my head, numbing my brain, freezing my soul. Just like the frozen yogurt that's entering my mouth.

We're sitting at one of the round laminate tables at the mall's food court, my emerald dress neatly folded inside a bag hanging from my chair. I wiped down the surface of the table, but underneath my forearms, I can feel the stickiness that clings to all food-court tables everywhere.

Unlike the relative quiet of the dress store, the food court is packed. Wall-to-wall people load up on grease-on-top-of-grease food. At the next table, a family with more ponytails and Band-Aids than I can count crowd around two large pizzas. Next to them, a couple barely older than us gaze adoringly into each other's eyes. The air is saturated with the scent of fried food. Like the stickiness of the tables, I'm pretty sure the smell has bonded with the air molecules. You could bulldoze this mall, and I'd still smell overly salted fries.

I take another bite of Froyo. And try to ignore the boy sitting across from me, the one who refuses to be ignored.

For example, I ordered lychee-flavored Froyo—my favorite. And of course, he has to get coconut—my second favorite. It's maddening. So what if he's not doing it on purpose? These are the flavors of our childhood. And now, all I can think about are the fresh kernels of corn they serve with coconut ice cream in Thailand and wish that I could take a bite of his yogurt.

Minutes pass. The family finishes their pizza—with only two tantrums that have to be bribed with freshly baked cookies—and leaves. The lovebirds have given up all pretense of cheesy coupledom and just attack each other's lips.

And we still don't speak.

Mat's eyes have lightened to a nice shade of dark brown, although that could just be the fluorescent lights. He pushes his half-eaten Froyo to the middle of the table and takes an all-too-familiar speckled notebook and measuring tape from his messenger bag.

I scowl. "You know keeping a record of our dates is a pointless exercise, right?"

He shrugs. "Tell that to your parents."

"Take the measuring tape," I persist. "Are we supposed to record the distance between us now? Or before?"

In the dressing room, I don't say. *Where the distance between us was not quite zero but pretty darn close.*

But if I'm trying to draw a reaction from him, an acknowledgment of what happened between us, then I fail. Miserably.

"Now's probably as good a time as any." He stretches the tape between his end of the table and mine, but when his fingers graze against my hand, I jerk out of his reach.

Indifferent, he releases the tape and jots the number in his notebook.

Infuriating, thy name is Mat.

"What are you putting under Topic of Conversation?" I ask. "Are you going to say we discussed kissing?"

He looks up, his eyes distant. "Is that what you want me to do?"

I clench my teeth. Clearly not. If he wrote that down, my life would be over. Forget dating. I wouldn't even be able to leave the house, period. It would be like being under quarantine. He knows this. Which is why I don't give him a real answer.

"That depends," I say, as sweet as the Froyo I have yet to take a bite of. Come to think of it, he hasn't eaten any of his, either. "What grade would you give me?"

He lifts his brow. "For promising a kiss and not following through? Hmm." He looks up at the soaring ceiling, as though searching for an answer among the scattered skylights. "C-plus."

"What?" I yelp. "Why is my grade going down? Some teacher you are."

"I'm not your teacher," he says. "Just your evaluator. Or your, um, dater. Er. Datee?" He shakes his head, puzzling over the term. No wonder. Such a concept shouldn't even exist. Leave it to Mama to dream up new scenarios for the English language.

"Doesn't matter," I say. "If Mama thinks you're making me *worse* at dating, then she'll yank you from the job. And then where will you and your three-month trek across Asia be?"

Even as I say the words, I want to snatch them out of the air. What am I doing? I *want* Mama to replace him.

I wish I could date someone else, such as Taran.

But it's too late.

"You've got a point," Mat says thoughtfully, scrawling a big, bold "B" in the notebook.

I huff out a breath. I'm so annoyed—at him and myself—that I grab a clean spoon and stick it in the middle of his Froyo, scooping up a gigantic bite and not even bothering to hide it.

"Hey! What are you doing?" he protests.

"Don't worry, I haven't used the spoon," I say testily. "You're not getting my germs. Besides, we always used to split our food. Remember? Not just with Froyo but also with pizza rolls. You preferred the plain cheese, and I liked pepperoni, but we'd trade a couple of pieces for variety's sake."

For a moment, all I hear is the loud din of conversation around us. A crumpled napkin lands squarely on our table, and a grade-school kid rushes up, a baseball cap turned backward on his head. He apologizes profusely and carries the napkin over to his true target—that trash can ten feet away.

Ignoring him, Mat leans forward, his hands clasped on the greasy surface. "Yeah. That was fun. I kinda miss trading with you," he says, so softly that I can't be sure I heard him correctly.

I miss you, I think. *I miss watching* Frozen *together for the millionth time. I miss how you would always give me the last Sour Patch Kid, even though I'd already had more than my share. I miss saving the red ones for you, even though I liked them, too.*

But I don't say any of this out loud. Instead, I take a deep breath. Give myself a pep talk. And try to remember the words that I've practiced on countless sleepless nights.

"I'm sorry I told everyone you had a crush on Denise Riley." Once I start, the words tumble out, one after the other. I've rehearsed this apology so many times that the speech comes automatically. "I'm even sorrier that I knocked your binder over so that everyone saw that you carried a picture of her. It was immature and petty, and I've regretted it ever since. I know my actions are pretty much unforgivable. But I hope you'll forgive me anyway."

He startles. "Oh, I had forgotten about that." He stares, unblinking, for several long seconds. "Is that why you think we stopped being friends?"

My mouth falls open. And stays open. "Um. It's not?"

"No. It didn't bother me, because I never had a crush on Denise. I just told you that because I didn't want to admit who I really liked. Carrying her photo was just part of the ruse." The tops of his cheeks redden to a rusty brick.

"You lied to me? Why? Who *did* you have a crush on?" My thoughts whirl like a hurricane. "Forget it. Not important. What I really want to know is: if it wasn't my betrayal, then why did you avoid me?" I lick my lips. "Why did you stop being my friend?"

He wants to answer, I can tell. His lips part, and the words are right there, on the tip of his tongue, in the depths of those opaque eyes. He just has to lower his walls, if only for a moment, and the truth will come rushing out.

But in the end, he just shakes his head, keeping his answers where he's always safeguarded them. Locked up tightly in his heart.

"Fine." I collapse against my flimsy plastic chair, frustrated. "You don't have to answer me. But are we really not going to discuss what happened?"

His forehead creases. "What do you mean?"

"The dressing room!" I exclaim. "Where we almost

kissed. Where we most certainly *would've* kissed if we hadn't been interrupted."

His eyes deepen. The air turns soupy once more. It's the only explanation for why I can't get a proper breath. The physical spark between us flares, and all of a sudden, I'm intensely aware of just how much distance separates our hands. And I don't even need the measuring tape.

"Winnie! Is that you?" A familiar voice invades my thoughts.

I blink, and my best friend materializes next to our table. Her long, elegant neck is draped with multiple strands of shiny beads, and her sleek bob curves around her cheeks.

Chib-peng. I totally forgot that I asked—okay, begged—Kavya to "bump" into us at the food court so that she could rescue me from what was sure to be an unbearable date.

"Kavya," I say weakly. "What are you doing here?" I don't even have the energy to make my question convincing.

Which is probably why she doesn't bother to answer. Instead, she turns to Mat, scanning him from his floppy black hair to his beat-up loafers. "Hi, Mat," she says demurely.

"Hey." He smiles at her.

She pauses a beat to melt under his attention—and then zeroes in on the shopping bag hanging from my chair. "Did you find a dress for Taran's party? Let me see."

Without waiting for a response, she picks up the bag and slides out the dress. "Oh, Winnie," she says, her voice hushed and reverent as she unfolds the garment. "It's gorgeous. Taran is going to *love* it. And get this. After some intense digging, I've discovered…" She pauses dramatically. "That his favorite color is green."

Mat snickers. "Those are some hard-core detective skills you've got. How many victims did you have to torture to get that top secret information?"

She tries—and fails—to hide her delight that Mat's actually talking to her. He's teasing, sure, but it's clear from his tone that it's out of affection, not malice.

"I don't believe in torture," Kavya says primly.

"Neither do I." His gaze searches my face until I meet his eyes. Until I know, as well as he does, that we're both thinking of that moment when he implied that it was torture for him to pick out clothes for Taran to enjoy.

"What's *your* favorite color, Mat?" Kavya asks.

He turns back to my best friend. "Are you giving me a firsthand demonstration of your supersleuthing?"

Her eyes twinkle. "Answer the question. Or I'll have to kill you."

"Who wants to know?" he counters.

"Winnie," my traitor of a best friend says.

"Hey!" I protest, hands up. "Leave me out of this."

"Well, it's not green. That's for damn sure." He picks up his Froyo, jabbing his spoon so hard that it goes right through the Styrofoam. I stare, fascinated. Are we still talking about favorite colors?

Regardless, he's lying. I know for a fact that emerald green used to be his preferred hue.

Emerald, as in the color of his cell phone case in middle school. And backpack. And winter coat.

Emerald, to reflect the day of the week on which we were both born: Wednesday. According to ancient Thai custom, each day of the week is associated with the color of the god who protects that particular day.

Emerald, as was the stone in the delicate necklace he gave me for my twelfth birthday. I still have it, packed away in a velvet box at the back of my drawer. Maybe it's not healthy to hold on to such a sentimental gift from my ex-friend. But I couldn't bear to get rid of the first piece of jewelry I ever received from a boy.

Kavya places a hand on her hip. "I'll be sure to file that away under classified information. Mat's favorite color: not green."

She looks at me, and I shrug. I wish she could help me sort through my confusion, but I don't think the Budha himself—the deity who protects Wednesdays, not to be confused with Buddha—could untangle this complicated web.

"I'll call you later, okay?" I say to Kavya. "I need to, uh, talk to Mat about something."

She nods and squeezes my hand. With a final lingering look at Mat, she departs.

She's barely out of earshot when Mat straightens. "You were asking me about the dressing room," he says abruptly. "By that, I'm assuming you want to know why I acted the way I did."

Caught off guard, I nod, my brain trying to catch up with this shift in conversation.

"I'll tell you," he says. "But you'll have to come closer."

"What?" I frown. In spite of the background din, I can hear him just fine. "I'm plenty close."

"No. Come *around*. I don't want to miss a detail of your reaction." He gestures impatiently for me to stand, and it's such an odd request that I comply.

As soon as I'm on my feet, however, he tugs me forward so that I fall sideways into his lap.

I yelp, but then his arms go around me. They're warm. As are his legs. And his chest. Any further protest dies in my throat. I've never been held like this, ever. So much of my body is in contact with his. His jeans-clad thighs are slabs of rock underneath my legs; his fingers sear into the small of my back. As if pulled by a magnet, my hands find their way back onto his chest.

Embarrassed, I smooth out his shirt where I creased it earlier. But that doesn't help my mortification because I end up sorta petting him.

He doesn't seem to mind.

"You want to know why we almost kissed?" he whispers, his lips brushing against the lobe of my ear.

I shiver. I can't help it. I have no more control over my reaction than an ocean has over its swells.

"It's because..." he continues. Voice, still whispering; lips, still brushing. "I made a bet with my buddies. That I could get you to fall for me before our fake dates are over."

The world tilts. It must, because I'm tumbling off his lap, gripping onto the sticky countertop to stop my descent off the edge.

Did I hear him properly? Did he actually say what I thought he said?

Vocabulary flees my brain.

"So all of this... It was..."

I can't even put a sentence together. But it doesn't matter. The smug expression on his face says it all.

I've been played.

Chapter Fourteen

"Holy crap. Is this target practice or a shrine?" Kavya sails into my bedroom later that afternoon, her hair flowing behind her like there's a fan held up to her face. I swear, she'd look like a model if she were on her hands and knees, digging in the dirt. I know because last spring, we overturned a garden at a retirement home as part of our junior service project.

"It's about to be a graveyard," I snarl, holding the sight of the Zombie Sidestrike up to my eye.

Pop, pop, pop.

A single picture of Mat isn't enough this time. A whole series of sketches lines my wall. His face. His long, lean body, which spans three pieces of paper. Next comes a close-up of his infuriating eyebrow. Guava of a nose. Lips like big, lumpy pillows. Biceps, chest—and abs. Can't forget those. Drawing those body parts evoked so many emotions that I broke several pencils. Which only serves to fuel my rage.

"There must be ten drawings here." Kavya surveys the

lineup. "Obsessed much?"

Instead of answering, I let loose a succession of foam bullets.

Detecting my mood or fearing for her life, Kavya retreats to my bed. She wisely keeps her mouth shut for the next few minutes while I demolish the sketches.

When I've done as much damage as my aching shoulders will allow, I slump onto the pink polka-dot comforter next to her. The Nerf gun lies limply on my lap, and her light, floral perfume engulfs me.

She turns to face me. "Wanna tell me why you're so upset?" she asks.

I do—from the yellow sweater with the floppy bows to the way Mat looked at me in the green dress. From the almost-kiss in the dressing room to his zinger of a revelation—that he'd made a bet with his buddies that I would fall for him.

Her jaw drops, as expected, but her ears don't steam next. Instead, she tilts her head, considering me.

"Winnie, do you like him?"

"What? No." My fingers twitch on the trigger of the Sideswipe, even though I'm out of bullets. "We hate each other—oh, excuse me, *loathe* each other."

"But you sat on his lap, right?" she persists. "Why would you do that if you don't like him?"

"Because I kinda fell?"

"I don't buy it." She faces me, her knees jabbing into my thighs. "You've been snarking at each other for years. But none of your comments was malicious. You never aimed to truly hurt him. In fact, when Delilah Martin told the girls last fall the exact details about Mat's underwear—that he wears boxers, that he prefers solids—you were the first person to tell her to shut up."

"Because I didn't want to hear it."

"No," she says softly. "Because the details were too personal. They weren't meant to be shared publicly. You were protecting Mat."

I open my mouth and then close it. And then open it again. Because she's right. "He was my best friend for my entire childhood," I say weakly. "What else was I supposed to do?"

The sun spills through the window, heating my neck, highlighting the clothes I've left draped over chairs and heaped on the floor. I get up and begin to clean, because I don't want Kavya to think I'm a slob—but also because I need something to occupy my hands.

"How *was* his lap?" my best friend asks. "Cozy?"

I gather an armful of leggings and T-shirts, the blush spreading through my body. Even my elbows are probably red.

She hoots. "Oh, Winnie, don't ever change. I love that you're so innocent."

"When I was ten, I used to want my first kiss to be with my husband at our wedding," I confess. "Goodness knows, that would make Papa happy."

"And now, at the wise old age of seventeen, how do you feel?" she teases.

I toss the dirty clothes into a hamper. "I'm not sure. But I'd like my first kiss to be genuine and not part of a bet."

She gestures for me to sit next to her. "I don't care if you have your first kiss when you're eighteen or eighty. No judgment here. All I want is for it to be right for *you*.

"I'll let you in on a secret. First kisses pretty much suck— and not in a good way. Too much slobbering. Too much thrust." She jabs her tongue out repeatedly to demonstrate. "I only have one word to describe mine: 'braces.'"

I giggle. Kavya's parents are as strict as mine, but that's never held her back.

"I'd love for your first kiss to mean something," she continues. "But I'd also love for it to be with someone who knows what they're doing." She waggles her eyebrows. "With Mat, there's a good chance you'll have both."

Is she right? There were some long, sticky moments, in the dressing room and out of it, when the connection between us was a weighty, palpable thing. Is my attraction to him real? Or was I just confused?

I lick my lips. I suppose it doesn't matter how *I* feel when he's made his feelings abundantly clear. He's flirting with me only because of a bet. Nothing more. "Bet me ten bucks that I can make him fall for me first."

She raises an eyebrow. "Those are some pretty hefty stakes."

"Seriously, Kav?" I grumble. "You're missing the point. I just have to *tell* him that I made the same bet. Help a girl out."

"Make it a dollar and you've got a deal."

I sigh. "Fine. A hundred measly pennies. You're a true friend."

She reaches over and squeezes my hand, accidentally depressing the trigger on the Nerf gun. A foam bullet flies out and hits pencil-Mat's knee, and we burst out laughing.

"Anytime, Winnie. Anytime."

*T*he following Friday, I pace my bedroom. What am I going to do? My bet with Kavya was hardly real. I doubt any money will ever change hands. Knowing my best friend, she'll make me repay her in single-serve chocolate chip cookies, the only kind I'm industrious enough to whip up.

But those were fighting words. I'd like nothing better than to make Mat fall for me. To make a fool out of *him*, when that's what he tried to do to me. The only question is: how?

An entire week has passed, and I've made no progress toward my goal, other than to beam a cheesy smile at Mat a few times during school. Each time, he gave me a strange look, as though wondering if I was coming down with a fever. Clearly, I need to sharpen my flirting skills, especially because we have a date tomorrow at the Songkran festival.

Groaning, I flop onto my spinny desk chair. That's the crux of the problem. This is not a fair fight. Mat has a ton more experience than I do. He's actually dated people. Even—gulp—kissed them. The most time I've spent in the back seat of a car is when I didn't weigh enough to activate the airbag.

I pull out my cell phone. There's only one place I turn when I run into school problems or friend problems or help-I've-lost-my-eye-mask-and-can't-sleep problems. My sisters.

Me: How do you make someone fall for you?

Bunny: Send nude pics?

Ari: Bunny!!!

Me: Bunny!!!

Ari: Seriously? This is our baby sister who's asking

Bunny: Yes and she happens to be 20 months younger, not 20 years

Me: Good thing, too. Because then I wouldn't even be born

Bunny: Neither would we. We'd be having this convo in the womb

Ari: Focus, please. Winnie asked a serious question. She deserves a serious answer

Bunny: Oh, so now you wanna talk about nude pics? Who's the pervert this time?

Me: LOLOL

Ari: Noted. And ignored. You're fabulous, Win. Just be yourself

Me: But I've been myself for seventeen years. And he hasn't fallen yet

Even as I type the words, I gnaw on my lip, remembering Mat's comments in the dressing room. According to him, I haven't been my true self for four years. Is there any basis to his claim? Or is he just messing with me once again?

Bunny: Holy guacamole. Are you talking about Mat?

Ari: She's totally talking about Mat

Me: I AM NOT TALKING ABOUT MAT

A minute passes, with no response.

Me: Ok. I might be talking about Mat

Bunny: Ha! I KNEW it!

Me: It's not what you think. I made a bet with Kavya—since he made a bet with his friends—basically, it's a race to see who can make the other fall first

Ari: That makes no sense

Bunny: And needlessly complicated

Ari: Why don't you just keep it simple? Tell him you like him. Maybe he'll respond the same way

Bunny: Oh, hey, I have an idea. Send a pic! Doesn't have to be racy. Never underestimate a photo of a nice pair of knees or a crumpled-up dress on the floor

Ari: Less is sometimes more

Bunny: Especially, you know, when it's LESS

Me: I have no idea what that means. But thanks. You've given me a lot to think about

I text them a row of heart-eye emojis. Are they right?

No clue. No doubt my sisters have more experience than I do. A better understanding of this whole romance thing. They might not have dated in high school, but they've been in college for seven whole months, without parental supervision, surrounded by gummy penises. I know of at least four kissing sessions—and those are only the ones they bothered to share with me.

Mat has more layers than the comic books we used to devour. There's no telling what will make him fall. Still, I don't have any better ideas, so I might as well follow my sisters' advice.

Taking a deep breath, I arrange my new green dress artfully on my carpeted bedroom floor and take a photo with my cell phone.

And then, before I can change my mind, I hit send.

Chapter Fifteen

The doubts start at the crack of dawn the next morning, when I sneak over to Mat's house to redecorate a certain Jeep in his driveway. I drape garlands of plastic jasmine and pink roses along the passenger doorframe. Was it silly to text a photo of my dress? I fasten a tall golden chada—a headdress worn in classical Thai dance—to the hood of the car. Is Mat laughing hysterically at my pathetic attempt at seduction? I even tape long finger claw nails, like the ones worn in the fingernail dance, to the sideview mirrors. Did he even receive the damn text?

He must have.

There's been no response, but a few times, I saw dots appearing on the screen only to disappear again, which means that he started composing a message—and then changed his mind.

Not that I was staring obsessively at my cell phone or anything.

A few hours later, Jeep decorated, I meet up with Kavya to go to the Songkran festival. By the time she turns into the parking lot of the wat Thai, my stomach's tied itself into macramé—and it has nothing to do with the orange cones (and a bumper or two) that she almost took out.

"Are you positively sure no one's going to dump water on me?" Kavya asks wistfully. Her chin-length hair is pulled into an itty-bitty ponytail, as though she's prepared for a torrential downpour. "Not even a cup?"

I smile, in spite of the churning in my torso. "If it means that much to you, I'll happily pour my iced tea over your head."

"That's okay." She sighs dramatically. "I just can't believe there's no rowdy water play at a water festival."

"It does take place at a temple," I point out. "And there'll be so much food, I promise you won't notice."

"I'll hold you to it." She pulls into a narrow parking spot, her brows creased in concentration. "How come you're meeting Mat here when you have a date with him?"

"Mama's very literal," I say ruefully. "In *Always Be My Maybe*, Randall Park arranges to meet Ali Wong at a farmer's market in San Francisco. It's the closest scene in a rom-com that Mama could find to a Songkran festival, so here we are. Fake date number three."

Kavya turns to me, mouth open. "Isn't that the scene where she tells him that she has insane, freaky sex with Keanu Reeves?"

I cringe. "Oh, please don't remind me. That detail must've slipped her mind when she was planning the date."

"She's using these movies as a dating instruction manual?"

"Something like that." I take off my seat belt. "I can assure you, though, that there will be no insane, freaky sex on this date, especially since our parents will be there."

"Is that the only reason?" Kavya teases.

I blush and change the subject. "The Songsomboons used to be fixtures at this festival. But that was before Mat's mom went to Thailand to take care of his sick a-ma. She used to make the best Thai curry puffs around," I say longingly. "Flaky pastry crust, stuffed with tender potatoes, curry, onions, garlic. Kinda like bajos."

Bajos are the Konkani word for pakoras, and Kavya's mom has made them for me often, sometimes using cauliflower, other times using bell pepper, or onion.

"Oh, look!" Kavya points. "Mat's already here."

My stomach flips as we stare at the Jeep tucked in the corner of the parking lot, the Thai flag, with its wide central blue stripe, bookended by narrower white and red stripes, on the rear window.

"You match," she says.

She's right. The Jeep and I are wearing the same colors. My pink sarong skirt is threaded with gold, cinched at the waist with a thick gold belt and paired with a simple, strapless pink satin top. My modesty is preserved by the lacy sabai thrown over my bare shoulder.

"I've always wanted to be twinsies with a car," I remark.

Kavya pretends to pout. "And here I thought you and I were twinsies." She's dressed in the traditional langa (skirt) and dupatta (scarf) of her culture. "Never mind. We can *all* match. But if you don't mind my asking, what emotion is Mataline supposed to be conveying?"

I smile. This feeling may not be overly deep or complicated, but it perfectly captures my heart at the festival today. "Pride."

. . .

*W*e approach the wat, and Kavya's eyes light up. I don't blame her. I've been here dozens of times, and my breath still gets short at the detailed architecture. The roof is made up of three ornamental tiers, a practice reserved for temples, palaces, and other important buildings. A long, thin panel, called the lamyong, decorates the edge of the roof in an undulating shape. This serpentine form evokes the Naga, while the bladelike pieces that protrude from the panel suggest both fins and feathers.

We slip off our shoes, making sure we step over the enlarged threshold. A hallway leads past a large open room, with a three-dimensional metal-cast image of the Buddha. Inside, a few people sit on the floor, praying. The air is tinged with the smell of incense.

Seven Buddha images line the hallway, one representing the god for each day of the week. I walk down the row, placing money into each donation box, and lead Kavya to another Buddha image, which sits in front of a basin of water. After a quick prayer over clasped hands, I pick up the ladle and pour water on the Buddha's forehead. This is exactly what I need today: a clearing of the mind.

"You can pour the water wherever you want," I whisper to Kavya. "The heart, the back. Wherever there's pain or confusion you want to wash away."

She nods and then resolutely trickles water onto the Buddha's chest.

We walk through the back door to the open lawn and put our shoes back on. The calm doesn't so much evaporate as it explodes. Hordes of people mill around two rows of food stands. Everywhere I look, I catch sight of my favorite dishes. Both my eyes and my nose are flooded with grilled meats and fish sauce, coconut milk and sugar. I was born into this cacophony of taste and color and scents, and it never fails to give me comfort.

"Where do we even start?" Kavya asks.

I laugh. "We just pick a spot and dive in."

I purchase some coupons at a nearby cash register, and then we step into the fray.

Before long, we're alternatively taking bites from bundles of sticky rice and skewers of moo ping, or grilled pork.

"This is the best." Kavya closes her eyes, as though that will allow her to better taste the food. "We should have Songkran every month. Every week."

I rip off a hunk of pork with my teeth. Food is not just a sliver of our culture but also a thread that connects the entire tapestry of who we are. We use it to socialize—and to take care of one another.

I'm still chewing, my mouth unattractively full, when Kavya nudges me. "Don't look now, but your favorite person is at ten o'clock."

I can't help it. I look. Mat strides through the crowd, wearing a long-sleeve Mandarin-collared shirt with gold buttons, along with baggy, light-weight trousers.

"Holy hotness, what is he wearing?" Kavya gapes.

"Traditional Thai clothes," I say. "Like mine."

She emits a low whistle through her teeth. "It suits him."

I can't argue. A phraratchatan *is* a good look on Mat. How come I've never noticed before?

He turns his head at that precise moment. Our eyes catch—and hold. Two seconds? Five seconds? I'm not sure how long we stare at each other, but he eventually rips his gaze away to greet an older woman. The fierceness on his face morphs into an expression of deference as he drops his head and gives a slight bow over prayer-clasped hands in order to wai the elder.

Respects paid, Mat raises his gaze and finds me once more. But he does more than stare this time. He heads straight in my direction.

I swallow hard. Uh-oh. Let the fake date begin.

Chapter Sixteen

*M*at stomps up to us. His brows are scrunched; his face is red. He's about as agitated as I've ever seen him. I instinctively tighten my shoulders, bracing myself, but Kavya speaks first.

"Hi, Mat." Her tone is sly, but her face is the pencil sketch of innocence. She even widens her eyes, blinking rapidly, in case he didn't get the memo.

He halts, in much the same way he paused to pay respect to the elder. Indecision wars over his face: annoyance at me versus ingrained politeness. Politeness wins out, as I knew it would. The attribute's only been drilled into us since the day we were born.

"Hello, Kavya," he says smoothly. "You look pretty today."

She rolls her eyes, since he's only glanced at her for the two seconds it took to make his statement.

"Are you having a lovely Songkran?" she asks, her voice extra-chipper. She's just messing with him now. My best friend loves nothing better than to thwart a person on a mission.

But Mat is a worthy opponent. "As lovely as the lod chong is long," he says, referring to the tapioca flour noodle that's served with crushed ice and coconut milk, two tables to our left. He hands a coupon to Kavya. "In fact, you should try it. You'll love it."

She's been effectively dismissed—and we all know it. "I'll leave you two to your date," Kavya purrs, "but it's going to cost you." She snatches up the coupon and holds out her hand for more. Mat gamely hands over the rest of his coupon book.

"Be good. Or, you know, don't be. Whatever suits you best," she says, backing away. I step forward to try and delay her departure. But it's like trying to catch water with my bare hands: she's gone.

"Come with me," Mat demands. When I just stare, he amends his statement. "Please? With a cherry on top?"

I sigh. Fine. But only because I used to say that all the time as a kid—and he remembered. "Lead the way."

We squeeze through the crowd, and Mat stops in front of a large willow tree, whose low branches droop all the way to the ground. He jerks his head, indicating that I should follow, and then disappears behind the thick curtain of leaves.

This guy is entirely too arrogant, and part of me loathes to do *anything* he asks. But I have to admit, the other, bigger part is dying to know what he thought of the photo I texted.

I take a deep breath. Square my shoulders. And walk in after him.

. . .

The leaves scratch over my arms and scalp. And then we're in our own world. In the shade of the tree, the midday sun has been muted to the shadows you typically find in the early evening, and individual conversations blend into soothing background noise.

In reality, the food stands are probably only thirty feet away from us. But the drooping branches block their sight—if not their scents, if not their sounds—so it's easy to believe that we're the only two people around.

Without preamble, Mat thrusts his cell phone in my face. "What is the meaning of this?"

I don't have to look to know the screen displays the photo I sent last night.

"Have your powers of observation fled?" I ask calmly. "That's a picture of my green dress on the floor of my bedroom."

"I know what it is," he grounds out. "I just don't know why you would text *that* to me, right before bedtime. Did you want to wreck my entire night's sleep?"

I try not to smile. "Why would it wreck your sleep?"

"Because I laid awake all night, trying to figure out if you were punking me!"

"You said you wanted a photo." My pulse is pounding. I'm not sure where I'm getting the courage to have this conversation. But Bunny's always telling me to ride the wave of adrenaline, so I just go with it. "Would you rather have a photo of the necklace that goes with the dress? Or maybe my high-heeled shoes? A wrap for my shoulders?"

Mat snorts. "Is this your idea of flirting with me? Giving me a rundown of your clothes and accessories?"

"Um, yeah," I say, hoping I don't sound as ridiculous as I feel. "Is it working?"

He shoves a hand through his hair. "Bizarrely enough,

it kinda is."

I grin. Oh. Now I get the reason for his annoyance. For those dark circles under his eyes. It's not because he's disgusted after all. He is most definitely…something else.

It makes me feel bold. Bolder than I've ever been in my life. Maybe even as bold as my sisters.

I take a step. Just one tiny step, probably no more than a few inches. But it has the impact of making the rest of our already limited world fade away. The willow branches rustling gently. The smells of fish sauce and lime juice that sneak through the curtain of leaves. The hard, packed dirt beneath my thin-soled ballet flats.

The only thing I notice, the only thing that matters, is the boy in front of me.

"What are you doing?" he asks, a strange gurgle in his voice. His chest heaves up and down, but he doesn't back away.

"Getting closer to you." I mean the words to be snarky, a restatement of the obvious, but his Adam's apple rolls along his throat.

All of a sudden, I'm painfully aware that we're not touching. His fingers, hanging by his sides, are a few hands' width away. His face, flushed above mine, moves nearer the longer we stand there.

"Why?" he whispers.

A live wire stretches between us. From his hands to my hands. From his lips to my lips. I desperately want to close the distance between us. To see what sparks we could produce if skin pressed against skin.

But I can't.

I shake my head—hard. What am I doing? I can't get lost in these feelings. I can't, for a single moment, forget what I'm doing and why.

He made a *bet* that he could get me to fall for him. Which leaves me no choice but to do it first.

"I like being close to you." I opt for the direct approach. But instead of strategy, the confession feels uncomfortably like truth. "Do you?"

"Yes," he says immediately. "I like it, too."

Ha! I want to shout. *Take that.* "My plan's working." I fight to contain my glee. "You're falling for me."

"I'm *what*?"

"You want to kiss me. All I had to do was recite a laundry list of my clothes."

"Right," he says dryly. "Try that with anyone else and see how far it'll get you."

But I'm so giddy that the sarcasm falls right off me. I poke my finger into his chest. "I made my own bet with Kavya. And this means: I've won."

His eyes narrow. "You know, you give up your best advantage in a bet by telling the other person about it."

"But you told me about *yours*," I protest.

"That was to keep you guessing."

"That's what I'm doing," I retort. "Keeping you guessing."

He stares at me for a long moment. And then he bursts out laughing. Any other time, I would've assumed he was making fun of me. But now, I actually think he finds me entertaining.

"Oh, Winnie. I don't think you could keep *anybody* guessing. That's what I like most about you. Your emotions are spelled out across your face all the time."

"Oh yeah?" I ask, oddly defensive. "What am I feeling now?"

He grins. "You're feeling that you'd really like to sit with me."

He settles on the grass, near the base of the tree, and

pats the dirt next to him. I squint. Even if I wanted to join him, my outfit's not exactly appropriate.

Seeing my expression, he pats his lap. "This seat's open if you're worried about messing up your clothes."

"No, thank you." I lower myself to the ground, crossing my legs in front of me. That's about the only way you can sit in this narrow skirt.

"You didn't have any problem sitting on my lap the other day," he points out.

"I made a monetary bet with Kavya," I say loftily. "You've admitted you're attracted to me. It doesn't seem fair to use your attraction against you."

He lifts his brows. "Since when did fairness enter into the equation? Besides, do you really think you can get me to fall for you without touching me?"

I let out a breath, insulted. Pretty sure both my body *and* my mind are crush-worthy. And I'm going to prove it to him. "Oh, I can definitely make you fall. Just look what happened last night. You could barely sleep, and all I did was send you a photo of a dress."

He narrows his eyes. And then the moment shifts, as though a challenge has been issued—and accepted.

"I really like this outfit on you," he says, his voice rumbly. "This color looks nice with your hair. And your skin."

Ha. Does he really think I'm that naive? Surface-level compliments are the fakest form of flattery. I learned that in the first grade. Back then, I had no idea how to fit in with the other kids. No clue how to giggle and gossip and chase one another around the playground. The only "in" I had was through flattery. I like your socks! I like your stickers! I like your Band-Aid! (Which, in the first grade, is a bigger compliment than you might think.)

"Is that all you've got?" I toss my hair back. "I'm

immune to compliments. Especially the fake ones."

He smiles, and I can't help but notice his teeth—and his lips. "As I was saying, pink suits you. But do you know what I really like?" He lowers his voice. "Your skirt with the cat heads printed all over it. I believe you wore it several times this last month. I wouldn't mind if you wore it every day."

I freeze. Because no one, absolutely no one—other than me—likes that skirt. Even Kavya doesn't bother to pretend. I can't believe he noticed either the print *or* the number of times I donned it. Let alone both.

With an effort, I swallow. "Now I know you're making fun of me. You think the cat heads are ridiculous."

"I do," he admits. "Beyond the fact that it's printed with heads, which is just creepy, you're allergic to cats."

"Exactly. *These* are the only cats I'm not allergic to." I shake my head. "Honestly? You're terrible at this game. I might as well collect my winnings from Kavya now."

He leans back on his elbows. "The skirt may be ridiculous, but I like the way it looks on you. Sometimes, when you turn too quickly, it flares out, revealing a couple of extra inches of skin." He looks at me through lowered lids. "It's worth all the time I spend staring, just for that brief glimpse of your thighs."

I'm hot all over—my cheeks, my neck, my ears. Okay, so I've underestimated him. He's better at flirting than I thought. Doesn't mean I'll give up without a fight.

"I dreamed about you last night," I lie. I *have* dreamed about him. Just not last night. "In fact, I've been dreaming about you disturbingly often."

The smile on his face turns plastic, and a rush of triumph spurts through me. Gotcha.

"Each night, we're somewhere new. Walking in a lush, green forest. Next to a rushing river with boulders. Playing hide-and-seek in a golden field of cornstalks."

"Note to self: all of Winnie's fantasies could be movie sets. No wonder your mom keeps setting us up on these rom-com dates."

He probably intends his words to be biting, but the crack in his voice gives him away.

"The setting is different," I say evenly, "but we always end up doing the same thing."

"Sex?" he croaks.

"No! Jeez. Get your mind out of the gutter." I flush. Apparently, I can't be that racy, even when I'm pretending. "Kissing," I correct. "I have kiss dreams about you, Mat."

He clears his throat. "Tell me about them."

"Well." I lick my lips, my mind racing. Problem is, I don't have any real-life experience, and my imagination's just not that good. Kissing scenes in movies are always a little too intense, and half the time, I end up averting my gaze.

Oh gosh, maybe I really am a prude.

"I always wake up just as your lips touch mine," I admit.

"That's it?" His disappointment is a tangible thing, skipping across the small space and infecting me, too.

"Yeah."

"So it's just as frustrating as real life," he says.

I look at him. He looks at me. The wind rustles the willow branches around us.

My eyes drop, for an infinitesimal moment, to his lips, and then I wrench my gaze away. My heart pounds, and the air around us has turned hot and thick.

This is all pretend. Two bets we made with our respective friends. Any resulting feeling is a manufactured by-product. Nothing more.

"You asked me a question in the food court," he says, leaning against the tree, fiddling with the grass. I can't help but wonder how those same hands would feel gliding over my skin. "When I confessed that I made up my crush on Denise Riley, you asked me who I actually liked."

"I withdrew the question. Because it was none of my business."

"I was going to tell you. Before my mom left for Thailand. Before everything fell apart. I swore to myself that I would confess before we got to high school."

His eyes are dark, hypnotizing gems. "Confess what?"

"My crush," he whispers. "It was always you. The person I had a crush on was...you."

My thoughts scatter. What? How? Why? Back then, I never even thought about romance. And even if I did, it wouldn't have involved him.

"I wasn't interested in *you*," I blurt. "Not like that. I mean, you were my best friend. I didn't think of you that way."

"I know," he says quietly. "That's why it was so hard to work up the courage to tell you."

I blink. How do I process this? What do I feel? It's like my entire world's been flipped upside down, and I have to reimagine every event from the last four years. Because if he *did* have a crush on me, what does it mean that we stopped being friends?

I grab my temples. Oy tai, I'm so confused.

Wait a minute. Maybe this is exactly how he wants me to react. Confused, vulnerable, *susceptible*. Oh, he's good. But I'm better.

"You're very clever," I say lightly. "You almost had me fooled there. But trick me all you want, I will never, *ever* fall for you."

His mouth parts. A series of emotions flickers across his face, one as unreadable as the next. And then he snaps his jaw shut. "You got me. I was trying to trick you."

Somehow, I didn't expect him to agree so quickly. "So you didn't have a crush on me?"

"Of course not." He laughs hollowly. "You were the most awkward person on the planet. Still are. You had frizzy hair out to *here*." He holds out his hands, shoulder-width. "Why would I crush on you?"

My face burns. I've long since tamed my puffy hair—albeit mostly with ponytails—but those embarrassing middle school memories come rushing back. "Okay, then."

"Okay," he repeats. If I didn't know better, I'd think he sounded miserable.

All of a sudden, I can't be here any longer. Underneath this willow tree, separated from the world by a curtain of drooping branches. His body is too big, the space inside too small. I'm suffocating.

I spin on my heel and march away from the tree. I'm outta here.

But judging from the heavy thuds of his footsteps, he's coming with me.

Chapter Seventeen

I burst out of the tree, and the outside world appears, as though I've crossed through a brick wall from Diagon Alley back into real life.

A couple trades coupons for bright-yellow desserts made out of egg yolk and sugar, while a group of young men slurps rice noodles and beef broth. In one corner, a teenage girl teaches her Caucasian and African American friends how to jeeb and wong, two basic hand positions in Thai dance. Down the middle of the aisle, a young boy pushes his grandmother in a wheelchair. She must be at least ninety, but she is impeccably dressed, her midnight hair arranged in a stately bun, diamonds flashing at her ears, fingers, and neck.

The scent of food floods my nose once more. It had never faded, of course, but it was subsumed under the sunshine smell of Mat's skin mixed with the woodsy fragrance of his soap.

"Winnie, wait!" Mat catches up with me just as I'm about to enter the fray.

I turn—but he must've misjudged his steps. He bumps right into me, his arms automatically encircling my waist. One hot second later, we spring apart.

"We've had our date," I say, a whole lot steadier than I feel. "In *Always Be My Maybe*, they talk for five minutes, tops, in the farmer's market. We've already passed that time limit. What do you want?"

"I still have to fill out the notebook," he reminds me. "What should I say we talked about?"

I'd forgotten about that damn notebook. Once again, our actual topic of conversation isn't fit for recording.

Mat's eyes snag on a group of high school girls dressed in traditional Thai dance costumes, complete with long, curvy fingernails. "How come you're not dancing this year?" he asks. "You were so good at the last festival. And, uh, the festival before that."

I narrow my eyes. The flattery is clumsy, halting. Nowhere near his usual smoothness. "I wasn't aware you saw my performances," I say stiffly.

"Oh, sure. You're like a different person when you dance." His lips quirk. "Not clumsy at all. Why aren't you performing now?"

"I don't know," I say slowly. Maybe I should be offended by his backhanded compliment, but he's only stating the truth. I am clumsy. "I mean, my sisters didn't dance their senior year."

It was a matter of course that I wouldn't, either. End of analysis.

"Not remotely the same," he says. "They applied to… what? Ten, twelve colleges? You were accepted into Northwestern early decision. So you have a much lighter workload."

I shift my shoulders. I've always liked to dance, mostly

for the reason he identified. I don't feel quite so awkward when I'm wearing those gorgeous costumes. My limbs feel less unwieldy when they're following a predetermined set of movements. For the brief duration that I'm on a stage, I feel like what a good Thai girl should be—graceful and poised. Pretty much the opposite of what I usually am.

But when Mama assumed that I wouldn't be participating this year, I didn't argue. After all, Thai dance isn't going to help me become an economics professor. Who cares if it's fun?

"You don't have to do everything like your sisters."

"I know that," I say, annoyed.

He raises an eyebrow. "Do you? Because from where I'm standing, your life looks like a poor copy of theirs. Why are you so hell-bent on following in their footsteps anyway? You know you'll never measure up, right?"

My anger flares. It's one thing for me to admit my insecurities to myself, in the middle of the night. Quite another for him to say them out loud. "That's very rude."

He blinks. "I'm sorry. I'm not trying to be rude. I'm just thinking of that Einstein quote. A fish judged by its ability to climb a tree will always think it's stupid."

"Are you calling me a fish? Or stupid?"

"Neither." He swats at an invisible fly. "I'm just saying, maybe it's time to pursue your own path. Be your own person, instead of letting your family dictate all your decisions."

I'm shaking now, I'm so upset. But I don't know if it's because he's crossed a line—or because he has a point.

At any rate, the festival's too crowded, and my mind's too jumbled for me to figure out the meaning and purpose of my life. "Like I said, the date's over," I say coldly. "We're no longer under any obligation to speak to each other. So why are we?"

His eyes shutter, and a memory flashes across my mind. Four years ago, Mama was dropping me off at school and insisting that I wear a coat in sixty-degree weather. I snapped at her, annoyed—but then I looked up to see Mat watching us, a wistful expression on his face.

Maybe he missed his own mother. Maybe he wished that she were nagging him instead of across the world in Thailand.

I never found out how he felt because we had already stopped talking. But he's wearing the same expression now.

A pang shoots through me. Was I too harsh with him? How many times did he hurt my feelings, not because he's a terrible person…but because he misses his mom?

Fueled by a sudden clarity, I reach out and touch his sleeve. I want to take back my words. I want to get past our sniping. I want to be friends again.

Before I can say anything, he rips away his arm and takes off.

In spite of his height, in spite of the exceedingly striking way he fills out his phraratchatan, he's swallowed in the crowd within moments.

Chapter Eighteen

After a few confused seconds, I start walking, too, putting one foot in front of the other without any clear aim. I should probably find Kavya. She's never been to a Songkran festival, and I should make sure she's having fun.

But I don't see her tall, slim figure or that itty-bitty ponytail anywhere. How long has it been since we parted? How much time passed while I was under the willow tree with Mat?

Too long...and not long enough.

I'm jerked out of my thoughts by the line of people stretched across the aisle. Ah. The khanom krok table. The smell alone should've clued me in. Designed to be eaten while hot, the snack is made up of two round caps of fried rice flour placed on top of each other, with coconut pudding oozing out of the middle.

Any other year, I'd wait in lines two, three, four times as long. But even as my mouth waters, I can't bear the thought of standing still, not when my nerves are trying to escape from under my skin.

"Winnie! There you are." Mama swipes the sweaty bangs off her forehead. "Take over for me, will you, ouan?"

"Ouan" means "fat" in Thai. But it's an affectionate, rather than an offensive, nickname. According to traditional Thai folktales, demons were believed to steal newborn babies from their cribs, and unorthodox nicknames were a way of tricking them.

Without waiting for a response, Mama sinks onto a folding chair and presses an icy water bottle to her forehead. She opens the bottle, takes a swig, and then replaces it on her head, as though she can't decide whether her thirst or her warmth needs more attention.

I step behind the portable griddle and flip a hoi tod. The battered oyster pancake sizzles on the hot surface. The sumptuous flavor will pair perfectly with the crunch of bean sprouts and the heat of the sriracha.

"Has Kavya stopped by?" I ask as the scent of the fried egg pancake teases me. I can just imagine biting into a hot, silky, buttery oyster. "I want to make sure she tries my favorite."

Mama shakes her head fondly. "They're *all* your favorites. Hoi tod. Nam phrik kapi. Yum pla duk foo. I don't think I can name a Thai dish you don't like. You're my spice girl," she says, without an inkling of the nineties pop girl group. "Eating massaman curry when you were two years old."

"Ah. But if he wants to be my lover, then he has to get with my friends," I quip.

The water bottle slips through her fingers, crashing onto the grass.

Aw, crap. What was I thinking? This is Clueless Parent 101. Do *not* quote unfamiliar pop songs to your overprotective mother.

"*What* lover? Are you referring to Mat?" Her voice rises in a hysterical pitch.

I stifle a groan. "It's a song, Mama. I wasn't talking about Mat or anyone else."

I might as well have not spoken. "Winnie," she says sternly. "Are you pregnant?"

Steam rises from my ears, and it has nothing to do with the oysters I'm cooking. "Seriously?" I grumble. "Must you always skip fifty million steps? I haven't even kissed him yet."

The "yet" slips out accidentally. I shut my mouth so fast that I bite my tongue.

Yelping, I drop the spatula and hold a hand up to my mouth. My elbow bumps into a stack of paper plates, spilling them to the ground, and the pancakes start burning.

Holy macaroni. This is not my day.

Mama takes a new, clean spatula out of a shopping bag and nudges me aside. Expertly, she removes the pancake from the heat and pours more batter on the griddle.

"I'm a pediatrician," she says calmly, which just figures. So like Mama to sound the fire alarm, only to revert to the voice of reason. "I can recite to you the statistics surrounding teenage pregnancy. So you can't blame me for asking the question. I have another. Do you need any contraceptives?"

I grit my teeth. "Oy tai, Mama. *No.*"

"I'm just asking," she says, still composed, still serene. "It's always better to ask."

Before I can respond, Papa emerges from the crowd. He deposits two plastic bags of fresh bean sprouts on the table and pulls out a pan to start grilling them. "Good morning to two of the four loves of my life." Glancing around furtively, he leans over and kisses Mama on the cheek.

I blink. "Hey. I saw that."

Mama turns chili-pepper red. "Papa!" she says furiously. Once upon a time, they must've called each other by their nicknames. But for as long as I can remember, they've used the same name for each other as their daughters use. "What are you doing?"

I understand her outrage. PDA is particularly un-Thai. Uncommon for adults and unheard of for a good girl in her teens.

I don't think I've seen any of the aunties and uncles of the older generation kiss each other, ever. They tell the filthiest jokes at the dinner table. They stay up until six a.m. on New Year's Day singing karaoke. But the lips of one spouse never touch another's in public.

Papa adjusts his wire-rimmed bifocals. "I just read this article," he explains. "A person needs at least twelve hugs a day in order to thrive. With the twins gone, our daily allotment of hugs has dropped significantly. And I thought this would be a good way to up our supply."

"That was a kiss, not a hug," Mama retorts. She begins to plate the hoi tod and gestures for me to flip over the sign that states that the station is open for business once more.

"Your hands were busy," Papa says practically.

I try not to giggle. I love my parents, as exasperating as they are. "Hey, can I hug people, too?"

"No," they respond in unison.

"Do you want me to shrivel up and die?"

"Of course not. That came out wrong." Papa darts a look at Mama, as though asking her permission, and then returns his attention to me once again. "I've been giving this a lot of thought. And, well, my first instinct is to suggest that you *not* hug, since I'm your father. But I have to face reality, too. You're dating now, and so it's not out of the realm of possibility that you *might* kiss someone. Among, uh, other things." He winces. I wince even harder. "Winnie. We need to have a talk."

"A talk?" I repeat warily. "About what, exactly?"

The tops of his cheeks turn pink. "I've been reading all sorts of articles, preparing for this moment. I've never had to do this before, you know. Your school offers sex ed, and goodness knows, the twins never seemed to want my help. Besides, they didn't date in high school, so it was never an issue." He whips out his phone, scrolling through the screen. "Hold on just one second. I've created graphics."

My eyes widen. Holy moly. The twins may never have had this experience, but this is a first that I *don't* want to have.

"Ah, here it is," he says. "So you see, a male has a body part, called a penis, while a female possesses what is called a vagina—"

"Ahhh!" I cover my ears. "Make him stop. Mama, for all that is holy in this wat, please make him stop."

"Now, now, Papa." She ladles batter onto the grill. "Is this absolutely necessary?"

"Those words never have to come out of your mouth, ever," I clarify.

He puts down the phone. "But I made a PowerPoint presentation so that I could be sure I got the explanation right. Don't you want to see my slides?"

"Not with a single cell in my body."

He blinks. "Are you sure? There's this one diagram that's particularly enlightening—"

"Oh, I see Dr. Song," I say, spying Mat's dad across the aisle. "He loves hoi tod. I think I'll take him some." I whisk up a plate and stride away.

"You forgot the sriracha!" Mama calls after me.

But I don't turn around. Dr. Song is just going to have to enjoy his oysters without the chili because I can't risk one more moment in Papa's company.

Chapter Nineteen

"Dr. Song!" I call, flagging down Mat's dad.

If Mat is my sworn enemy, then his father is the opposite. I've known him my entire life—literally—since he was the obstetrician who delivered me. He's as close to me as a real uncle, and the only reason I call him "doctor" is because the title holds more reverence than "uncle."

"Orrawin," he says, my full name warm and affectionate on his lips.

There's a moment of awkwardness as I lower my head over the plates I'm carrying, in an attempt to wai him. If I were a true Thai girl, instead of the Americanized version, I'd know the proper etiquette. Do I put down the plates first before greeting him? Where? On the ground, as there's no nearby surface? Or do I hand him his plate and *then* wai him?

I don't know the answer because I'm just a bumbling Thai American, who doesn't belong fully to either world. And so the plates go up with my hands and kinda get smashed together as I pay my respects.

He smiles indulgently. "Hoi tod is my favorite. How did you know?"

"Because you were the one who taught me to eat it," I remind him.

I remember the moment as if it were yesterday. I was five years old and on the verge of a tantrum because I didn't have any champagne to toast, like the adults. Dr. Song swooped in, handing me a plate of hoi tod. He showed me exactly where to stab, to procure an entire oyster, and we held our seafood high in the air so that we could "chaiyo" like everyone else.

It was the first time anyone had treated me like a grown-up. His example set the bar for how I should act, rather than the way I wanted to act.

He gobbles down a bite now. "This dish always makes me wonder how Mat is my son. Refused to go near oysters ever since he was a kid, that one."

"One of his many faults," I say, forgetting that I'm speaking to his father. Oops.

But Dr. Song's not insulted. "You always did keep him on his toes."

We both pause to chew and swallow. I hand him a napkin, and he pats his lips and regards me quizzically. "So. How do you like dating my son?"

I almost spray out the final bits of mashed-up oyster. "Er, okay. I guess." My mind whirls. Does he read the composition notebook along with my parents? Maybe he thinks I'm a dating disaster. I wouldn't mind if he pulls Mat from the project—but will that make *my* parents consider me a failure? "I mean, it's going really well. I'm having such a wonderful time." Great. Now he'll think I'm in love. "The truth is—it's…" I let out an exasperated breath. "The truth is, I don't know what it is. What does Mat say?"

His eyes twinkle. "You know Mat—he doesn't say much. But last Saturday, I caught him trying on half a dozen shirts before going to the mall with you."

Wait, what? He changed his clothes before seeing me? Why?

I rack my brain, trying to even remember what he wore. Black jeans. A navy thermal shirt that hugged his solid chest. All in all, the outfit was pretty nondescript, even though he looked good. I mean, he always looks good.

I shake my head, but the muddled thoughts refuse to clear. "We're not dating for real. It's just a favor he's doing for Mama. You know that, right?" I peer at him. "Since you gave Mat permission to trek across Asia? Another day for his trip for every day he fake-dated me."

Dr. Song chews thoughtfully. "That's right. As much as I'd like to, I can't just hand over the funds for that trip, you know. Gotta make him work for it, even though we're all each other's got."

I blink. "What do you mean, you're all each other's got? What about Auntie Nit? I know she's in Thailand, taking care of her dying mother. But you still *have* her. I video call my sisters once a week. Don't you do the same?"

Seconds pass, and the silence turns the ordinary conversation into something extraordinary.

I shift my weight. Now that I think about it, Auntie Nit's been gone an awfully long time. Four years. The same duration that Mat and I haven't been friends. Isn't that a hefty amount of time for a person to be dying?

"Shouldn't Mat's a-ma be dead by now?" I blurt. Oh, pra Buddha cho, forgive me. That was disrespectful. "I'm so sorry," I gasp. "I didn't mean—"

He places a hand on my shoulder, stopping me. "It's okay."

But shame is a many-clawed crustacean crawling up my throat. The last thing I want is to hurt this kind man's feelings. I've more than fumbled the etiquette; I've damn near obliterated it.

"I've always liked that about you," he continues. "The way you speak your mind. Saying the things other people are too scared to put out there."

"That's not being brave," I say miserably. "That's called having no filter."

He shakes his head, as though I've insulted someone dear to him rather than myself. "One of these days, I hope you'll recognize your true worth. I see your value quite clearly. And it appears my son does as well."

He gestures over my shoulder. I startle. Ten feet away, Mat is chatting with Kavya. I had no idea they were standing there. As I watch, Mat glances up and frowns. He's probably wondering why his father is fraternizing with the enemy.

What he doesn't understand is that there are no lines in this sand. Our conflict has always been between the two of us. Not our friends, not my sisters. Never our parents.

"I don't know that Mat recognizes very much," I say, smiling to take the sting out of my words. "But I've gotten the impression lately that he misses his mother. When is she—is she?—coming back?"

"It seems that Mat is truly my son after all," Dr. Song says gently. He gathers both of our plates and tosses them in a nearby trash can. "Turns out, we're both liars."

With that odd statement, he turns and walks away, leaving me to stare after him.

Chapter Twenty

I'm still puzzling over Dr. Song's words when Mat and Kavya approach. He said they were both liars. What does that mean? What were they lying about?

"Why were you talking to my dad?" Mat asks.

"None of your business," I say automatically.

"Of course it's my business," he says. "He's my dad."

"And it's my conversation."

"Were you talking about me?"

I roll my eyes, falling back into our usual pattern. Why do I do this? Why is it easier to be snarky, rather than risk being honest?

Maybe I'm as much of a coward as Mat says I am.

"Yes, Mat. Because the entire world revolves around you. I haven't seen your dad in months, but instead of asking about his welfare, I decided to pump him for super top secret info about you."

Kavya winks at me. "Oh. I can get any info from Mat you want. He's child's play to crack." Her short black bob bounces along with her feet.

"She's pretty devious," Mat says grudgingly. "You know, she scored an invite to Jessica Tananunkul's wedding reception tonight? Jess didn't even invite *us*, and we've known her all our lives."

Wow. Jess is a decade older than us, but we've been in the same community as long as I can remember. When she got engaged, she announced that she would marry in a small, intimate affair. One that apparently includes vivacious strangers she meets at Songkran festivals.

"I can't wait!" Kavya twirls in a circle.

Mat grins. How can I blame him? My best friend certainly follows her own path. She doesn't linger in *anyone's* shadow, no matter how large.

"There's going to be a live band," she continues. "And dancing. The groom danced ballroom competitively in college, so he's going to give a lesson during the reception."

And then the implication of my best friend's spontaneity sinks in. "You were supposed to come with me to Taran's party." I fight to keep the panic from my voice.

"Oh." She wrinkles her nose. "You don't really need me, do you? Practically our whole class will be there."

She has a point. But I'm not like her *or* my sisters. I can't waltz into a party by myself. Those moments before I find someone to talk to are excruciating.

"I know. Mat can take you." Kavya turns to him. "You're going to Taran's party, right? Can you give Winnie a ride?"

He startles. Our eyes meet, and for a moment, he looks like he might agree. But then he stiffens, like her words are a raw mango with a sour aftertaste. "What do I get in return?"

"Forget it," I say coolly. "I'm perfectly capable of getting myself to the party."

Any further discussion is interrupted by a familiar

Thai folk song piped through the loudspeakers. All around us, the people who were wandering the food stands pair up and organize themselves into a large circle. As if pre-orchestrated, they begin to dance, old and young, their hand movements and footwork more or less synchronized.

Kavya's eyes widen. "Holy crap. It's a flash mob."

Mat grins. "Hardly. It's the ramwong—a circle dance performed at festivals and parties. We all learned it as kids. They'll definitely perform this ritual at the wedding tonight."

"Gotcha." My best friend nods. "It's like the stick dance we do at Indian weddings."

"Exactly. We might as well teach you now so that you'll be prepared." He looks at me, his eyes a little hesitant and a lot vulnerable. "Should we show her?"

I swallow hard. The partners never touch in the ramwong, but the dance is extremely flirty. If I pair up with him, I'll have to look over my shoulder and into his eyes every fourth beat.

I'm just not ready for that level of intimacy. Not when my brain is stuck in the spin cycle. Not when I have no idea how I feel, much less what he's thinking.

"You don't need me to demonstrate," I mumble. "Go ahead. Partner with Kavya. She'll pick it up immediately. I have to go."

I trip away. They stare after me, probably confused by my sudden departure. But my only thought is to leave them, to leave the awkwardness of the situation.

Instead, I run directly into Taran.

• • •

"*H*ey there." Taran's smile is bright and immediate, making me feel like I'm the center of his universe — even though I'm pretty sure I didn't enter his mind until I almost knocked him over. "Afraid the ramwong will start without you?"

"Afraid you'll find another partner before I could grab you." Um, wow. Did those words really come out of my mouth? I'm never this brave. Never this flirty. But my thoughts aren't with him but with the boy from whom I just walked away.

A dimple peeks out of his cheek. "You're the only partner I'd ever want."

Smooth words. Maybe too smooth. But his manner is light, easy. After the morning I just had, I could go with pleasant right about now.

We assume the position, his front to my back, his arms outstretched around my body. We begin to dance, falling into step with the line that circles around the food stands and proceeds inside the wat for the official dance performances.

I look over one shoulder, catch his eye, and smile prettily. Four beats later, I look over my other shoulder, finding his gaze once more.

I have never, ever danced the ramwong with a cute boy before. Usually, I pair up with Papa or one of my sisters. There's even a long-ago photo of five-year-old Winnie and Mat dancing together. Our mothers swore that they would display the photo at our wedding someday.

Of course, that was before we grew up. Before our hormones had our parents shaking in their pha thung chang kben that wraps around the lower body. Before romance became a danger, rather than an aspiration and a dream.

"That's it," I blurt as I meet Taran's eyes for one

electrifying moment.

"What is?" To his credit, he doesn't even blink at the fact that I'm picking up a conversation I'm having inside my own head.

"Why my mother is the way she is," I explain. "She went from not allowing my sisters to date to expecting them to be engaged in the span of six months. It's because she wishes she could fast-forward through that part of our lives. The hurt, the angst. She'd like nothing better than for us to get to happily-ever-after without enduring the heartache."

"Sounds like a caring mother to me," he remarks.

"Yeah," I say quietly. "She is."

Mama didn't institute her practice-dating scheme because she's irrational. She's not a caricature of a controlling Asian mom. Rather, she only wants to protect me.

All of this flashes through my mind in the span of four beats. And when I turn my head, supposedly to meet Taran's eyes, I glance past him. I sweep my gaze over the next five couples, and when my eyes meet Mat's, I don't think either of us is surprised.

The look we exchange is so intense that it makes me stumble.

Our eyes hold for half a beat, and then I'm turning once more.

And yet...and yet...I don't think I'll ever forget that look for as long as I live.

*A*fter that one glance, however, I lose track of Mat. The ramwong turns a corner, and the next time I glance over my left shoulder, he's not where he's supposed to be. A few beats later, Taran and I enter the wat and proceed to a hall where a raised platform has been erected.

"Now, let's see how the real professionals do it." Taran smiles sweetly as girls with tall chadas and long fingernails take the stage.

Each girl wears a lavender blouse and sinh, a printed tube skirt. Ornate gold jewelry circle their biceps, and necklaces cross their torsos like armor.

I try to curve my lips. I *should* smile. Taran's being cute and funny—but his remark reveals that he doesn't know me at all. He doesn't understand that I should be up there, too. That I *would* be up there, if it weren't for my unquestioning obedience to Mama's opinion.

Of course, it's not Taran's fault that he just moved to town. I haven't given him the chance to get to know me. So I just nod, and we both turn to watch the performance.

The beautiful fabrics rustle and the gold fingernails flash as the dancers execute their intricate movements. My mind is so cluttered, however, that it's hard to pay attention.

Taran touches my arm. Maybe he's taking advantage of the dark, but I'm surprised at his boldness. Our parents are not only present, but there are spies everywhere, in the form of their friends.

I turn and look into his dark eyes. His smile holds a secret that only the two of us share. "Are you coming to my party tonight?"

"I bought a dress," I confess. "The first new outfit I've had in ages."

He lifts his brows. "Deets?"

"Green. Silky. Swishy."

"Stunning," he says gravely.

"What, the color?"

"All of it." Heat passes through his eyes. "Especially the person wearing the dress."

My lips wobble. There's got to be an appropriate response to his blatant flirtation. I just don't know what it is. Maybe Mama is on to something with this practice dating. These skills sure as hell don't come naturally. At least not to me.

We continue to watch the dancers. He doesn't touch me again, but I can feel the warmth of his presence against my bare skin. When the performance ends, he turns me to face him and lifts a hand to graze my ever-present ponytail. "Wear your hair down tonight."

He beams—always handsome, ever angelic—and then strides away. Good thing, too. My parents might tell me what to do, but I don't appreciate being ordered around by anybody else—not even cute and flirty boys.

Tamping down on my annoyance, I wander back outside the wat. But my irritation flares once more when I notice that some of the food stands have already packed up—including the khanom krok station.

Chib-peng. I can't believe I missed my favorite dessert. Who knows when I'll have the chance to eat it again? That winding line was long for a reason: because that crisp and melty goodness was worth the wait.

"Hey." Kavya materializes beside me and throws her arms around me. "You're my best friend on the planet, you know that?"

I hug her back. "I take it you enjoyed your first Songkran festival?"

"*Love*. Pretty sure I'm coming back every year." She shoves a paper-wrapped package at me. "A present for you. Well, it's from Mat, not me. He was afraid that you didn't have the chance to pick it up."

My hands shaking, I unwrap the package to reveal four perfect half-spheres of fried rice flour placed against one another, coconut pudding spilling from the sides.

Khanom krok.

Chapter Twenty-One

Hurry, hurry. I urge the Prius forward. I was able to wheedle the car from Papa, after much begging, but it's not doing me a whole lot of good in this Saturday afternoon traffic. Where did all of these cars come from anyway? What could these people possibly have to do? I need to get to the mall *now*, before someone else snatches up my prize.

Unlikely. But you never know.

I pull up to the final traffic light before the shopping mall. What Mat did—procuring my favorite dessert—just isn't fair. We placed bets that we could get each other to fall and agreed that physical affection was off-limits. Emotional manipulation should be as well.

Argh. I jerk the steering wheel, and it's a good thing the car's not moving. Mat's a good-looking guy. I admit it. Doesn't mean I *liiiike* him. Doesn't mean I want to date him for real.

Which makes the khanom krok even more inexplicable.

I turn into the parking lot and wonder, not for the first

time: did our friendship break apart so that we could come back together in a new and different way?

That's precisely what I intend to find out.

After way too long in the lot, I finally find a parking space and rush, huffing and puffing, to a store in an isolated wing of the mall.

"Oh!" the salesperson behind the cash register exclaims. "It's you."

"You remember me?" I glance around, certain it's because they don't have many customers. And yet, several moms and daughters are surveying the new arrivals along the wall, and a group of teenagers is pawing through a pile of T-shirts. The place actually seems quite bustling for having such a terrible selection of clothes.

But I can hardly fault their taste when I'm a returning customer, too.

"Sure," the salesperson says. Her name tag says "Anita," and in spite of her blond dreads and light-blue eyes, she reminds me of Kavya. "You were here last week, trying on our ugly sweater collection with your boyfriend. Whew." She fans herself. "If he were a few years older, I'd totally go for a hottie like him."

"Arghuym." The sound that exits my throat is barely human. Not even close to English.

"Don't worry," she continues, misinterpreting my reaction. "I wouldn't make a play for him, even if I did see him again."

Even nonsensical noises escape me now. Instead, I look around wildly—and suck in a breath. Because it's not here. The item I was after. The hideous yellow sweater with the strategically placed loops.

"Oh no," I whisper. "Don't tell me someone bought it."

"What?" The silver ball piercing in her brow twitches.

"You mean the green dress you tried on? Sure was a stunner. Didn't you already buy it?"

"I did. I meant the yellow sweater."

"The yellow sweater," she echoes. "The one with the picnic baskets. And the unfortunate ribbons?"

Her voice gets higher and more pitchy with each sentence. I'm not sure what's happening here, but I nod.

She lets out a whoop. "I won! Lindsey, get out here," she calls into the storage area. "And *bring the yellow sweater.*"

A girl, whom I assume is Lindsey, comes out, carrying an armful of loosely stitched yellow yarn. I wince. The sweater's even more hideous than I remember.

"Please tell me this isn't a false alarm," Lindsey says.

Anita gestures impatiently. "Quick, ring her up before she changes her mind."

Lindsey heads to the cash register, her movements quick and economical. "May I ask?" She pauses, as if searching for the least offensive wording. "Why on God's green earth would you buy this?"

I blink. I mean, *they* stocked the sweater. "There's this boy…" I begin.

"Always a good start," Lindsey says enthusiastically.

"If it's the same delicious guy who came in with her last week, sign me up," Anita chimes in.

I let out a slow breath, trying to understand my own intentions. "Long story short, I bought the green dress to impress someone else. But now, I don't know if he's the right guy after all."

Anita shrieks, clutching her heart. "So you're buying the sweater to show the first guy that it was him all along? Oh, that's so sweet. It must be the l-word."

I blanch. No, not love. But definitely not loathe, either. Maybe something in the middle.

"That will be $55.13," Lindsey says to me.

"Wha-at?" My mouth drops. "For this monstrosity? I thought we just agreed that it's the ugliest sweater on the planet."

"It is." Anita smirks. "But we don't set the prices. Corporate does. No idea what they were thinking, but we placed bets whether anyone would actually buy one. I can't believe I won."

"It was kinda a joke," Lindsey adds. "I mean, what kind of fool would plunk down fifty bucks for *that*?"

Me, I guess. I'll raise my hand. I'm the fool.

But it remains to be seen exactly how foolish I turn out to be.

Chapter Twenty-Two

Walking into Taran's house is like walking into a wall of noise. Chatter roars around me, a dozen decibels higher than is comfortable. Rock music blares in the background, which makes people yell even louder.

Even the smell is loud. Human sweat, tinged with sweetness. The origin of the first is obvious. And the scent of berry-fruit syrup? Must be from the reddish liquid that everyone's carrying around in purple plastic tumblers.

Taran's parents, if they were ever here, are nowhere to be seen. They probably escaped as quickly as my parents did after they dropped me off.

I move farther into the party. The girls wear cute dresses with heels or tight jeans with tank tops. Nobody, absolutely nobody, has on a sweater—and certainly not one as ugly as mine.

And yet, conversation doesn't come to a screeching halt like I feared. At most, a few eyes skim my offensive attire and then turn away, dismissing me. I guess I'm not that important. Which suits me just fine. As Mat is so fond of pointing out, I much prefer creeping along in someone else's shadow.

Now what? my mind screams as I stand alone. Desperately, I recall the advice from the video call with my sisters.

"Get something to drink," Bunny instructed, her eye makeup dark and dramatic. "Doesn't have to be alcohol. A drink will give you something to do with your hands."

"Make sure it comes from a closed container," Ari added, her features softer but just as lovely. "Drink straight from the can so no one can slip any drugs inside."

Squaring my shoulders, I make a beeline for the kitchen island, cluttered with cans of pop and an enormous punch bowl.

I pick up a Coke Zero, my feet bumping into a couple of empty glass bottles under the island. A girl from my trig class smiles at me, her eyebrows arched curiously.

"Winnie! You look so cute." Is it just me, or was there a nearly imperceptible pause in Anjelah's compliment? "What's the occasion?"

"Oh, the sweater's an inside joke," I say weakly.

"Ah. Say no more." She gives a sage nod. "Whoever they are, I hope they're worth it."

Again. Like the salesperson, Anjelah's assuming there's a romantic motive behind my sweater. And that's only maybe—hopefully?—true.

"Nice bows," a male voice says in my ear. It's Steve from history. We've never actually spoken, but he leers at my chest now. How will he feel, come Monday, when we have to sit next to each other in class? Or will he not even remember that he ogled me, since he hasn't bothered to look at my face?

He stretches out a hand, as if to untie a bow, and I slip

nimbly out of his reach.

I walk through the party, searching for a friend—or at least a friendly face. My smile is beginning to feel like one of the wobbly Jell-O shots some guys are downing in the corner.

This is awful. No doubt Kavya's having a better time than I am at a wedding with people she doesn't even know.

And then I see him.

Mat, magnetic and compelling in a simple black T-shirt and jeans. Playing Flip Cup with a bunch of his friends. He performs a successful maneuver, and the group around him erupts into cheers. A guy pounds him on the back, and Delilah Martin kisses him on the cheek.

I freeze. The movement is easy and casual, as though she kisses him all the time. And maybe she does. As far as I know, they never dated after homecoming. But maybe they got together recently. Or maybe they don't need to date in order to do…whatever it is they do together.

Cheeks burning, I walk swiftly out of the room before he sees me *or* my ridiculous sweater. I don't know what I was trying to prove. Not only is this top ugly as sin, but its heavy stitches are freaking hot. Shoulda worn the green dress. Maybe I'd still blend into the foliage—Taran's parents have potted kaffir lime plants just like mine—but at least I wouldn't be sweating.

I retreat to a staircase at the back of the kitchen and sit on the darkened steps. The air is cooler here, but more importantly, I'm alone. I yank the sweater over my head, grateful that I'm wearing a black camisole underneath, and lower my flushed face to my knees. My parents are having dinner with their friends. How soon can I interrupt their evening to ask them to pick me up?

I don't know how long I sit there, but eventually, I hear

heavy footsteps on the stairs above me. I scoot to the edge of the step, hoping the person will sail right past. Instead, they sit next to me. Startled, I look up.

It's Taran.

"What are you doing here?" I blurt. "It's your party. Shouldn't you be in the center of it?"

He tilts a purple cup into his mouth. "It's terrifying out there," he admits. His hair is neatly combed, his eyes glazed—but that only contributes to his vulnerability.

"I don't know anyone, outside of the million people who introduced themselves to me last week," he continues. "I'm terrible at faces. Worse with names. I've already insulted three girls because I didn't remember who they were. So I thought I'd take a break before I make anyone else mad."

My cheeks soften. I may not always feel like I belong, but I've been going to school with these people for years. I can't imagine starting over a few months before graduation. "You're doing great. Everyone is already enamored by you—by your charm, by your smile. You have nothing to worry about."

He tilts back his drink again, the ice cubes rattling against the plastic. And then he grins at me. "Thanks for the vote of confidence, Winnie. It means a lot."

"So you remember *my* name?" I tease.

"You're impossible to forget."

"Because I poured jalapeño vinegar on my shirt?"

He bumps my shoulder. "Because you look really good *without* a shirt. Er, sweater. Er, what the hell is this thing?"

He frowns at the Franken-yarn on my lap. Even balled up, the sweater is monstrous.

"I thought you were going to wear a green dress," he continues. "One that's tiny and silky and looks like lingerie."

"I didn't describe it like *that*," I choke out.

"No," he agrees. "But that's how I imagined it. Doesn't matter. I like this little thing, too." He turns his attention to the thin straps of my cami. "You could rock anything you decide to wear."

He slips his hand around my neck, warm and enticing, and leans forward so that our lips are inches apart. Goose bumps pop up along my skin. Is he going to kiss me? Holy macaroni. This is just like my dream. I'm about to have the first kiss of my life.

Even if it's not with Mat. A small, secret part of me wanted my first kiss to be with him. But he's busy playing Flip Cup with Delilah, and for all I know, my former enemy loathes me as much as ever. Mat Songsomboon has wrecked a lot in my life, and I'm not about to let him destroy my chances with this perfectly cute guy, too.

Taran moves even closer, and I wonder if I should ask him to slow down, so that I can take better mental notes. My sisters are going to want every detail.

Let's see. One hand cradles my neck, while the other one is splayed on my hip. *My* hands are still hanging by my sides. Should I leave them where they are? Or put them on his body?

He licks his lips, as though he knows *exactly* what he's about to do with them. I shiver, and his breath wafts across my bare skin, hot and…alcoholic? Huh?

I jerk up my head, narrowly missing his chin. All of a sudden, I remember the empty bottles underneath the island. *Not just any old bottles*, I realize now. Containers of hard liquor, whose contents were probably poured into the punch bowl.

"The punch," I say. "I think it's been spiked. How many cups have you had?"

He scrunches his forehead. "Not sure. Maybe five, six

cups? Thirsty tonight."

For the first time, I notice his words are a little slurred. I can't believe I didn't pick up on it sooner.

"You're drunk." I'm not such a prude that I don't know that teenagers sometimes drink alcohol at parties. Especially when there's a big punch bowl, just inviting people to add their own contributions. I've even had champagne with my parents once, during Chinese New Year.

I'm not judging him, but I can't help the disappointment that flows through me. I want my first kiss to be genuine—and that means I'd like it to be with someone who hasn't had too much to drink.

"I'm only a little buzzed," he assures me. "Just enough to lower my inhibitions so that I can approach pretty girls who would otherwise intimidate me."

He begins to lower his lips again, but then he stops. "I thought I asked you to wear your hair down."

"I like ponytails." The dangerous tone in my voice doesn't seem to penetrate his haze.

"You have such beautiful hair," he says. "I want to run my hands through it when I kiss you."

Without warning, he threads his fingers through the loop of my ponytail holder and pulls it out.

I leap to my feet, outraged. "What the hell? You have no right to do that."

"Oh, sorry." He blinks, the black elastic dangling from his hands. "Did I hurt you?"

No more than a vigorous brushing—and I'm used to that. It's how I attack my thick, wavy hair every day. "That's not the point. You have no right to interfere with my hairstyle. With my *body*."

He frowns. "But in the movies—"

"The movies are wrong!" Too late, I realize I'm yelling.

Rapid footsteps thunder toward us, and someone pokes his head through the open door into the stairwell. He takes one look at my arms crossed defensively across my chest, and he tightens his hands into fists.

"What is going on here?" Mat growls. "If you laid one unwanted finger on her, I'll kill you."

Chapter Twenty-Three

"Relax, dude. It was just a misunderstanding." Taran holds up his hands in the universal gesture of peace. Too bad he's still holding my hair tie.

"That's mine," I snap. "Give it back."

"Take it." He pushes himself off the step and flicks the black elastic at me. I catch it and gather up my hair in a sloppy ponytail. The jumbled mess is a far cry from the sleek 'do I achieved earlier — but at least the new hairstyle reflects the chaos roiling my insides.

Taran looks from me to Mat and then back again. "I was leaving anyway. I was supposed to meet Julie Kwa in one of the bedrooms. She was quite eager to…get to know me. But I got sidetracked when I saw you sitting here, looking so dejected."

I thought my anger had peaked, but there it goes, soaring to new heights. "You were on your way to see another girl, but you made a move on me?"

Mat shoves forward so that he's blocking Taran's path. "You made a move on her?" he repeats, his voice low and threatening.

"I wasn't successful, so does it really matter?" Taran neatly steps around Mat. "Now, if you'll excuse me. I have to go." He turns, seeking out my eyes in the darkened alcove. "I really am sorry, Winnie."

He ducks through the doorway, leaving Mat and me together. And alone.

"I didn't need your help," I say stiffly. "I had the situation handled."

Mat raises his brow. "I'm sure you did. But you don't really think I would hear your voice raised in panic—and not do anything? Not many people could ignore a cry of distress. Least of all me with least of all you."

I slump, the tension flowing from my shoulders. I didn't realize until now how tightly I've been holding them. "You're right. I'm sorry. I'm just taking out my anger on you. Thanks for coming to my rescue, even if I didn't need to be rescued."

"You're welcome," he says, his lips twitching. "Thanks for validating my decision, even though you don't want me here."

"We're good at that, aren't we? Willfully misunderstanding each other?"

He looks directly at me. His expression is so steady, his eyes so clear, that I know he hasn't been drinking from the punch bowl. "I don't want to be," he says quietly. "I don't want us to misunderstand each other anymore."

The statement is so big, so packed full of meaning. And yet, it's also incredibly vague. I don't know what he means. Is he as sick of our game play as I am? Does he want to clear the air so that we can go back to being friends…or something more? Or is this just another strategic move to get me to fall for him?

My head officially hurts.

"Do you want to go outside?" I ask.

He draws back, surprised. I'm just as taken aback by my words. This is about the first conversation we've had that hasn't been loaded with insults or hidden meaning. It's just me, issuing an invitation. Not because I have an ulterior motive. But because I want to.

"Sure," he says.

A single word, a simple answer. I like that, too.

He holds open the back door for me, and I walk into the night. The cool air wraps around me, fresh and inviting after the stifling heat. We cross the wooden porch and descend the stairs.

Mat inclines his head, as though asking if I'm willing to risk another set of steps, with another boy.

I am. At least with *this* boy.

My pulse in my throat, I sit. He arranges himself a few steps below mine so that my head towers over him and his shoulders are by my knees.

I don't know if he's putting distance between us on purpose, but I appreciate it. After the interaction with Taran, I need space, and Mat's given that to me, without my even asking.

When we were younger, he had an uncanny knack for anticipating my wants and needs. I guess I shouldn't be surprised that he still has this same ability.

A sudden gust of wind has me shivering, and I shake out my sweater and put it on.

When my head emerges from the scratchy yarn, he sucks in a breath. "You're wearing the sweater. You didn't buy it that day at the mall. Did you go back?"

"This afternoon, after you gave me the khanom krok," I admit, suddenly shy. Am I revealing too much? It's just a sweater. How can such a badly stitched pile of eyesore make me feel so bare?

I lick my lips. "You remembered my favorite dessert. And it seemed to bother you that I bought the dress with Taran in mind. I, uh, no longer felt right wearing it, after you were so nice to me. So I went back and got the sweater."

His eyes widen. "Don't tell me you returned the green dress."

"Um, no. You'd have to rip that dress out of my cold, dead hands."

"Good," he says roughly. "Because that dress belongs with you. Although I'm glad that Taran doesn't get to see it tonight. I hope he *never* sees it."

A thrill shoots through me, but I opt for the safe response. "Thank you for the khanom krok."

"Thanks for the sweater." His lips quirk. "Although, if this big, bulky thing is part of your arsenal, your seduction routine could use some work."

I narrow my eyes. "Oh, really? For your information, big, bulky sweaters are *plenty* sexy. They leave something to the imagination. They're begging to be taken off."

"My bad." Mat's eyes glow, as bright as the stars in the night sky. "Prove me wrong, Winnie. I need to be put in my place."

"Ha. You wish."

Our gazes meet briefly, and then we both look away.

I don't know how to respond to this Mat. The one who's just as witty as my former enemy—except it's not at my expense. The one who teases me, same as always—but because he seems to like me rather than scorn me.

Because I can't chance another collision with his gaze, I look up. I was both right and wrong. Mat's eyes do shine, but they can't compete with *these* stars, which twinkle like diamonds against a jeweler's black cloth. I draw in a long, icy breath, and it feels like I'm swallowing the stars themselves.

My senses flood with this moment. The music pulsing at our backs. The splintered wood under my jeans. The scent of pine mixed with booze. And last, but not least, those brilliant, burning stars. Dazzling me with their beauty. Showing me that the world is bigger than my thoughts, my problems.

In their starkness, I find the courage to voice the words that have been locked inside my brain, rattling against its bars, since this afternoon.

"Mat, have you been lying to me?"

He leans back on his elbows, as though to get a better view of the sky. But I can tell he's just stalling. "What do you mean?"

"This afternoon, when your dad and I talked," I say haltingly. "He said you were both liars. I kinda thought, well…it seemed to be about your mom."

Mat studies his shoes, although I'm not sure how much of his black laces he can distinguish from the night. He doesn't turn his head, doesn't meet my eyes. Maybe this seating arrangement benefits him more than just giving me space.

"It's complicated." He picks at the soles of his sneakers. "So many years have passed since she left. My dad has long since told his friends the truth. He was surprised that I had never cleared the air with you."

"You didn't have much opportunity." I don't know why I'm defending him, but every minute we spend under these stars brings him closer to the boy he used to be. The boy my heart wants to protect. "Every time we were together, we were sniping at each other."

"Four years." He yanks at a piece of rubber that's become detached from his shoe. "I probably could've found an opening during that time. I'm sorry I didn't."

"Hey." I put my hand on his shoulder. It's the first time we've touched since our *Pretty Woman* date. "I'm fairly sure we're *both* responsible for being at odds."

He looks at my hand for so long that I begin to question. I begin to doubt. I start to pull my fingers away, but he reaches up and catches them with his own.

His bare skin is a jolt to my system. I've held hands with guys before. There have been stolen dances at homecoming (where I of course attended stag). Harmless flirtations at parties. But the connection has never felt quite this warm. I feel like he's touching not just my hand but also my heart.

I slide down a step. I'm still sitting above him, but our heads are now more or less level. Our eyes—and our lips—line up.

He swallows, his thumb moving in light circles against my skin. "There's no easy way to say this, so I'll just stick with the facts," he says. "Fact: my mother didn't go to Thailand to take care of her sick mother. Fact: my a-ma is pushing ninety, but she still walks in the garden every morning. Fact: my mother abandoned us. She met a man online and moved to Oklahoma to live with him and his kids. Fact: the divorce became final last year. Fact: I haven't spoken to her since my birthday ten months ago."

My mouth drops. "Oh, Mat. I'm sorry." The words are hopelessly inadequate, but I don't know how else to offer comfort. "Why didn't you tell me from the beginning?"

"My dad asked me to lie. At the time, he was hurting so much. We were both reeling, and he just couldn't deal with the dishonor on top of everything else." His eyes tilt down. "You know as well as I do what a big scandal the truth would've been in our community. It was much easier to say she went home to take care of her mother, since it's a common enough scenario."

He stops talking. His thumb ceases to move. I count ten whole heartbeats before he speaks again.

"I can understand why Dad wanted to hide the truth. But I don't think he understood what he was asking of me at that moment. What it cost me to lie. What I lost."

"You were a kid," I protest. "You did what your father asked. Your sins, as it were, are plenty forgivable."

He fixes his eyes on our hands. "But I did much more than just lie. I also pushed you away."

I blink. And blink again. I then pull my fingers out of his grasp. Not because I'm angry, but because I need to think, and I can't do that while he's touching me. "Are you saying that this is the reason our friendship ended?"

He nods miserably. "I didn't plan it. If I had known our friendship would fall apart, I would never have agreed to lie. But I didn't know that being around you would be so damn hard. Every day, at lunch, you would chatter about how much you missed my mom's cooking. How she would be back before I knew it. When I finally stormed off, you followed me and apologized. You said you should've known that talking about her would make me miss her more. And I couldn't look you in the eyes any longer. I just couldn't."

He takes a shaky breath. "I only wanted some distance. I didn't mean for our break to be permanent. I thought maybe we'd go our separate ways for a couple of weeks. But you were so angry. So hurt. Our resentment of each other spiraled out of control, and I didn't know how to stop it."

I stare. Part of me feels so much for the little boy who lost his mother. That part wants to wrap him up tightly and hold him close, so that he can never be hurt again.

But I can't forget the tears I cried. The countless nights I didn't sleep. The loss of his friendship was the single most devastating event of my childhood. And he could've prevented it all with a few honest words.

"You didn't know how to stop it," I repeat. My voice is so brittle that it might shatter. "Oh, I don't know. Maybe *I'm sorry* would've done the trick. Or *let's be friends again.* Or even: *scoot over, that's my seat.*"

"I did try," he says. "After a few months, I was desperate to make things right. I had a speech all prepared, but when I came up to you, I panicked. Instead of apologizing, I pointed out the hole in your pants. Which was nothing out of the ordinary, because you *always* had a hole at your knees, from all that running and tripping you did. But you got really mad, and everything else I said just made it worse. We fell into this awful pattern, and, well…you know the rest of it."

I scrutinize his straight eyebrows, the unfairly long lashes, and struggle to recalibrate the past. "Wasn't it obvious that I wanted our friendship back?"

"Not to me. I was convinced you hated me. Anything I could say or do seemed too little, too late. Childhood friendships always end, they say. I guess that's what I thought happened. We grew up and grew apart."

He looks up, his eyes as black and fathomless as deep lake water. "I assumed you had abandoned me, too. Maybe that was the wrong conclusion, but after my mom left, it was hard for me to trust anybody. So I didn't look too far beneath the surface. You told me, with every word and every action, that you didn't want to be my friend anymore, and I believed you."

"You underestimated both me and your mom," I say

quietly. "She loved you. I saw it in every lunch she packed, every time she pulled you in for a hug. I don't know what your relationship is like now, but her leaving doesn't negate the past. It doesn't erase what you once had.

"As for me…" I take a deep breath. The words are harder now. The sentiments riskier. "I cried. More times than I want to admit. Because I lost you. I *missed* you."

I drop my face into my hands, overwhelmed by the rush of emotions. Everything I've felt in the last four years crashes over me now, and I don't know how to reach the top of this wave. I don't know where to find the strength to fight this current.

Turns out, all I ever needed was a little help from him.

Gently, Mat pries away my hands and lifts up my chin so that we're looking at each other. "I cried, too. If I listed every session, we'd be here all night."

I choke out a laugh. "We were so awful to each other."

"The worst." He traces his finger along my cheek, scooping up a stray teardrop.

"The things I said to you." I shake my head. "I made fun of everything—your clothes, your hair. Your mannerisms. Nothing was off-limits."

"You don't know how often I would try on a shirt and wonder what you would find to criticize."

"I *always* found something wrong," I say. "No matter what. I made up flaws if I had to. Which I did half the time."

"Only half?" he teases.

My lips twitch. This banter is familiar territory. But with the removal of the barb, the absence of any malice, it feels wholly new. "Even monkeys get every fourth answer right on a multiple-choice exam."

"So you're saying my fashion sense is better than a monkey's?"

"Only on Tuesdays and Thursdays."

"Finally. A compliment from Winnie." He clutches his heart. "I'll take it."

We smile at each other, and then we lean back against the steps, studying the night sky. The silence is both awkward and nice.

I have no idea what the future holds. I don't know what kind of friendship we can salvage. I'm even less sure how our fake dates will proceed. But I know one thing.

I'm very glad I wore the world's ugliest sweater tonight.

Chapter Twenty-Four

The doorbell rings on Monday morning, just as I'm arranging a couple of slices of toast on my plate. Mama had an early shift at the hospital, and she's no longer trying to butter me up—which leaves me buttering my own breakfast.

"Can you get the door, Winnie?" Papa calls from upstairs. "I'm expecting a package."

I stick a piece of toast in my mouth. Yum. I've prepared it the Thai way—buttered and sprinkled with sugar. Most of my American classmates think that's weird, with the exception of Kavya, who doesn't find anything weird. She'll pop a fish eyeball (mm, both crunchy and tender) into her mouth without blinking—her own eyes or the fish's. In comparison, my sweet-and-salty combo is much more innocuous. Waffles are served with butter and syrup. Biscuits pair with butter and honey. Why not sugar?

With the bread hanging from my lips, I open the door.

Ack. The toast falls from my mouth, and I hastily catch it, leaving my fingers both greasy and gritty. It's not the mail after all, but the guy who has a habit of showing up where he's least expected.

"Taran. What are you doing here?" I chuck the bread in a trash can and wipe my fingers on a tissue.

But I hardly need to be self-conscious. Taran looks like hell. His bloodshot eyes sit above ink-dark smudges, and his hair sticks out in every cardinal direction. Even his bark-brown skin appears wan—a feat I didn't realize was possible. He looks like he's been hungover for the last day and a half. And maybe he has.

"I'm sorry, Winnie," he says without preamble. "I almost *don't* remember my behavior on Saturday night. But long, terrible sequences came back to me yesterday, while my head was hanging over the toilet. I'm absolutely mortified."

I cross my arms, more to stiffen my resolve than because of any anger. He deserves every bit of my annoyance, but I can't help but soften at his obvious misery.

"Did you get in trouble?" I ask. The reason I never saw his parents Saturday night was because they weren't present. Mama informed me that she ran into the Tongdees at a local restaurant. I don't blame them for wanting a quiet meal, but their absence at a wild high school party seems awfully trusting.

Taran nods sheepishly. "By the time my parents got home, I was passed out on the bathroom floor. They didn't even try to move me. My mom just threw a comforter over me, and I spent the night on the cold tile." He shrugs. "It was the first time I ever drank. My dad said my hangover was probably punishment enough, but they grounded me anyway. Otherwise, I would've come over yesterday."

"Seems reasonable enough," I say, my voice as stiff as my spine.

"The punch doesn't excuse how I treated you. I'm not

saying that."

I sigh. The alcohol's definitely not an excuse, but I'm suddenly so tired of being mad. The amount of energy it took to maintain my animosity toward Mat was exhausting. Now that Mat and I have finally crested the hill of forgiveness, the last thing I want is another enemy.

Besides, Taran *did* apologize. And it only took him thirty-six hours, instead of four years. That's something.

I drop my arms. "I hope you apologized to Julie, too. I don't know what went down between you two, but it probably wasn't appropriate, given the circumstances."

"Nothing happened, I swear. She was never waiting for me. I just said that. The truth is, I stumbled to the bathroom and went to sleep." He shakes his head. "My first party at Lakewood, and not only did I get trashed, but I wasn't even awake long enough to enjoy it."

"Serves you right." A smile ghosts over my lips.

"The important thing is: do you forgive me?"

"Might as well. I mean, life's too short to hold a grudge." My words may be flippant, but the wisdom cuts deep. That's a lesson I wish I learned four years ago. But I can only move forward now and not back.

"You're still mad." He places his hand on the jamb, which makes me realize the door's been open way too long. Mama's a stickler for closing entryways — a lingering habit from her years in Thailand, where homes are cooled room by room — so I gesture for him to come inside.

"Is it because of that Julie comment?" he asks once I shut the door. "I swear to you I just made that up to make you jealous. I'm interested in *you*."

I give a short laugh. A few days ago, I would've died to hear such a confession. Now, I feel almost nothing. "The point is moot. You're too new in town to know about the

Tech girls. Like I alluded to the other day, I'm not allowed to date. At least, not for real."

He raises his brows. "Really? You and Mat seem awfully close. I know you said there was nothing between you, but he's always around."

"It's complicated."

"I like complex." His eyes are warm, his face earnest. I can't help but smile. For all his faults, Taran has an uplifting effect on people.

"Long story short. My sisters and I weren't allowed to date in high school. But then they got to college and refused to consider the notion of getting engaged. So, Mama decided that I need to *practice* my relationship skills." Never have air quotes been so exaggerated. "And Mat's the person she's picked for me to practice with."

Laid out like that, the situation sounds ridiculous. But that's Mama for you. "So unless you want to sign up to fake-date me, I'm a lost cause," I say wryly. "I appreciate the interest, though."

He leans against the wall, unfazed. "In that case, would you like to be friends?"

"Friends?" I test out the word on my lips. "I could go with that."

He sticks out his hand, and we shake on it.

Papa walks by the foyer at that precise moment. He halts and does a comical double take. "Touching," he gasps, as though he's having a heart attack.

I jerk my hand out of Taran's grasp. "Breathe, Papa. It's just a handshake. You said you were facing reality, remember? So you'll have to accept that I'll have cause to touch someone sometimes."

My throat rattles with the need to laugh. Taran, on the other hand, looks like he's been caught pilfering the donation box at the wat. *I'll explain later*, I mouth to him.

Composing himself, Taran lifts his hands into a prayerlike position and waies Papa. "Sawatdee krup. You must be Dr. Tech. I'm Taran Tongdee. My father says you went to med school together."

Papa rubs his chin like he's sizing Taran up.

"Papa," I say sharply, hoping I don't die from embarrassment. "Taran stopped by to say hello. What you saw was a *friendly* handshake. Because we're *friends*. And that's what *friends* do."

"That's right." Taran nods vigorously. "When I see Winnie, all I can think is *sister*. Which is kind of weird, 'cause I only have brothers, and all I know is torment. Not that I want to torture Winnie." He swipes a hand across his brow. "God, no. Nothing could be further from the truth." He looks up at the raised beams on our ceiling. "I'd, uh, like to color pictures with her," he bursts out. "With, you know, crayons."

I giggle. He's kinda cute when he flails. "Only if we were seven."

"*Whatever* brothers and sisters do," he corrects. "That's what I want to do to her. I mean, with her. I mean…" He flushes. "Just give me crayons. Please."

I crack up. This guy is *exactly* like me. How, oh, how does he exist?

Papa snaps his mouth shut, and color finally seeps back into his face. "What do you want to be when you grow up?" he barks.

Taran's face relaxes, as though he's spotted familiar ground—and is making a mad dash toward it.

"A doctor, sir. Specifically, I would like to be a radiologist, like my father."

Good answer. According to the Thai parent handbook, maybe the *best* answer he could have given.

"What did you score on the SATs?" The interrogation continues.

"Perfect on math. Seven hundred on the verbal section."

Papa's eyes flicker, as though he's impressed but doesn't want to be. "How many AP exams have you taken?"

"None, sir. They didn't offer APs at my tiny school in Kansas. But it doesn't matter, because I've been accepted early decision to Harvard."

Papa's eyes widen. He backs up a few steps. Hell, even *I* back up a little. Taran's completely won him over now.

"Harvard, huh?" Papa scratches his chin. "You know, when we first came to this country, I stood on the steps of Widener Library and prayed that one day my children would attend school there. Why? Because that would mean I was right to move to this country. Right to uproot our lives. So that my children would have better opportunities than I did."

His tone is soft, nostalgic. And one that I've rarely heard before.

"Really, Papa?" I ask. "You never told me that."

"Because I didn't want to give you the wrong impression," he says. "Harvard is just a symbol of a better future. Nothing more. The truth is, I couldn't be any prouder of the twins for going to Wash U. Couldn't be any prouder of you for getting into Northwestern. You're all such incredible young women. Whatever I had to sacrifice to get you here, I would make again. In a heartbeat."

"Oh, Papa." My eyes misty, I hug him. He can be gruff. He might be absentminded, and he's hugely overprotective. But he loves me through and through.

With one arm still around me, Papa nods at Taran. "Congratulations. And good luck to you." He turns to me. "I got called in to the hospital. Can you take the bus to school or ask Kavya for a ride?"

"I can take her, Dr. Tech," Taran offers. "I'm already heading there."

Papa blinks rapidly. Even his newfound approval didn't prepare him for this scenario.

"But the people," he manages. "What would they say?"

I roll my eyes. The people *again*. For as long as I can remember, these anonymous, faceless people have dictated what I can or can't do. I'll have to invite them to my wedding, since they've played such a central role in my life.

"Pretty sure the *people* will never find out unless you call and tell them," I say archly.

Papa chews on the inside of his mouth and then looks at his watch. "Fine," he says reluctantly. "But remember—"

"I know, I know," I interrupt. "We already shook hands, but if it will ease your mind, there will be no future touching."

I scoop up my backpack. Taran wisely doesn't say a word. We trip out the door and down the steps, hoping to get away before Papa can change his mind.

I'm just opening the door to Taran's Honda Accord when Papa comes out on the porch.

"Winnie, wait." He throws something at me. A pair of black leather gloves slaps me in the arm, tumbling to the ground.

"It's almost sixty degrees," I protest.

He adjusts his glasses. "Somewhere in the world, it's cool enough to wear gloves."

"But—"

"No buts," he says firmly. "If you want that ride, put them on."

Sighing, I pick up the gloves from the grass. And I put them on.

Chapter Twenty-Five

The gloves don't stay on for long. I peel them off thirty seconds into the ride, and by the time we pull into the parking lot at Lakewood High, the black leather is stuffed into my backpack, largely forgotten.

"Got you here, safe and sound." Taran turns off the ignition and directs his gleaming smile at me. "And no *people* even saw us."

"Oh, really?" I gesture at the clumps of students walking past our car. It's still fifteen minutes before first bell, but the lawn is already crowded. "What do you call these creatures walking around on two legs?"

"Those are people, all right. Just not the kind our parents like to invoke."

I give a mock gasp. "Don't tell me these so-called people live in your world, too. I thought they were a pure invention of my family."

"Oh, sure. Any time I forgot to cut my fingernails or practice the piano—"

"Any time I was late to class or stayed up past my

bedtime—" I chime in.

"What would people say?" we conclude together.

Laughing, Taran turns to face me, his biceps brushing against the steering wheel. "When I was little, I was terrified of these people. I thought an army of spies was hiding under my bed and around each corner, waiting to leap out and catch me doing something wrong."

"And now?" I tease.

"Now, I think people are pretty great." He grins. "You just have to spend time with the right ones."

He lifts his hand, and his fingers hover in the air, inches from my face. "May I?"

I don't know what his intention is, but I nod.

He smooths a piece of hair from my face very, very gently.

I clear my throat. "That was…nice."

"I've learned my lesson, Winnie." His fingers linger on my cheek. "I won't touch you again without your permission. I know I've already apologized. But words mean nothing. It's the actions that count."

I agree, in theory. I've heard this sentiment a million times. But I don't think it's wholly accurate. Words do count. They can hurt, and they can heal. Look how much a few words changed the relationship between Mat and me the other night.

Maybe it's neither words nor actions alone that have an impact. Maybe we need both.

"Will you let me drive you to school again?" Taran asks, pulling away his hand.

"I wish." I make my tone light. I've already shot the guy down once. No need to do it again. "But I'm pretty sure this was a one-off. Papa would never let me be seen riding in the same guy's car on a regular basis."

He frowns. "Didn't Mat give you a ride when I first started school here?"

"That was the scene of our very first fake date."

"Ah," he says. "That explains things."

"What?"

Taran taps the steering wheel in a nervous tic. *Rat-tat-tat.* "That explains why he's staring at us right now."

"Huh?" I glance up, distracted. My gaze flits from one corner of the windshield to the other, taking in the rack of bicycles, a group of giggly freshmen, and a football arcing high in the sky.

And then I see Mat. He's wearing his beat-up black jeans and one of the thermal shirts that I secretly like so much. This shirt is light gray, and the color makes his skin even darker, his eyes even deeper.

I'd be hard-pressed to find anything wrong with his outfit. Back in the day, I'm sure I would've come up with *something* to criticize. But today, the clothes look pretty much perfect.

A handsome outfit for a handsome guy. Too bad his handsome face is scowling at us through the windshield, ten feet away.

My stomach drops to my knees. How long has he been standing there? Did he see Taran touching my face?

Our eyes meet for the briefest of moments, and then Mat turns and walks away.

I finally catch up with Mat at his locker. I'm aware of its exact location—main floor, second corridor to the right, adjacent to the gym. Don't ask me how, since I've never visited him here before. No doubt my sisters and Kavya would have a plethora of explanations.

All I'm willing to admit is that I've been paying more attention than I thought.

Around us, students jostle one another, apply lipstick in front of mirrors, and even make out against the central bank of lockers. It smells like gym class—old sneakers, slick floors, and overpowering perfume.

But the scene and the scents fade in comparison to the boy in front of me.

Mat's head towers over his locker. His movements are jerky, his lips pursed in fierce concentration.

I don't know if I'm brave or foolhardy, but I go up to him cautiously, as one might approach a slumbering crocodile.

"Good morning," I venture.

He turns to me, his eyes carefully blank. He's not at all surprised to see me. Does he know that I've been trailing him since the parking lot?

"You have a stain on your shirt," he says blandly.

I look down. Imagine that, I do. I'm not sure how he noticed the stain so quickly, but maybe he's equally aware of every detail about me. "I dropped a piece of toast on my shirt this morning."

"Of course you did." But he doesn't snicker, and he's not amused. There's no light in his eyes. This exchange is neither our earlier antagonism nor our newfound teasing. This exchange is…nothing.

"I don't have an extra shirt." Five-ray chula kites, the kind that Thai people fly in the annual competition, flutter in my stomach. "Otherwise, I would change."

"Take this." He reaches into his bag and then tosses me a T-shirt. It's light blue and emblazoned with the school logo, a shirt that he wears for gym class.

At least it's freshly laundered and smells like fabric softener.

I crush the cotton underneath my fingers. What does this mean? Plenty of students wear the oversize sports jerseys of their significant others, tied up in the corner with a rubber band, maybe even exposing a bit of midriff. Is that why he's giving me his shirt? Or is he just implying that my stained shirt is worse than his old gym attire?

Since the warmth emanating from him clocks in at about a negative two, I'm going with the latter.

"No thanks." I hand him back the shirt. "No one will be surprised to see me with a stain."

He shrugs and flings it into his locker. "Suit yourself."

He slams the locker door, and the finality of the sound makes me wince.

"What's going on here?" I ask. "Why are you mad at me?"

"I'm not mad." The slash of his gaze belies his words. "I just don't understand you. After what happened, why are you riding in Taran's car? Why did you let him touch you?" He shakes his head, although I'm not sure if he's disgusted with me or himself. "Did I completely misread the situation on Saturday night? I thought he was harassing you. Was I wrong? Maybe you were having, I don't know, a *lover's spat*." He pronounces the words as though they're poison.

My jaw drops. "Mat. Are you jealous?"

He snaps his mouth closed. Straightens his spine. And then, instead of answering, he just leaves.

Chapter Twenty-Six

The warning bell rings. Mat's striding in the opposite direction of my first class. If I follow him, I'll be late. I'm never late. But if I *don't* follow him… Well, we've already lost four years of friendship by not communicating. I don't want to lose four more.

I hurry after his imposing figure, but the sea of students prevents me from breaking into a flat-out run. He must know I'm behind him, but he doesn't slow and he doesn't pause.

We're halfway through a courtyard set between two buildings when he finally stops. "You're still here?" he asks, leaning against one of the weathered picnic tables. A dozen of them are scattered across the green lawn. The open air means that the sun shines brightly overhead, providing a welcome shot of vitamin D for students during lunch and in between classes. "You have trig at the other end of school."

I reach the picnic table, dropping my backpack at my feet. I want to pant—because the pace he was setting was kinda brisk—but *he* hasn't broken a sweat. He's not even breathing hard. "How do you know my schedule?"

"The same way you know where my locker is."

He's got me there.

We stand, looking at each other, as the courtyard empties, students disappearing behind the double-glass doors on either side of the open space.

Brrrrrrrrriiiiiing.

It's the sound that I've been both dreading and expecting: the bell that signals the beginning of first period.

"Late," Mat says mockingly. "You're officially late."

"There are worse things." To prove my unconcern (lie— already, I feel the sweat gathering in between my fingers), I sit casually at the table. Surreptitiously, I wipe my palms against my skirt. No cat heads this time but a perfectly unobjectionable plaid.

He sits across from me. "Who are you, and what did you do with Winnie the Rule Follower?"

"You say that like it's a bad thing."

"It's not, generally." He runs a hand through his hair. "But in your case, it's like you're afraid to do something wrong so that no one will notice you. I bet that's one of the reasons you're friends with Kavya. Without your sisters to provide a shadow, you need someone else to draw the spotlight."

"That's quite a speech," I manage to say.

He leans forward, his deep eyes bracketed by straight eyebrows. "Tell me I'm wrong."

I take a deep breath and release it, one beat at a time. It's not easy to listen to someone's assessment of you, especially when it's critical. Not a simple thing to separate your feelings from the observation, to set aside the opinion from the objective truth.

But those words sneak into my chest. They ricochet in

my heart, ringing louder with each bounce. And so I try.

"You're not wrong," I say slowly. "But you're not fully right, either. There are a billion reasons why I love Kavya. She's kind and loyal and fun—"

"I'm not disputing any of that," he says, his voice soft.

"And I'm not afraid to shine." I stop. My thoughts take another lap around the twisty track that is my mind. "I just don't know how."

"Be yourself." He shrugs. "That's it. That's all."

"How?" I look at him, my heart in my throat, and on my sleeve, and in the butter stain on my shirt.

He considers me for a long time. And then he gets to his feet. "Good luck figuring it out. I have to get to class."

"Wait." I rush around the table and put my hand on his wrist. He goes perfectly still. And I get an inkling of what it means to be myself. "Could you help me?"

His eyes flash. "Why in the eighth level of hell would I want to do that?"

The words should hurt. They should send me running to a quiet corner, as so many of his cutting comments have done over the years.

But his voice shakes on the last syllable, and that's when I know. I can see right through the walls he erected to protect himself. I can read the feelings that he's not voicing.

Most of all, I've figured out how to be myself.

I just pray to the pra Buddha cho that I'm right.

"Because you like me," I say softly.

The wood of the picnic bench bites into my thighs. The grass tickles my ankles, and the sun slants over the courtyard in long, lazy rays. I lift my hand from his wrist and place the pads of my fingers on his bare forearm. Slowly, I skim my fingers up his arm, over the bunched sleeve at his elbow, and onto his shirt-covered biceps. Here, I pause, feeling the solid rock through the waffle-patterned cotton. Holy hotness, this boy has muscles.

My neck is all of a sudden too warm, and I'm light-headed from the sensation underneath my fingers.

Mat clears his throat. "Well, yeah. I mean, we used to be friends a long time ago."

"You like me more than just a friend, Mat," I say.

"I do?" His voice is gruff, approaching strangled.

I run my hand over his shoulder, up his neck, and onto his face. He stands there, completely rigid, a bronze statue under the glow of the sun. I can almost believe he's stopped breathing.

I continue my exploration, tracing his jaw, chasing his warmth. The moment I touch his mouth, however, my world narrows to the single tip of my finger. I rub my index finger gently over his lips. Full, fascinating. I could stay here all day. The entire week.

"Winnie?" My finger moves with his mouth, his hot breath moistening my skin. I stare at his lips, entranced. He could read aloud the entirety of *Paradise Lost*—what we're currently studying in English lit—and I wouldn't get bored. "Why do you think I'm interested in you?"

I swallow hard. This is it. The biggest leap I've ever taken. Let's just hope that if I fall, the pra Buddha cho has conjured up a net to catch me.

I take away my hand. My fingers ache where they've been touching him, but I know that this separation is necessary. Hopefully temporary.

"The reason I know," I whisper, "is because of this."

And then I wrap my hands around his neck and pull him down, until his lips meet mine.

Chapter Twenty-Seven

The moment that my lips touch his, I panic. What am I doing? How am I the aggressor here? I've kissed exactly nobody in my life, and he's tongue-wrestled with how many? Twenty? What if he thinks I suck? Or worse yet, *don't* suck. Are you supposed to do *that* in a first kiss? How the hell would I know?

I jerk up, just as he moves forward. Somehow, someway, the top of my head bangs into his cheekbone, and I see stars. Not the good kind.

"Owww!" he yells.

"Sorry, sorry," I gasp, shooting back. "I don't know what I was thinking."

He recovers enough to grab my arms, steadying me before I fall to the ground. "You don't have to apologize. Just give me a second here." He gingerly touches the bruise that's already forming on his cheek, grimacing.

"This is just perfect," I moan. "My very first kiss, and I give you a black eye."

"It's below my eye." His tone is eminently reasonable.

If he's surprised at my admission that this is my first time, he doesn't show it. No doubt he figured as much. "And really, can that even count as a kiss? You touched my lips for what? Point two seconds? Did you even feel anything?"

"I remember every detail *before* it happened. And afterward," I say stubbornly. "That has to count for something."

He sits down and pats the bench next to him. "Maybe we'd better try that again. I can't have you thinking that's a proper kiss."

I look at his hand. And then at his lips. I want more than anything to see if he's right. To see if there's *more*. But what if I mess up a second time? "Are you sure that's something you want to risk?"

"Hell yes." He lifts his brows cockily. "My reputation's at stake here."

I huff. "*That's* why you want to kiss me? Because of your reputation?"

"That's right. My reputation," he repeats. "It's not because you understand me better than anyone else at this school. It's not because your eyes always seem to be laughing, even when your mouth isn't. And it absolutely, positively has zero to do with the fact that I've been thinking about nothing else since you tried on that green dress at the mall."

He beckons with his fingers. This time, I move forward to peer at his bruise. It's going to need ice. But before I can say so, in a move as natural to him as walking, he scoops me up and lays me across his lap. My skirt hikes up a few inches. He glances at my bare legs and seems to stop breathing.

The air electrifies. I'm aware of every movement, every sensation. The rough texture of his jeans under my thighs. The cool air flirting with our lips. His warm, large hand settling on my knee.

He drags his gaze from my legs to my face, and I feel an almost tangible click when our eyes meet.

"Did it hurt?" I ask hesitantly. I lay my fingers on his cheek, right under the discoloration.

"Yes." His voice is low and scratchy. "But it feels better already. If you'd told me all I had to do was get a bruise to get your hands on me, I would've beat myself up a long time ago."

"I really am sorry." Before my nerves desert me, I replace my fingers with a gentle kiss.

"Even better." He taps his cheek, a couple of inches closer to his mouth. "How about here?"

I comply, my lips aching from the rough texture of his skin. And then he taps again, this time on his mouth. "And here?"

My heart is a caged bird, flapping its wings, almost too big for my chest. Each frantic and distinct beat thunders in my ears.

Swallowing hard, I lean forward.

"Winnie?" he murmurs. "Take your time, okay?"

"Just promise me you won't move."

His lips part, as though he's about to protest. But then he just nods. "If that's what will make you comfortable, fine."

I move closer. And then I press my mouth against his. And stay there. Oh my. This is nice. One thousand one, one thousand two. He must've misunderstood me, though. I meant no sudden movements to avoid any accidental black eyes. Not: stop moving altogether. One thousand three, one thousand four. Still, I can't complain. Fireworks aren't exactly going off here, but I can see why a kiss has become a symbol for affection.

One thousand five.

I draw back, triumphant. I did it! I had my first kiss. And it wasn't even terrible, like Kavya warned.

I smile at him. "That was really lovely."

His eyes fly open. "Lovely?" he croaks.

"Well, yeah." Doubt begins to sink in. Did I do it wrong? How is that possible when I wasn't even moving? "Didn't you like it? I stayed there for five whole seconds."

"You counted?" he asks incredulously.

Okay, I've definitely messed something up here. Clearly, the kiss wasn't as torrid as I've seen at parties—or even in the school's corridors—where the participants look like they're about to climb into each other's mouths. But this was a *first kiss*. Even Kavya said they're awkward as hell. What does he expect?

"I'm sorry it wasn't up to your usual standards," I say, my words as stiff as the bench we're sitting on.

He scrubs a hand down his face, wincing as he brushes against the bruise. "Listen, Winnie. I'd rather have a kiss from you than anyone else on this planet. And I *loved* it. But you know what they say. Third time's a charm. Can we try again, on my terms?"

"What terms?" I ask warily.

"For starters, I'd like to be able to move."

I choke out a laugh. "That was a misunderstanding—"

"A paralyzing one." His lips twitch. "Come on. What do you say? I promise you'll like it."

"Fine," I say. "But if I *don't* like it—"

He leans forward and kisses me.

Holy moly. So this is what… Wow. Okay. *This* is a kiss. Lips moving. Slowly. Sweetly. So hot, this give-and-take. A hint of teeth. Oh, hello, tongue. I could do this all day. All night. The sun would set. The cold would creep. And we'd stay right here, creating our own warmth.

His hands glide over my shoulders, caressing my back. But he doesn't need to urge me closer. I move in of my own volition. More. I want more. More kissing. More Mat. More of his orange Tic Tac taste. We used to gobble them by the handfuls when we were kids. I can't believe he still eats them. It's been years since I've tasted one…until now.

I run my hands up his arms and onto his chest. I have no idea what's appropriate. If there's a handbook on what to do with your hands during a kiss, I must've missed it. How could my sisters fail to prepare me for this? They have seven months of college dating experience. They should've coached me. In the absence of their advice, I decide to do with my hands what I want. Move them where I want.

Mat doesn't seem to mind.

We're leaning, so gradually, so steadily that I don't realize it at first. I must be the driving force, because all of a sudden, he's on his back, balancing on the narrow bench. I'm sprawled on top of him, listing to one side. He puts his hands on my hips and straightens me.

"Come back here," he murmurs.

And then we kiss some more.

Minutes or hours later, a wolf whistle slices through the air. I leap off him like he's on fire—and, well, he kinda is. For one ridiculous second, I don't know where I am. All I remember is Mat. Forget a single firework. His kiss is like the whole damn finale on the Fourth of July.

And then it registers.

I'm at *school*. Cutting class. In the courtyard, for anyone to see. Talk about PDA, something I swore I would never do.

My face flaming, I peek in the direction of the whistle. One of Mat's friends, Ramon, is leaning against the double glass doors, smiling broadly. At least it's not a teacher. "Didn't mean to interrupt," he yells. "But that was so hot, I couldn't help myself."

Mat sits up on the bench. "Mind your own business," he calls back good-naturedly.

Ramon gives us a salute and disappears back inside the building.

I perch on the bench, a foot away from Mat. I am dying. *Dying*. I don't even like holding hands with a guy in public. And here I am, caught in a horizontal position with Mat on a picnic bench. Oy tai. I can't decide whether to laugh or cry. The gossip will spread faster than our internet connection. What will my classmates say? Even worse, what will my parents think?

Good Thai girls don't engage in PDA. Well, good girls don't kiss in the first place, not while they're in high school. But if they're going to, then they should at least find a place a hell of a lot more private than the school's courtyard.

"Hey." Mat reaches over and taps me on the nose. "Don't worry."

I deliberately relax my shoulders. "Why do you think I'm worried?"

"Because I know you. And I know that when you're stressed, you get a crease…right…there." He draws a line down my forehead.

I fight back a shiver. *Get it together, Winnie. It's just a single stroke.*

But I've never been touched so much by any guy before, let alone Mat. I don't know if I'll ever get used to his casual caresses. I don't think I want to.

He has a way of making me forget about my parents. Forget what they might say. Forget if they'll approve.

"Ramon's a stand-up guy." Mat holds out his phone,

showing me the screen. "I just texted him to keep his mouth shut." His throat gurgles with a laugh. "Said I would tell everyone that he still sleeps with a stuffed bear named Lightning Storm if he indulged his need to gossip. He won't be telling anybody anything."

Oh. My insides get kinda melty. Because Mat's not stressed about his reputation. His name has probably been linked with four different girls this year alone. He asked Ramon to keep our entanglement quiet for me. Because he knew the talk would bother *me*.

"Thank you," I say.

He scans the knotted wood in between us. "Maybe you could tell me again without this foot of space between us?"

I flush. "I can't, Mat. I'm just not comfortable with PDA. I may have lost my head for a few seconds—"

"Minutes," he interrupts, checking the time on his phone. "Definitely minutes, and very nearly an hour, since first period is almost over."

The corners of my mouth curve. "Okay, minutes. But that doesn't change my point. My parents can be ridiculous, but I'm very much their daughter. As much as I liked the last *minutes*, we can't touch each other again. At least not in public."

The girl who engages in PDA doesn't fit my parents' image of me. *My* image of myself. And if I want to maintain that, I need to be a lot more careful from now on.

He searches my face. "But you *did* like it?" he asks, young, vulnerable.

I can't believe it. The cockiest guy in the senior class is suddenly unsure.

Both my heart and my lips ache. I wish I could slide over, negate this space between us, and show him just how much I liked it. But I can hardly break my rule sixty seconds after I set it. Plus, I was lucky today. Next time, someone less innocuous than Ramon might see us. And if that happens…well, I don't even want to think about the consequences.

Instead, I kiss my fingers and press them on the table, an inch from where his hand is lying. "Yes. I liked it very much."

He stares at my fingers, as if they might be able to untangle the thoughts in his head. "Okay. I can live with that. But on two conditions." He lifts his eyes, and they are as deep, as black, as I've ever seen then.

"First, I do get to kiss you again when we're in private."

I nod, my mouth dry. I shouldn't say yes. But how can I resist? "I'm counting on it."

"Second, Taran doesn't get to kiss you, either," he says darkly.

Really? After our last *minutes*, he's still jealous? But since he is—and maybe, probably, definitely because he's such a good kisser—I can reassure him.

"Taran who?" I ask sweetly.

Chapter Twenty-Eight

The rest of the week passes in a whirlwind of equal parts flirtation and frustration. Although we haven't talked about our status, Mat certainly acts like my boyfriend.

He waits by my locker every morning. He sits with Kavya and me at lunch, in the open courtyard, where his gaze drifts, ridiculously often, to a certain spot on the bench. And he calls every night, so often that I haven't had time for my weekly conversation with my sisters. Mat and I have four years to catch up on, after all. Four years of jokes and observations and confidences. His voice is the last one I hear before I fall asleep, and his face is the first one I imagine when I wake up.

But we don't touch. Not a friendly hand on the shoulder. Not the inadvertent bumping of hips. Not even a graze of our fingers.

One day, he grabs the loop on my backpack strap, inches from my collarbone, when we turn the corner and enter an empty corridor.

"Is this private?" he murmurs.

The backpack strap rubs against my shoulder, and I imagine the pressure as his hand. "I wish."

The look he gives me is so molten that I nearly combust.

Another day, he boxes me against a tree on the edge of the school's property, my back pressed against the bark, his hands on the trunk on either side of my head. I'm cradled inside his embrace—but we're not technically touching.

"What about now?" he demands. "Is this private?"

He's so close that I can feel the warmth emanating from his skin. If I moved my hand an inch, I could feel the softness of his T-shirt against the hardness of his torso. I want—but I refrain.

"I hear people laughing on the other side of this tree," I say.

"I can't see them," he retorts. "So they must not exist."

Now it's my turn to giggle. "You don't see them because you're only looking at me."

"Let's find an empty classroom," he begs. "A supply closet."

I regard him sternly, which isn't easy, because what I really want to do is take his face between my hands and kiss him. "No, Mat. Nowhere at school is private."

He walks his hands closer to my head, which should make no difference. An inch between us might as well be a hundred if we don't actually touch. But his fingers brush a few strands of my hair, and the heat flares between us.

"See me outside of school, then," he suggests.

"You know we can't." We've been over this a dozen times. My parents can't know that our dating has crossed the line from fake into real. They can't suspect that we're actually interested in each other. Otherwise, we wouldn't be allowed within a football field of one another—a restraining order à la Mama and Papa Tech.

So we just have to wait patiently until Mama arranges another date.

"Saturday," I say. "You can wait until Saturday. That's two days away."

"*If* she sets us up then."

"She will," I say, more confidently than I feel. "We've had pretend dates each of the last two Saturdays. You know how Mama likes her routines."

Sighing, he drops his hands from the tree, releasing me. "The least you can do is send me photos to get me through the next two days."

"Um." This is a new one. I've never—and will never—send nudes. No matter what Bunny says. "What do you mean?"

"I want one with your eyes crossed. And flat on your ass in the middle of the sidewalk, after you've tripped on nothing. And oh! If you can get one where you're laughing so hard, you're squirting milk out your nose, that would be super."

"You're such a dork." I raise my hand to smack him, and he ducks out of range.

"No touching, remember?" he says, his eyes bright.

I shake my head, pretending to be exasperated, but I can't quite stop my lips from curving. Saturday can't come soon enough.

*S*aturday morning finally arrives, and we sit down to our monthly Family Breakfast—Mama, Papa, my sisters, and me. Well, my parents and I are at our oval kitchen table, and my sisters are in their dorm room in St. Louis, since they won't move into their sorority house until next year. Propped at the edge of our table is an iPad, where we've set up the video call.

The tradition started when the twins left for college. Mama complained bitterly about missing my sisters, about the absence of family meals, about the split in our lives reflecting the fracture in her heart. So Ari proposed Family Breakfast as a way to appease her—but it's become *my* favorite morning of the month.

For starters, Mama always prepares an enormous spread of khao tom (boiled rice soup) and side dishes, and today is no exception. The table is crowded with a Thai omelet, chicken stir-fried with ginger, palo (five-spice stew), deep-fried catfish, pickled mustard greens, kunchieng (Chinese sausage), and sautéed bean sprouts.

On the other side of our call, my sisters have created their own spread, although it's much less impressive. Just regular steamed rice with various pickled vegetables from the can and a selection of store-bought nam phriks, which are spice mixtures made from chilies, garlic, shallots, lime juice, and either shrimp or fish paste. Mama's horrified that my sisters are eating the Thai equivalent of rice and condiments, I can tell. But the last time she pointed this out, the conversation ended with Bunny picking up a container of dried chilies and pouring it straight into her mouth.

"So," Mama chirps instead. "Any marriageable prospects?"

Ari starts choking on her rice, and Bunny whacks her on the back. I don't know why my sister's surprised. I mean, we've already covered their classes, sleep patterns, and clothes. (Mama's convinced the twins aren't dressed warmly enough, even though they're wearing leggings and a tee, just like me, and there's only a four-degree temperature difference between Chicago and St. Louis.) We were bound to get to Mama's favorite subject sooner or later.

Ari recovers, and the twins exchange one of their famous looks. My heart gives a swift, sharp pang. Even on the best days, it's hard enough to be a spare to their pair. But the distance is only reinforced when we're three hundred miles apart.

"Yes, Mama," Bunny says dryly. "I met a guy last night at a frat party. First name, Brian. Never got around to a last name. Not sure about marriageable, but he *is* a very good kisser." She waggles her eyebrows.

"Bunny!" Mama gasps. "Show a little respect. You may be in college now, and Papa may blurt out whatever pops into his mind. But that doesn't mean *you* have to."

"You are narrowing the blood vessels in your mother's heart," Papa says firmly. Typical Papa. He can't just refer to a heart attack like a regular person.

"Mama, she's kidding." Ari shoves her twin in the shoulder, and Bunny pushes her back. My foot kicks forlornly underneath the table, but there's no ankle for me to connect with.

"We attended no such party last night," Ari continues. "In fact, we stayed home and studied. Isn't that right, Winnie? Didn't I spend an hour quizzing you on biology?" She finds my gaze through the screen and winks.

We *did* talk for an hour last night—but our conversation consisted of my sisters shrieking about Mat kissing me. "Finally," Bunny pronounced, while Ari concluded, "Very impressive, little sister."

"Did you wink?" Mama demands.

Ari rearranges her smirk into a neutral expression. "Huh?"

"You winked just now," Mama says. "At Winnie. What

does that mean? Are you not telling us the truth?"

"Um. Pretty sure I had dust in my eye." Ari winks again.

"There!" Mama cries. "I saw it again." She turns to Papa, who is painstakingly separating the bones from his fish. "Papa. The girls are winking at each other."

"Better than sharing needles, I suppose," he says.

Mama huffs out a breath. Her shoulders turn inward, as though the world—or, at least, *her* world—is banding against her.

"Come now, Mama," Bunny cajoles. "You know how glitchy these video feeds are. I can assure you, there was no wink, no conspiracy, no plotting whatsoever." She grins wickedly. "Unless you count me plotting how I'm going to see Brian again. I probably should've gotten his number, but we were busy doing…other things."

Mama starts hyperventilating, and Papa abandons his fish to guide her head between her knees.

I take the opportunity to text my sisters under the table.

Me: Seriously, Bunny? Whatcha doing? If they keel over and die, I'm gonna have to dispose of their bodies. Maybe wait for this kind of talk until you're home and can help me?

Bunny: Just setting the stage. If I'm outrageous enough, by the time Ari confesses, it won't seem so shocking

Me: Confess what? Ari?!

No response appears for an unending minute. Finally:

Ari: I met someone

Me: WHAT? You couldn't have mentioned this last night?

Ari: Last night was about you

Bunny: *snorts* Right. The truth is, she's having a hard time telling the family

Me: Hey, I resent being grouped with the rents

Ari: Sorry, Winnie. Of course I'll tell you. It's just that this person is not exactly expected

I frown. Expected? What does that mean? It's not like Mat is expected, either. Or is he?

"Are you texting under the table?" Mama asks.

I look up guiltily, tucking away my questions for Ari. "No?"

"This is Family Breakfast!" she exclaims. "That means you must give your family your full and undivided attention. Texting your friends is not a quality use of this time."

Somehow, I don't think explaining that I'm texting my sisters will make her feel any better. "Because breathing with your head between your knees *is* a quality use?"

"It was a bonding experience between your mother and me." Papa returns to his fish. "I read an article on how extreme situations can bring two people closer."

"Do you need any more intimacy?" I tease. "I mean, you already have three children. And that's not even taking into account the kiss I saw earlier."

My sisters' heads snap as Mama's cheeks flush kunchieng red. "Kiss? What kiss?" Ari demands.

Mama ignores us. "I was just going to tell Winnie about her date today."

My ears perk up. Finally. A date with Mat. An unintended—but very welcome—side effect of teasing Mama.

"You do know that Winnie is practice-dating, don't you?" she asks my sisters.

"Is she now?" Ari asks, the picture of innocence, while Bunny grumbles, "Of course we know. We were there when it happened."

Mama bulldozes ahead. "I'm taking it up a notch. You know that adorable scene in *How To Lose a Guy in Ten Days*, where Kate and Matthew spray lobster juice at each other?" she asks, as though the actors are old friends. "So

I've decided that Mat and Winnie will drive into the city tonight to go to Lowcountry."

"Uncle Pan's restaurant?" Bunny asks. Uncle Pan is Mama's brother and my favorite uncle. I also like to think that I'm *his* particular favorite, since we're both the babies of our families.

"You do know that they make out after that lobster scene?" Ari grumbles. "Is that what you want to happen, too?"

"I can't believe this." Bunny knocks over one of the pickled vegetables in her haste to get closer to the screen. "When Uncle Pan opened his restaurant, we *begged* to go there with our friends. You wouldn't even consider it."

"Oh, stop." Mama jabs Papa in the ribs, her words applying to both the twins' complaining and her husband's fiddling with the bones. "The situation's different, and you know it. You twins were always pushing the boundaries, and I have never once had to worry about Winnie stepping out of line."

She beams at me. I usually live for these moments—but this time, I can't even enjoy her praise, with the guilt of kissing Mat hanging over me.

"I have complete faith in Winnie to conduct herself with decorum at all times."

Ah. Mama's harping on the point. And now I know why.

She's not complimenting me. She's *warning* me. About how I should act on this fake date. About how I must pretend to be on a date during this foray into the city—but not too much. And certainly not the way I "pretended" in the courtyard.

"She is the epitome of what a good Thai girl should be," Mama concludes. "Isn't that right, Winnie?"

All I can do is smile weakly.

Chapter Twenty-Nine

"You can look now," Kavya proclaims.

I open my eyes, and the reflection in the mirror stops my breath. My best friend, genius that she is, has applied my makeup so that I still look like myself—but the very best version. My eyes sparkle; my lips shine. My hair is in its usual ponytail, but Kavya has curled the thick waves so that it cascades to my shoulders.

I'm wearing, of course, the green dress. It's Mat approved, and yet...

"What if he changes his mind?" I ask. "About the dress. About *me*."

"Um, that's not going to be a problem. The way he looked at you this week? I thought my brown lunch bag was going to burst into flames."

"What if I spill something on my dress?" I persist.

"Honestly, Winnie? You probably *will*." She tugs at my skirt so that it lays more smoothly. "But that's not going to surprise anyone. Especially Mat."

I gnaw on my lip. "We might not have anything to talk

about. There might be this awful, looming silence between us, and I'll be so hard-pressed to fill it that I'll start babbling about, I don't know, the comfort and care of hermit crabs. And my hermit crabs died five years ago."

Kavya regards me through the mirror. "Didn't you talk on the phone all week?"

"Yes, but that's part of the problem. Maybe we've run out of topics to discuss." I wrap my arms around my waist. "Romance changes things, and going on an actual date creates all sorts of pressure. I'm not like the other girls he's dated, you know? I don't know how to flirt. I have no experience whatsoever."

"That's why you're going on this date," she says gently. "Relationship skills take work, just like anything else. And who better to learn them with than someone as hot and funny as Mat?"

I take a deep breath. She's right. I just need to get out of my head. To not overthink it. To have fun. Piece of mo kaeng cake.

The doorbell rings.

"Wait!" Kavya shouts, even though I haven't moved an inch. "Here." She fastens an emerald pendant around my neck. It's a simple necklace, one that a twelve-year-old boy once gave to a twelve-year-old girl. But the gemstone is pretty, and Sentimental Me wanted to wear it tonight, even if odds are he won't remember it.

"You're ready," she says when I still don't budge.

Thirty seconds later: "Don't want to keep him too long. Your parents are probably interrogating him as we speak."

This rouses me. I'd better get downstairs before this date is completely ruined before it begins.

...

*W*hen I descend the stairs, my parents and Mat are sitting on the leather couches. Mat has a glass of water in one hand and balances a plate of peanut-sesame brittle on his knee. No doubt Mama shoved both at him the second he came through the door, never mind that we're about to go to dinner.

Mat's telling a story about his father trying to order a vanilla cone at an ice-cream parlor. After several iterations of "What?" "Huh?" and "Can you repeat that?" Dr. Song switched his order to chocolate.

Mama and Papa are both laughing so hard that they're holding their stomachs. Because, you know, that's better than crying. This is the kind of story that our parents and their immigrant friends love to tell, finding humor in the pain of their assimilation. I should know. Mat and I have spent hours crawling under the table during dinner parties, listening to them talk.

"To this day, I still prefer chocolate," Mat says, "because that's all my dad ever ordered for me as a kid. Who knows what my favorite flavor would be if he'd ever figured out how to pronounce 'vanilla'?"

"He never told us this story." Mama pats a tissue to the corners of her eyes.

Mat grins. "Ask him next time."

"We will," Papa says. "In fact, I'll call him right now. Invite him to dinner. He's by himself tonight, yes?"

Mat nods. "He'd love that. He was just taking out a frozen pizza when I left."

So much for the interrogation.

I forget, this is why Mama picked Mat for me to fake-date in the first place. Because they've known him since he was in diapers. Because he's safe. Because Papa appreciates him, and Mama's always had a soft spot for him.

Better call him "Ugly," I remember Mama advising Auntie Nit. *This child is too pretty. With those big eyes and perfect lips, the demons will whisk him away for sure.*

I get to the bottom of the staircase, not that anyone notices. Nothing like a failed entrance to boost a girl's confidence.

"I'm here," I say.

They turn. An expression crosses Mat's face, but it's gone so quickly, I can't decipher it.

"Why, Winnie," Mama says. "You look so pretty. Almost as pretty as your sisters."

I'd roll my eyes if the kites weren't back in my stomach, this time the long-tailed pakpao that traditionally battles the chula.

"Doesn't she look nice, Mat?" Mama demands.

"Not *too* nice, I hope," Papa says, a note of warning in his voice.

Mat doesn't miss a beat. "Sure." His smile could charm a snake back into its basket. "I mean, she does remind me of Dr. Pat," he says, referring to Mama.

She lets loose a peal of laughter, and the wrinkles in Papa's forehead smooth out.

"What an upstanding young man." Papa slaps him on the back. "Any other boy, I'd worry that hormones would take the place of better judgment. But I trust you implicitly, Mat. I hope you know that. You have always treated Winnie with the utmost respect. I don't expect that to change tonight."

"It won't, Dr. Tech."

Smiling, they walk him to the door—and by extension,

me, although no one's bothered to give me a second glance. Mat raises his hands to wai my parents, but Mama hugs him instead.

I push down my annoyance. So it's okay for *Mama* to hug him but not me?

I look up at Kavya, who's watching from the second floor. *You've got this*, she mouths and flashes me a double thumbs-up. And then we're out the door.

Mat and I march down the sidewalk, stiffly and one foot apart. He stares straight ahead. He doesn't utter a word to me, much less admire my appearance.

Every step makes my spine a little straighter, my heart a little harder. Was I wrong? Was *Kavya* wrong? Is he completely indifferent to me? Will he treat me in this cool and civilized way for the rest of the date?

Ack. I'll never get through the night.

I'm beginning to wonder if I should call off the whole thing when I get a look at the Jeep.

He's decorated his car. Bright-red lobster claws are fastened to the rearview mirrors, and the headlights share space with a pair of wooden mallets. Even a long, stretched-out bib hangs under the grille.

"You hadn't changed the decor in a while, so I thought I'd help you out," he says. "Do you like it? I call this emotion 'hungry.'"

Both his tone and his expression are solemn, but my heart leaps just the same. I've been so caught up in our new relationship that I hadn't given my art project a second thought. But *he* did. And his thoughtfulness settles right in the center of my chest.

"I love it. Mataline's never looked better."

He opens the passenger door for me and then rounds the car to climb into the driver's seat. "Are your parents still watching?"

I glance at the front porch, where they're standing, smiles on their faces. Blissfully unaware that they're sending their daughter on a date with a boy she can't wait to kiss again.

"Yes," I say.

"Then I suppose this car can't be considered private." He turns, looking at me directly for the first time this evening.

In an instant, the air comes alive, as though it's simply been waiting for the moment that we're alone. Goose bumps erupt on my skin, and I'm having a hard time drawing a breath in the swampy interior of the Jeep.

"You look stunning," he says.

"As stunning as my mother?" I can't resist teasing.

He grins. "I only said that because they don't want to know how I really feel."

Ten minutes of going unnoticed makes me bold. "And how's that?"

Heat flashes across his eyes. "I'll be happy to show you later."

I swallow hard. "Mat?"

"Yes?"

"Start the car. They're going to wonder why we haven't left."

He starts the car.

*W*e begin our trip, falling into a comfortable silence. I watch his hands for a while as they deftly pull up the directions on his phone and maneuver the steering wheel. His fingers are so long. So elegant. And yet, even as

I'm enjoying the view, something's not sitting quite right with me.

I don't figure out what it is until we get on the highway. "I didn't realize you and Mama were so chummy."

His forehead creases. "Well, yeah. I've known her since I was a kid. And—I hope you don't mind my saying this— but since my own mom took off, she's been like a mother to me."

"I don't mind. But that doesn't make sense. You've barely seen her in the last four years."

"That's not quite true." He slides a glance at me. Focuses back on the road. And then looks my way again. "She used to bring us meals, once or twice a week, in those early years after my mom left. Looking back, I think she always knew the truth. At any rate, we talked a lot, your mom and I. She helped me through my anger and hurt." Another sideways glance. "I always wondered if that made you resent me more. That maybe you didn't like how much time she spent with me."

I fall back against my seat, floored. I had no clue. My parents and the Songsomboons have always been close. That's why Mat and I spent so much time together when we were little. But I assumed that Mama's relationship with Mat faded when mine did.

I'm not mad, though. Pretty much the opposite. What kind of a selfish, narrow-minded person would I be to begrudge a grieving boy this small amount of comfort?

I reach over and pick up his hand. It's the first time we've touched since the courtyard. There's a spark, of course. I don't think I could touch Mat and be completely ember-free. But more than the fire, there's also the warmth and refuge of friendship.

"I'm glad she could be there for you when I couldn't."

"I would've preferred *you*," he says, squeezing my hand back.

"You have me now," I say simply, and there's no shyness, no uncertainty.

It's funny. The Mat with the deep eyes and the biceps is so new, so exciting, that sometimes I forget he's the same Mat I've known all my life. My best friend for more than a decade. The boy whom I declared I was going to marry when I was six years old, *not* because he was a good kisser but because even then, I could see straight into his heart. I loved that boy. I'm not sure I ever stopped.

He brings our interlocked hands to his lips and kisses my knuckles. "I wish I wasn't driving."

I narrow my eyes. "And if you weren't, we'd be doing *exactly* what we're doing right now."

"I can always hope." He grins.

But I'm not ready to let go of the subject. "It's weird, you know? To think about you and Mama plotting behind my back. It's like, you were *conspiring* with her. She discussed the dates with you; for all I know, she even consulted you. I only found out about each date at the last minute."

"I get why that would feel strange." He's quiet for a minute. Outside, the guardrails, the oversize highway signs, and the rolling hills whiz by. "But I promise, it wasn't an 'us versus you' situation. She just feels comfortable with me, and your dad never wanted to be involved in the planning. So she talked to me."

I turn this over in my mind. "How does she think you feel about me?"

"Well, I make fun of you. A lot." He shoots me a teasing glance. "How you're always ripping your tights. How you can't wrap an egg roll to save your life. How you tried to impress the new guy by pouring jalapeño vinegar on your shirt."

"You told her that?" My face burns. "No wonder she thinks I'm a dating disaster."

He smirks. "She *also* thinks I'm a dating phenom."

"Don't tell me you gave her a list of all the girls you've ever kissed," I say dryly.

"Nah. That would take too long." He laughs, and I smack him across the shoulder.

"Ow!"

"You deserve it," I grumble.

His eyes are still smiling, but he arranges his mouth into a suitably solemn expression. "The real reason she trusts me is because I told her that I would never let anyone hurt you." He takes his eyes off the road and gives me a brief, searing glance. "Least of all me."

Chapter Thirty

My five-year-old niece has dubbed Lowcountry, "My favorite place outside of Disney World!" And I couldn't agree more.

Red-and-white-checked tablecloths cover long communal tables, and red stools snuggle up to the wooden bar. A handwritten menu is painted on the dark-brown columns, while fairy lights and greenery drape across the ceiling. The center of the room is dominated by a long, metal trough sink, an encouragement to get your hands dirty. But the food, of course, is the main event.

Patrons dig into the seafood boil, spilling over with succulent lobster tails, king crab legs, shrimp, mussels, even crawfish. A cloud of steam bursts in their faces when they cut into the plastic bags, whetting their appetites. Paper food trays boast heaping sides of jalapeño corn bread and red curry mac-n-cheese, crab hush puppies and garlic noodles. The handful of people who have already moved on to dessert bite into deep-fried Oreos—and moan.

Mat's mouth drops as soon as we walk inside, as much

from the garlic-and-butter scent as the lush spread on each table.

I grin. "You'll be dreaming about the Everythang sauce for days."

"Good." He waggles his eyebrows. "I could use something new to dream about. My recurring dream was getting a little…"

"Boring?" I demand.

"I was going to say obsessive," he says, his eyes dancing. "But boring works, too."

I slap him playfully, and he catches my hand and pulls me against his chest. My breath gets clogged in my throat. He *might* be making these comments just to give me an excuse to touch him. If he is, I'm not complaining.

"This restaurant isn't exactly private," I warn.

"Nobody knows us here," he says, the height of reason. "So it might as well be."

There's probably something wrong with his logic. I just don't want to figure out what.

When I check in at the front, however, I realize that his premise is not fully correct. People do know us here. As soon as I say my name, the hostess's eyes light up. "Oh! Your uncle's at our second location tonight. But he left strict instructions to treat you like VIPs."

Mat and I exchange a look and follow her through the restaurant, past all the communal tables, to a private corner booth. It even has a circular raised wall that stretches most of the way around the table.

This table's a mistake. It's got to be. No way would Mama—and by extension, my uncle—have approved of this VIP table, hidden from the other patrons' eyes.

"Actually, I'm not sure—"

Mat cuts me off. "This is perfect, thank you."

I stare at him, and he smiles back angelically. Which is just comical. I may be feeling a little (okay, a lot) more favorably toward him, but that doesn't mean he won't always have more in common with the devil.

The hostess holds out white plastic bibs, almost apologetically. "We offer these to all our customers. It's a shame to cover such a pretty dress."

"We'll take them." Mat accepts the bibs from the hostess, tying one on as soon as she leaves. "Do you want to put yours on, too?"

We haven't even ordered yet, which means there's no hurry. But he's smirking big-time, having way too much fun. I know I'm good company—but not that good.

I narrow my eyes. "Did you know they had bibs here?"

He grins. "That *might* have been one of the reasons I was all for this restaurant when your mom suggested it. I mean, I wanted you to feel comfortable. In your natural habitat. Wearing your regular accessories."

I pick up my straw and blow the wrapper in his face.

In response, he scoops me up and tugs me closer. Not an inch separates us on the bench. He leans forward until his forehead touches mine. "I really like you, Winnie Techavachara."

"Even at this angle?" I ask, since his face is charmingly distorted from this perspective.

"Especially here."

He backs up, looks around slyly at the wooden booth walls, and then pecks my lips.

The contact is over in half a second. It might even be quicker than the first kiss we had in the courtyard. And yet, I melt anyway. This peck just shows me what I should've learned the first time. There are different kisses for different contexts. And each one is special in its own way.

Footsteps approach, and I leap away from Mat. This booth might create a false sense of privacy, but we can't be lulled. This restaurant is no more private than our school. I have to remember that.

By the time the waiter appears in front of our booth, I'm diligently studying the menu.

We order a wide variety of items because I want Mat to sample the restaurant's repertoire.

"What heat level would you like?" the waiter asks, pen poised above his order form. "The Everythang sauce ranges from weak sauce, level one, to ridiculously hot, level four."

"Oh, ridiculously hot for sure," Mat says, ever cocky.

"Um, Mat?" I venture, having dined here—and burned my tongue—on a number of occasions. "You might want to reconsider. Even level three is pushing it for me."

"Nah." He smiles at me playfully. "Ridiculously Hot is my namesake. I *have* to go for it."

My lips tug. He's cute. I'll give him that. Even if he has no idea what he's dealing with. "I don't know about you, but I find it hot when my date's head remains intact."

"I'll be fine," he insists.

I turn to our waiter. "A little backup, please?"

"No way." He continues jotting down our order, a smirk on his lips. "It's a perk of my job to watch my customers cry."

But even *that* doesn't convince Mat to budge.

After the waiter leaves, my stubborn date rubs his hands together. "You wanna discuss stakes? How about: if I can handle the ridiculously hot sauce, then I get to kiss you."

"You don't need to win a bet for that," I protest. "And I'd really rather not go to the emergency room tonight."

"Oh, come on." His eyes gleam. "Where's your sense of adventure? This will be fun."

It *is* fun already. His enthusiasm is infectious, and I can't help but smile, even though I know this many chilies can't possibly end well.

"What is it with you and your bets?" I ask in mock exasperation.

As soon as I say the words, however, I remember another bet. Or rather, a *pair* of bets—the one he made with his buddies and the follow-up wager I placed with Kavya.

I haven't thought about the bets all week, because quite frankly, they no longer seemed relevant. The connection between us is so real, so genuine, that it rises above any juvenile action we've taken in the past.

Or so I thought.

The best cons, after all, are the ones that play the long game. Maybe Mat's engineering the biggest deception in the history of time.

An image of Ramon flashes across my mind. His wide smile when he caught us in the courtyard. The exuberant thumbs-up. I assumed it was the normal reaction of a guy finding his buddy in a compromising position. But what if the gesture was much more than that? What if it was the victory cheer of a guy who had chosen Mat's side in a bet among his buddies? If the bet involved more than one of his friends, they would've picked sides, right?

I drop my face into my hands as doubt slithers through me. I hate that I'm insecure. I hate even more that I'm suddenly questioning our every interaction.

"What's wrong?" Mat asks, alarmed.

I lift my face. "The bet you made with your friends." The words come out hoarse, each syllable pushed through a cheese grater. "Did you win?"

"What are you talking about?"

"You said you could make me fall for you," I say between clenched teeth. "Is that why Ramon looked so thrilled when he caught us? Was he on the right side of the wager?"

I'm not sure what I expect. Maybe embarrassment, denial, even deflection.

Instead, he leans over and kisses me on the cheek.

"Stop that. We're having a serious conversation," I say.

"You're cute," he says.

My temper spikes. "First of all, that's incredibly patronizing. And second, you're avoiding the question."

"Oh jeez. I didn't mean to say, you're cute when you're mad," he says, stricken. "I was stalling, and that came out totally wrong. I also think you're cute when you're happy. And nervous. And frustrated. You're *extremely* cute when you're hungry. I just...I'm messing this up, aren't I?"

I soften. "You don't have to stall. Just be honest."

He lets out a long, slow breath. "There was no bet," he says sheepishly. "How's that for smooth? You asked me why we almost kissed, right after you and Kavya were gushing over the dress you bought with Taran in mind." He looks pointedly at my necklace. "*This* green dress, which exactly matches the emerald I got you in the seventh grade."

"You remember," I murmur.

His eyes flash. "Of course I remember. I remember everything about you. I could hardly admit that *I* wanted to be the person you wanted to impress. So I made the bet up."

"My bet was with Kavya," I confess, "and I made her wager a whole dollar. Couldn't convince her to go any higher. The only purpose was to tell you that I had made a bet, too."

I don't know who moves first. But all of a sudden, his arms are around my back, and mine circle his neck.

Our location, our circumstances, haven't changed. We're still in a quasi-private booth in the corner of Lowcountry. Still on a date that my parents believe is fake. Still shouldn't engage in PDA, for both my own comfort and my parents'.

And yet, those things fade next to the boy in front of me.

"It worked, you know," I say. "You achieved your goal. I did fall for you."

He smiles, and then he tells me the same thing, but without any words.

Chapter Thirty-One

Around one a.m. that night...

Me: How's the tongue?

Mat: Pretty sure my taste buds = scorched beyond repair

Me: LOLOL. I did warn you

Mat: Which means it's probably also your duty to soothe me

Me: Glass of milk. Dr Pepper. Both will coat your tongue

Mat: I was hoping for something a little more...personal

Me: You could use the mug I painted for you in 7th grade. That's personal, amirite? It has flowers on it. And butterflies

Mat: *grumble* Thanks

Me: *big, cheesy grin* Anytime

Mat: Do you think your mom planned for this to happen?

Me: She didn't exactly pour chili pepper down your throat

Mat: She sent us there. Think about it. Tons of garlic. Enough chilies to breathe fire. Not a bad way to prevent two people from kissing

Me: Garlic's not a deterrent if we're both eating it

Mat: *jots note to self* Good to know.

Me: You should've seen yourself. Nose flaring, eyes bulged. Now THAT'S a deterrent

Mat: Too bad you didn't get a pic

Me: Oh, don't worry. I did

Sends photo

Mat: Huh. I didn't notice you taking this

Me: You didn't notice much, other than gulping down your water and knocking over mine

Mat: Just saving you from Chicago's terrible tap water

Me: Sure you were

Mat: I actually look hot here. Check out my biceps. Hello, granite

Me: Figures that's the first thing you would notice

Mat: Happy to notice more. Send me a pic of you

Me: Not following your logic?

Mat: It's only fair. Quick. Take one now

Me: Are you sure? I'm wearing my glasses. Eye mask on forehead. Ratty T-shirt

Mat: Stop getting me riled up and do it already!

Me: Fine

I sit up and take a ridiculous selfie. I stare at the girl in the picture for an endless moment. Why does this feel like leaping into the abyss? But if Mat's at the bottom, then I'll risk it. Taking a deep breath, I hit Send.

Mat: I'll keep it 4evah

Me: Shut up

Mat: No, really. I especially like the cat face on the eye mask. What is it with you and cats anyway? It's like you're overcompensating for your cat allergy

Me: I like cats

Mat: I got that part

Me: Just because I can't have one as a pet doesn't mean

I don't like looking at them. Speaking of things I like to look at...send me of pic of you

Mat: Thought you'd never ask

Five seconds later, a photo arrives. Of Mat. Without a shirt.

Mat: Well. What do you think?

My entire vocabulary has fled. I'm surprised I can even make sense of his words.

Mat: Have you fainted from all my hotness?

Good question. Do red cheeks, a pounding heart, and a dry mouth count as fainting?

Mat: Winnie? This isn't a come-on, promise. That's just how I sleep. I didn't even show you my boxers. We'll have to save that for next time.

I'm laughing now. I can't help it. I don't think I've ever met anyone like Mat—and I probably never will, ever again.

Mat: Kidding, kidding! Seriously, are you there? Can you respond, please?

Me: I'm here. Thanks for the pic

Mat: Are you going to keep it 4evah?

Me: First I have to figure out how I'm going to sleep

Mat: *cackles* OK. Sexy dreams—I mean, sweet dreams

Me: Brat

Mat: It takes one to know one. Talk tomorrow?

Me: Definitely. Nite

I throw down the phone and flop against my pillows, the smile practically splitting my face. I don't know how I'm going to face him tomorrow, or any other day for that matter. But for now, I'm just going to revel in another first.

Mat Songsomboon just sexted me.

Chapter Thirty-Two

I wake with the same smile on my face. Bits of sun stream around the closed blinds, which means my room is bathed in a perfectly muted light. I snuggle into my comforter, soft and cozy. A minute passes before I remember what day it is and what happened last night.

Sunday, which means I can sleep in. And yesterday, I had my first real date with Mat. My lips stretch even wider as I recall the moment his forehead touched mine, the way I laughed until my stomach hurt when he tasted the Everythang sauce, even the photo of him without a shirt.

It's been a long time since I was this carefree. This—dare I say it?—happy. Since I could completely let go and give myself to the moment. It feels good. Every second in Mat's company feels right. And I can't wait for more.

I reach for my cell phone, but I haven't received any more text messages. Little wonder. I kept him up late last night, and he's probably still sleeping.

What does he look like when he's asleep? Does he curl his hand under his cheek, the way he did as a little boy?

Or is he a sprawler—his long arms and legs taking up the entire bed?

I refuse to think about what he wears—or doesn't wear. My cheeks hot, I determinedly close my eyes, preparing to drift off again.

But then the doorknob rattles, and Mama walks inside. She heads straight for my blinds, twisting them open with a snap of her wrist. "Rise and shine."

Groaning, I pull the comforter over my head. Classic Mama. No soothing music to ease the transition into wakefulness, the way Papa rouses us. (He read an article once about the most effective way to wake a person up.)

"It's past eleven," Mama says. "You have a date in forty minutes."

My eyes pop open, and I sit up, throwing back my blanket. "I do? But it's Sunday. And I just had one last night." Not that I'm complaining. Far from it. The prospect of seeing Mat again has me giddy.

But Mama's usually the type to create a schedule—and stick to it. With the exception of the car ride home, we've had practice dates: 1) once a week, 2) on Saturdays, which, 3) re-create a scene from a classic rom-com.

Mama crosses her arms. "You're going to Parkway Deli. It's about time we give a nod to *When Harry Met Sally*."

"Um." How do I say this politely? To my *mother*? "That iconic scene at the deli. Meg Ryan—well, she was faking an orgasm. Are you positively sure that's the moment you want us to reenact?"

Mama blinks, her arms dropping. "Oh. Is that what happens? I must not remember the movie very well. Wasn't there just a lot of screaming and a really good pastrami sandwich?"

"Oh, Mama." I don't know whether to laugh or cry. "Are

you telling me that you've been planning all these movie dates with only the vaguest idea of what actually happens in them?"

She shrugs. "It's Papa who loves romantic comedies, not me. He used to make me watch them when we first came to the States. I'll never forget him bawling at the end of *Father of the Bride*. And we didn't even have children yet."

My lips twitch. I can totally see that happening. Papa's always been the sappy one in their relationship, while she's the epitome of practicality.

"Romance isn't going to get you where you want," she says. "It won't give you a good husband, a caring father. Someone who will take care of your family. Instead, it just seduces you away from your duty, tricking you into abandoning the people you love for a foolish, unattainable ideal."

My mouth dries. "Are you talking about…Mat's mother?" That's the only possibility, really, since no one's abandoned anyone in our family.

She doesn't respond. Instead, she surveys my collage of photos—of my sisters and me making goofy faces, of Kavya and me with our arms linked—and that's answer enough.

Auntie Nit was her best friend. They would take turns watching each other's kids or retreat to the kitchen and drink chrysanthemum tea if we were playing nicely. Mama must've mourned when her closest friend left. I know, from what Mat said, that she tried to atone for Auntie Nit's actions in the only way she knew how.

And I never even noticed.

I was young, sure. I was grieving the loss of my own friend. But I probably should've seen that something was amiss with Mama. That's the burden of parents, I suppose— that their children will always think of themselves first.

That doesn't mean that I can't try to do better.

"She's only one person," I say softly. "You should know, from firsthand experience, that there are other stories of romance that end happily. Look at our family. Look at Papa. He takes care of all of us — and he loves you to pieces."

She brushes away the notion. "Not in a foolish, romantic way. We're a good match. Partners in every sense of the word. But he's mostly devoted to our family, to you girls."

"No, Mama," I say stubbornly. "He loves you, too. I know it."

"You can think what you want." Her face softens, and she places a hand on my cheek. "I love *you*, romantic daughter of mine. But you'd better get up. You have exactly twenty-five minutes before your date arrives."

*T*wenty-three minutes later, I skip down the stairs. I could've used the extra seconds to primp, but I'd much rather have that additional time with Mat, on the off chance that he arrives early.

Besides, I've never needed much time to get ready. A quick shower, the usual ponytail for my hair. Ripped jeans, a simple T-shirt, a bit of gloss, and I'm done.

The one thing I'm *not* wearing is the emerald necklace. I looked for it on my nightstand, on my dresser, even the floor. But I can't seem to find the piece of jewelry anywhere. Oh well. I lose something at least once a day. It's bound to turn up. My misplaced items usually do.

Mama's sitting on the sofa. I expected Papa to be next to her, reading one of his articles, but he's nowhere to be seen.

"Where's Papa?" I ask.

Mama purses her lips. "He went to the gym."

"Really? Without you?"

It's one of my parents' traditions, attending the gym together on Sunday mornings. And she thinks they're not romantic.

"He had some extra energy," she says vaguely.

I tilt my head. She's acting weird, even for Mama. But before I can ask her what's wrong, she gestures at a composition notebook on the coffee table, the same one Mat was using to record our dates.

"Mat forgot the notebook when he picked you up last night," she says. "The ruler, too."

Oh. That's right. It never even crossed our minds to fill out an entry. I guess we got so caught up in the realness of our date that we forgot to keep up the illusion that it was fake.

"Sorry about that." I pick up the notebook gingerly. "I'll take it with me, and we'll make a record for our dates yesterday and today."

The doorbell rings.

"He's here." My heart dances, and my breath is short. It's only been a dozen hours since our date—and even less time since we've texted—but I can't help my body's reactions.

I get to see Mat again.

Hugging the notebook to my chest, I run to the door and fling it open.

A supercute Thai boy stands on the stoop. But it's not the boy I was kissing last night.

Instead, it's Taran.

Chapter Thirty-Three

I gape. Am I dreaming? Why is he here? There's no way Taran's my date this morning. Maybe, by coincidence, he just happened to show up at the same time that we're expecting Mat.

Taran steps over the threshold, offering me a bouquet of flowers. They're gorgeous, bright blooms of yellows, purples, and pinks. I must really be in shock if I'm only now noticing this gift.

"Hi, Winnie." He flashes his dimple. "You look nice today."

I don't, not by his standards. My jeans are ripped, while his are freshly pressed. My hair's up in a ponytail, and I know—from painful firsthand experience—that he prefers it down. But my head's spinning so much that I accept both the flowers and the compliment.

"What are you doing here?" I ask.

"I'm your new boyfriend," he says, his cheeks a dull brick. "That is, I'm the person you're practice dating."

I turn very slowly to Mama. She's risen from the sofa,

her hands clasped in front of her. She studies me. Not Taran but me.

"Mama?" My voice echoes against the vaulted ceilings. "Is this true?"

Shaking herself, she walks forward, takes the flowers from me, and begins to arrange them in a vase. "Yes."

"What about Mat?"

She shrugs. "He's no longer interested."

"Like hell," I blurt, although I never curse—or even *speak without respect*—around my parents. "He was interested last night—" I cut myself off, realizing my mistake.

Mama's lips tighten, but she doesn't comment on my admission. "Mat's taught you everything he can. It's time for you to date someone new."

She knows. The awareness is in the rigidity of her spine, the betrayal in her voice. I'm not sure how. But someway, somehow, she knows about the kiss from last night.

Or, if I'm being honest, *kisses*, plural. Not just in our corner booth at Lowcountry but also walking to the car. Up against the car. *Inside* the car. Once I gave in to temptation, it was impossible to resist him. My willpower was a sandcastle constantly swept away by an onslaught of waves. I didn't stand a chance.

I skim my fingers along the speckled notebook, attempting nonchalance. But inside, I'm trembling, cracking, falling apart. A puff of air would knock me off my feet. What was I thinking? Lowcountry is my *uncle's* restaurant. He may not have been present, but he had eyes everywhere, in the form of his servers, the hostess, the bartender. I doubt Uncle Pan asked them to spy—that's not his style. But all it would've taken was one stray comment to him about the lovebirds…and a subsequent phone call to my mother.

"Mama," I say as calmly as possible. "I don't know what you've heard—"

"We'll talk later," she interrupts. "Believe me, we have a *lot* to discuss." She shifts her gaze from me to Taran. "For now, your date is waiting. Go on. Go eat some pastrami sandwiches. Just…maybe not like the movie."

I poke at my Reuben sandwich. The rye bread balances on top of thinly sliced corned beef, piles of sauerkraut, and slathers of Russian dressing. No Swiss cheese, because I'm not a fan. Any other week, this might be the perfect Sunday brunch.

The deli looks remarkably like the movie set of *When Harry Met Sally*. Are all delis more or less the same? The long metal counters lined with swivel stools, the flashing neon signs that spell out words, even the delicious smells of rich meats and fresh bread that saturate the air and our clothes.

I half-heartedly pick up my sandwich and take a bite. I managed to slip into the bathroom before we left for the deli, in order to send Mat an SOS text. I can't remember the exact words I used. Something along the lines of: "Help! Mama found out about our kissing!! Now she's sending me on a date with Taran!!!" But I do remember the effusive exclamation points.

He hasn't responded. Either he's still sleeping…or he's not very happy with me.

I cram another piece of corned beef into my mouth, even though I'm the opposite of hungry. I need this date to be over, like, five minutes ago. Should I fake food poisoning? Nah, don't want to give these yummy sandwiches a bad name. Maybe just a stomachache? I'm not up to a fake orgasm, but if I find a way to incorporate lots of screaming about my Reuben sandwich, will Mama forgive me for kissing Mat?

"Winnie, are you okay?" Taran asks.

I swallow. I'm not being fair. Taran's been a wonderful date so far. Gentlemanly, entertaining. He's kept up a steady stream of conversation since we left the house, regaling me with his adventures as a Thai kid in Kansas.

The most awful incident concerned a school photographer who argued with him about retaking his class photo. The do-over should've been a clear-cut case, since his eyes were closed. But the photographer maintained that his eyes were simply small.

I laughed in sympathetic outrage—but then, in spite of his engaging stories, my mind must've drifted.

"I'm sorry. I'm really distracted." I stir the paper straw in my iced tea, watching it disintegrate. "It's just…how did this happen?" I gesture between us. "You. Me. This date."

He leans forward and grabs one of my fries, being careful to touch only one. I stare. He can't still be hungry, since he's already finished his burger and the accompanying fruit salad. More importantly, this is our first date—and a fake one at that. Awfully presumptuous, isn't he?

"You said the only way I could date you was to be part of your mom's schemes," he explains. "I told *my* mom, which was just as awkward as it sounds." He grins boyishly. Put a hundred girls in my position, and I'd bet half of them would fall for him at this precise moment, grabby fries and all. "She called your mom. Lucky for me, they had already met at the party at your house. At first, your mother politely declined, but this morning, she called back and said she changed her mind. So here we are."

"But this isn't what you think," I protest. "It's not *real* dating. Mama will make us reenact every rom-com made in the last thirty years, and we'll have to record everything—down to the distance between us—in this notebook." I nod toward the composition notebook, which is snuggling up with the salt and pepper.

"Sounds fun," he says impishly.

I wrinkle my forehead. Is this guy for real?

"Listen, Winnie. I like you," he says. "I'll enjoy hanging out with you, no matter what the circumstances."

"But dating me is pointless. Don't you see? The moment our feelings become even remotely real, she'll just replace you with someone else." Just like she did with Mat.

"So we'll pretend."

"I *have* been pretending." My voice rises. Cracks. The couple at the next table glance at us. Maybe I'll pull a Meg Ryan yet and convince them to order my sandwich. "It was a miserable failure."

He steals another fry. It takes all of my effort not to slap away his hand. "Are you talking about Mat? Because you two sucked at faking. Pro tip: you can't look at each other like *that* if you're trying to hide your feelings. You and I just met, so what we feel for each other isn't nearly as deep. I'll do a much better job pretending."

"But why?" I shake my head. "Why would you want to date someone if you feel so little for them?"

He reaches for another fry. I push the whole plate toward him, because that seems nicer than telling him to stop. Once he has the whole pile, however, he just ignores it, proving my initial theory. He's not actually hungry.

"You're a nice girl," he says finally. "Pretty. Easy to be around. But the truth is, I'm not actually interested in you."

I grab my plate back. The fries are pretty much contaminated, but I can still eat my Reuben. Who knew relief could make you so ravenous? "Oh, good. Now I don't have to let you down easy."

He eyes me as the sour sauerkraut and sweet and tangy Russian dressing explodes on my tongue. *Yum.*

"You could pretend to be a *little* disappointed," he says.

"Why? I'm not hurting your feelings. You said yourself that you don't like me."

"I might have been interested," he says evenly. "If you weren't so obviously into someone else."

Huh. I didn't realize my attraction to Mat was so apparent. But it's hard to argue with the observations of a newcomer, so I just take a gulp of my iced tea. "If you *don't* like me, then why did you go to so much trouble to date me?"

He slouches in his chair. "You wouldn't understand. It's my parents."

"Try me." I let go of my straw, and sure enough, there are bits of paper in my mouth. Ick. I wipe my tongue on a napkin, thankful this isn't a real date. "I'm the girl whose parents are making her fake-date, remember? Pretty sure I have a fair shot at understanding."

"You're right." He looks up, a new light in his eyes. "I mean, we're at a *deli*. Because of some movie that's, like, twice as old as we are. And I was supposed to order a pastrami? Or something?"

I grin. "Have you really not seen *When Harry Met Sally*?"

"Nope. Sounds old."

"It is. But the story's also really cute. We'll have to watch it together sometime." And who knows? Maybe we will.

"They want me to marry a Thai girl," he blurts.

Ah. The statement is more surprising than my classmates might think. Even in the suburbs of Chicago, there just aren't that many Thai people around. So when my parents and their fellow immigrants came to America, many of them accepted that their children probably wouldn't grow up to have Thai spouses.

"I know." He winces. "We were living in this tiny town in Kansas. Good luck with that, right? There weren't even any Asian girls at my school, let alone Thai. My mom resigned herself to taking photos of me with my falang homecoming dates. None of them knew what a sabai was, much less wore one."

He stirs the ice cubes in his glass, almost violently. *His* straw hasn't disintegrated. Am I doing something wrong here?

"But then we moved to Chicago, and she was so damn *hopeful*. I overheard her telling my dad that her dearest wish might actually come true. I might marry a Thai person. She even cried." He stops, the background hum of other people's conversations filling the silence.

"Maybe it's silly," he continues, not looking at me. "But she's done so much for me. And I just wanted to make her happy, if only for a little while. Even if our dating is fake."

My heart squeezes. I reach out and pick up his hand. "It's not silly at all, Taran."

He lifts his head. Our gazes tangle in a moment of true understanding.

I'm not sure how long we sit there, holding hands. But the next thing I know, I hear a strangled cough next to our table.

I turn—and look right into the face of Mat Songsomboon.

Chapter Thirty-Four

"Aw, crap." Damn. Did I say that out loud? I totally did. Some thoughts—scratch that, *most* of my thoughts—are better off locked inside. Especially now, when Mat's appearance has fried my brains like the eggs cooking on the nearby grill.

"This isn't how it looks," I blurt. "I can explain."

Said every cheater caught in the act ever. Could I seem any guiltier?

Chib-peng. Chib-peng. Chib-peng.

Mat clears his throat. And looks pointedly at my hand, still encased in Taran's. "*What* isn't how it looks? You holding hands with him?"

Cheeks blazing, I snatch away my hand, glaring at Taran. My ability to think may have temporarily gone up in a cloud of smoke and grease—but his hasn't. *He* could've extracted his fingers if he wanted to help me out.

But by the way he's smirking at Mat, helping me is the last thing on his mind.

"So you got my text. I didn't say where we were. How

did you know to come to the deli?" I wince. The words—unnecessarily defensive—leave my mouth before I can stop them.

Mat stiffens, giving me his aloof, superior face. If I didn't know better, I'd think he hated me—as I did for four long years. The problem is, I do know better. And I know that this expression only means that he's hurt.

"I wanted to talk to you," he says quietly. "When I found your necklace in the Jeep this morning, I thought I could kill two birds—return your necklace and see you. Your mom said I could find you here."

He holds out his hand and drops a delicate coil of gold onto my open palm.

The necklace slithers against my skin. But before I can thank him, he turns and walk out of the building.

For a few seconds, I just stare. And then a couple of my brain cells finally connect, and I push myself to my feet. "I have to go after him," I mutter, not sure if I'm telling myself or Taran.

My date crosses his arms, snickering. "This I've got to see."

Really? I shoot him my blandest expression, the goodwill he's built up evaporating in an instant. But I don't call him on his insensitivity. I have more pressing matters.

I throw a couple of bills on the table (courtesy of Mama), tuck the necklace carefully into my pocket, and hurry into the parking lot. I come up behind Mat just as he's arriving at the Jeep. Mataline's still wearing her bib and brandishing her mallet from last night. The silly costume makes me feel even worse.

"Mat," I say hesitantly, not sure what he's angriest about. The date or the hand-holding? Maybe both. "Let me explain."

"You don't like PDA," he says coolly. "Well, I don't like public drama. If you want to talk, we're not doing it here, where anyone can hear."

"Fine." I swallow my pride because I'm the one who's in the wrong here. He just brought me my necklace. I was holding hands with another boy. "Whatever you want."

Emotions flicker through his eyes. If we had stayed close these last few years, maybe I would've been able to read them. But as it is, they're as opaque to me as the waves of Lake Michigan during a turbulent storm.

"Okay," he finally says. "Let's go inside my car."

*B*y the time we climb inside the Jeep, however, the momentum has been disrupted. I was desperate to talk before, but these past few seconds have blocked my throat and sealed my lips. I have so much to say that I don't know where to start—and how.

The leather seats squeak as we settle onto them. I don't need a ruler to measure the space between us. He's squashed against his car door, and I'm jammed up against the other—but the distance separating us is infinite.

The harsh rays of the sun are bisected by the car's roof, softening the light and creating an atmosphere that's mellow, even romantic. If only the air weren't saturated with so much tension.

Squeak. Squeak. Squeak.

How long can we sit here without speaking? Will we be here all afternoon, changing positions in an attempt to find comfort, each ensuing squeak a substitute for our words?

I'm sorry.

Squeak.

He's only a friend.

Squeak.

I like you, not anyone else.

Squeak, squeak. Squeak, squeak.

But these sentiments belong to me, not him, so it's up to me to break the silence.

"You're mad." Maybe not my most inspired opening, but at least it's a start.

"How would you feel if you were in my shoes?" Mat asks, his head lowered.

"Not good," I admit. "But it's not what you think."

"Oh, I think the situation's pretty clear," he says. "I walk into a deli, and you're on a date with another guy, holding his hand. True or false?"

"True," I say, because there's no denying the facts. "But you know it's a fake date. I texted you—"

He grips the steering wheel, since it's right in front of him. But then he slowly releases his fingers, one by one, as though reminding himself that Mataline's not his target. "I guess your reservations about PDA don't apply to Taran? 'Cause last I checked, a deli is a public location. You weren't even in a booth. Or did you just not want to touch *me* in public?"

"That wasn't PDA." I struggle to find the right words. "There was nothing romantic about me holding his hand. He's not interested in me. He said so himself. And I'm certainly not into him."

At least, I'm not anymore. We both know that once upon a time, I *was* crushing on Taran. I have a jalapeño-vinegar-soaked shirt to prove it. But that was before. Before Mat and I reached our new understanding. Before we kissed.

"He told me something about…his mother." I stumble, not wanting to betray Taran's confidence. "I reached out, took his hand in a gesture of friendship. End of story."

"Interesting," he says in a tone that conveys the opposite. "Because I wanted to talk to you about *my* mother. Only I didn't get the chance."

I look up. Really? Last I heard, he hasn't spoken to her in nearly a year. "What happened?"

"She called the house this morning, wanting to reconnect. Apparently, you told my dad that I missed her?" He moves his shoulders, managing to inject anger, disgust, and indifference into one simple gesture. "Well, I don't need a pity phone call. So I didn't take it."

"Oh, Mat." I reach out, intending to touch his shoulder, but he jerks away.

"Don't. Don't touch me the way you touched him. Because you feel *sorry* for me."

I clasp my hands in my lap. "I feel a lot of things for you. *Sorry* isn't one of them."

He leans his head back, looking up at the car ceiling. One minute passes. And then another. "Okay, fine," he says finally. "Let's say I buy your explanation, that the hand-holding was nothing. Why did you agree to the fake date in the first place?"

"I told you. Mama found out about our kissing." My voice is calm, even. I wish I could say the same about my quivering insides. "I don't know *how* she found out. Uncle Pan must've called her. So she decided to replace you with Taran as my practice boyfriend. Taran, for his own reasons, agreed."

"And you just went along with it?" he asks incredulously.

I stare. "Well, yeah. What else could I have done?"

"You could've told her no."

I blink. And then blink again. "Since when is *no* a feasible answer with my mother?"

"Since always. You just have to be willing to say it."

Seriously? I can't tell if he's being stubborn or deliberately obtuse. "Listen, I get that there's a different standard for guys in our culture. I also get that your mom hasn't been around in a few years. But you have to see how ridiculous that stance is. You know what my mother's like."

"I do. Which is why I think you're not giving her enough credit. She's way more reasonable than you assume."

I love sharing Mama with Mat. I love that someone outside of our family gets to benefit from her affection and warmth. I love that she was there to ease his suffering, if only a bit.

What I don't love: that Mat now believes he understands my mother better than I do.

"She sent you to the deli," I say, my voice low and controlled. "She knew I was there with Taran. She knew it would hurt your feelings to see us. But she did it anyway, because she wanted to drive us apart."

"Wrong," he counters. "She didn't *want* to tell me. I insisted."

I wrinkle my forehead.

"Really," he says. "She even warned me that I might not like what I see but not to jump to any conclusions."

My mind's spinning. I don't understand. What is Mama's goal here? Whose side is she on? "Did she ask you about kissing me?"

He shakes his head. "I think she started to, but she cut herself off. I'm not sure why. Maybe she wanted to come to an understanding with you first?"

Ha. This is where he's completely off base. Mama's never come to an understanding with me, ever. The normal course of our interaction is that she dictates and I follow.

"So you want me to refuse to date Taran," I recap dully. "Why? I really don't think she'll buy that we're fake-dating anymore."

"I don't want to fake-date," he says, his eyes glittering. "I want to date for real."

Oh. *Oh.* These are the words I'd been waiting for. The ones that would've sent me straight into bliss, if they'd been uttered twelve hours earlier. But now, they feel more like fish sauce rubbed in my wounds.

"I can't ask my parents if we can date for real," I say regretfully. "They'll never agree."

"Why not? You just need to try."

But I'm no longer hearing him. An image seizes me with startling clarity, and I lean forward, drumming my fingers on the dashboard.

When Papa was twelve years old, he snuck a cigarette from an older boy's pouch. He got violently ill after he smoked it, he explained to us. So ill that he swore off cigarettes from that day forward.

"What if we admitted that we kissed but only because we were curious?" I ask excitedly. "And then we decided it wasn't for us. Because first kisses are awful. Everybody knows that. We realized, the moment our lips touched, that we saw each other as brother and sister. Still, I want to keep dating you because I'm comfortable with you." My fingers drum faster. "What do you think? This could work. I think she might actually buy it."

He hasn't so much as blinked. "And then what?"

"Then we get to date. We'll be able to spend time together."

"Sneaking kisses when we can?"

I flush. "No. We *don't* sneak kisses. That's what got us

in trouble in the first place. I've already lost Mama's trust once. I won't do it again."

He opens the door and gets out of the car, even though we're in the middle of our conversation. Even though he said he doesn't like to fight in public. It's as though his feelings, his thoughts, are so big that they can no longer be contained by the Jeep.

I hop out of the car, too, walking around the bumper to meet him.

"You want us to lie," he says.

"It's not lying—"

"Pretending? Practicing? It all amounts to the same thing." His lips are parallel chopsticks. His eyes, clear and utterly solemn. "I've already had one person I loved not fight for me. I'm not interested in another one."

I feel like someone punched me in the gut. I am nothing like his mother—*nothing*. But if he can't see that, I don't have the slightest idea where we stand. "If you trusted me, even a little, you wouldn't put me in this position."

"This is hard for me, too," he says quietly. "I've had your parents' good opinion all my life. That's not easy to come by. The last thing I want is to jeopardize my relationship with them. But my feelings for you are so strong that I'm willing to take the risk. Are you?"

I shake my head, not just in response to his question but to this entire conversation. "We don't need to put an official title on what we are to each other. I'm not going to abandon you like your mother did."

He turns away from me. "That's not what this is about."

"Of course it is," I say. "If your mom hadn't called this morning, you wouldn't be doubting me."

"No, Winnie," he says. "This isn't about my mom. This is about us. We can't control your parents' rules. But we can control whether or not we even try. The Winnie I thought I knew, the one who made me fall for her without even trying—*she* may be a rule follower, but she also fights for what she wants. At least, the Winnie from four years ago would have. Isn't that the real reason why you opened my binder to embarrass me? You were trying to make me notice you again." His voice is as certain as I've ever heard it. "But if you can't fight for me now…well, maybe you're not the person I thought you were."

My eyes sting. My heart aches. My body feels like it's been wrapped with barbed wire. I can't take a step in any direction without getting cut.

"You don't mean that," I whisper helplessly. Ineffectually.

"I'm going to leave now," he says. I can't think of any reason to announce his departure other than to give me an opportunity to stop him.

I want to stop him. I do. I just don't know how.

He gives me one last searching look. His eyes are pained, but so is my chest. So is my breath. There's nothing about this moment that doesn't hurt.

"I didn't want our friendship to end like this," he says. "Don't be a stranger. Okay?"

I nod, no longer capable of speech. And then he gets back in his car and drives away.

Chapter Thirty-Five

I slip inside the front door without making any noise, placing my shoes soundlessly inside the built-in shelves. I take the stairs two at a time. And finally, finally, I make it inside my room and fling myself on my bed. Without my parents seeing. Without breaking down.

I'm used to swallowing my feelings, to letting the tears rain inside me. I don't think even Taran guessed how upset I was, and he was the one who drove me home. (Proving, once and for all, that he *is* a good guy.)

But now that I'm alone, I let the cries come in huge, shaking gasps. So loud, in fact, that I have to shove a pillow against my mouth to keep my parents from running up the stairs.

You're not the person I thought you were.

Eight words. A simple sentence. One that's not even intrinsically unkind, if you take it word by word.

How can they hurt so damn much?

Those words slice into my heart, severing my arteries, piercing my soul. I've cried over Mat before, from the silly squabbles we had as kids to the very real loss of our friendship four years ago. But never like this.

The ache sits on my chest like a tangible toy, useless and broken. I wish it were an object, because then I could remove it. I could put it somewhere far away, so that I don't have to feel this way anymore. So that I don't have to endure this pain any longer.

Our good times play through my mind like a movie reel. The moments he made me laugh, the looks that warmed me from the inside out. The way he kissed me like I was someone more than I ever dreamed I could be.

I don't know if he's right. Or if I am. Or, hell, maybe, probably we're both wrong.

The realization doesn't help. My heart doesn't hurt any less because the assignment of blame doesn't change the situation. It won't bring Mat back to me.

Later—twenty minutes? an hour? *two* hours?—there's a soft knock at my door.

"Winnie, are you okay?" Mama's voice drifts through the wood. "I made tea for you."

I attempt to sound like a human being. "Thanks, Mama. You can leave it at the door. I'm not feeling well."

"I knocked earlier. You didn't answer."

"I must've been asleep." I was most definitely crying. We must both know that. But, as always, it's easier to tell a white lie than to wade into the messy truth.

"I'm coming in." She doesn't usually give a verbal warning. Usually, she barges in after a quick knock. I think of Mat, announcing his departure, and my eyes sting once again.

Mama walks inside, places a mug of tea on my desk, and sits on my bed. For a moment, we consider each other in the dim light. And then I dive into her arms.

I don't know if she's mad at me. I'm not sure where we

stand, because we still haven't discussed the kissing. But she's Mama, and she's here, and at this moment, that's all that matters.

"Shhhhh," she says into my hair, rocking me gently. "Shhhhh."

When I was younger, I used to respond to her shushing with, "But I'm not saying anything!" Now, I know that this is just her way of soothing me.

"I'm sorry, Mama," I mumble against her shoulder. "You and Papa trusted me not to kiss him. And I did it anyway."

"I'm sorry, too," she says simply. "My entire goal was for you to avoid feeling this pain. If I contributed to your heartbreak by choosing the wrong person…well, then I've also failed you."

I lift my head so that she can see my eyes, bloodshot and all. "You didn't choose wrong. Mat's always been a good guy. He still is. We just didn't work out."

I wish I could say more. I want to unload to her everything that's happened. But that's not how our relationship works. That's never been the way it functioned.

I still remember Ari patiently explaining to me, in our early teens. *Keep your mouth shut when our parents lecture you. The only thing you're allowed to say is "chai, ka" or "kao jai, ka."*

"Yes" or "I understand." Didn't matter if I meant it. These answers merely symbolized that I'd listened. That I'd heard their instruction. That I'd shown the proper respect.

Sometimes, I get so bored of this respect. Yes, it's important, and yes, it's my parents' due. But respect also prevents us from admitting our infractions—and talking about them. That's what I want. For us to talk. Not as friends, exactly, but certainly without this yawning chasm between us.

Wishes are pointless, however. She's the only mother I have, and we love each other. That has to be enough.

"What did Papa say?" I wet my lips, a little surprised I have any moisture left in my body. "Is he very mad?"

Mama might be the loud one, but it's Papa's reaction that concerns me more. He withdraws when he's angry, and that's a whole lot scarier because you don't know what he's thinking. You don't know if you've disappointed him—permanently.

Mama sighs, her entire body deflating. "I didn't tell him about you kissing Mat. So long as you and I can clear the air, I don't think he needs to know."

My heart swells. Not telling Papa is huge. I've never crossed the line before, not like this. I'm not sure if he would ever forgive me. It's a testament to Mama's love that she's willing to keep my deception a secret.

"Thank you, Mama," I say quietly. "I'm sorry I broke your trust. The kiss didn't mean anything. It was just an experiment, I guess you could say. It won't happen again."

The lie sits on my heart, weighing me down, trying to pull me into the abyss. Who knew I'd get so good at fibbing? But the truth won't make a difference now. At this moment, my priority is repairing my relationship with Mama.

She nods, giving me one more hug. "Drink your tea," she says, dropping the subject. This, more than anything, tells me that she does trust me.

And I cannot, I will not, let her down once more.

Chapter Thirty-Six

*D*on't be a stranger.

Those were Mat's last words to me, and the cliché could refer to any number of relationships, from the intense loathing we previously had for each other to the way Kavya embraces everyone she meets with jazz hands and a jazzier heart.

Four days after our fight, it's become increasingly apparent that Mat didn't mean any of those relationships. Because strangers can still treat each other with courtesy. Strangers can exchange banal comments about the weather, such as, "The rain in Spain falls mainly on the plain"— Bunny's standard response to just about any question when she was cast in *My Fair Lady* her junior year. Strangers don't speed-walk in the other direction when they see you coming. And they certainly don't brace themselves when you pass in the hall, as though you might be carrying an infectious disease.

So, yeah. Mat's not acting like a stranger, all right. He's acting way, way worse.

I slam my locker door. Hell, I shouldn't even be at school. I should be wallowing in my bedroom, with the blinds closed and the lights off, feeling sorry for myself.

But Mama wasn't having it.

"The best way to get over puppy break is to distract yourself," she said Monday morning. "So get up. Get dressed. And get to school."

"First of all, it's puppy love, not puppy *break*," I said indignantly. "And second, what I'm feeling is most certainly not that." Now, cat love, I might've considered. Especially if it was symbolized by the cat heads printed on my skirt.

"You shouldn't have any problem going to school, then." She pointed a finger at my door. "Move."

Student of the year, I am not. But I obeyed my mother like the good Thai girl that I am.

It's Thursday morning now, and I'm still here, at least physically if not mentally.

Kavya materializes by my elbow. "What's up, zinnia?" she says cheerfully.

"What?" I grunt. "That doesn't even rhyme."

"I know. But why should buttercups get all the attention? There are *lots* of yellow flowers, many of which are just as cute, and they never get mentioned, much less have songs written about them."

I sigh. "You are seriously weird, you know that?"

"So are you," she says, and I can't even argue.

My best friend stops in the middle of the hallway and turns me to face her. We're now a pair of interconnecting boulders in the school's natural current, forcing students to flow around us.

"You've been crying." Her tone is almost accusatory.

"A little." I attempt to smile. "The only good thing about this whole affair is that I got to try the waterproof mascara that Ari swears by. And she's right. It totally works."

"You don't need him," Kavya says. "I mean, you've got me. I can walk you to class, just like he does."

She curves her arms out to either side—I guess to look broader?—and rises onto her tiptoes. Then she saunters down the hall in an exaggerated version of Mat's swagger.

I giggle for the first time in ninety-six hours.

"What else?" she muses. "I don't need to hold your hand, since you don't believe in PDA. How about I just look at you longingly instead?"

She turns her topaz eyes to me, resting her chin on interlaced fingers and blinking rapidly.

The giggles morph into a full-on laugh. "Are you supposed to be me or Mat?"

She shrugs. "Either, really. You both were pretty gone over the other."

"Yeah." Sobering, I close my eyes. Kavya puts my hand on her shoulder and keeps walking, leading me through the throng.

My life is surreal. A week ago, I had a boyfriend. Sorta. Our relationship came together quickly and dissolved just as rapidly. If I spaced out, I would've missed it.

"Cheer up." My best friend marches us to class. "At least you can say you got the full high school dating experience. The falling-in-lust bit, as well as the requisite heartbreak. If your mom's goal was to give you practice, then she certainly succeeded."

I sigh. "I think Mama will only be happy if I also *practice* getting over him."

"You could try kissing someone else," Kavya suggests.

I open my eyes just as we walk into trig class. We take seats next to each other. Coaching me through heartbreak is just one more reason why Kavya and I should always have the same schedule. The administration should take notes.

"Does kissing someone new actually help?" I ask curiously.

"Who knows?" Kavya stretches her long legs into the aisle, admiring her silver toe polish. "Believe me, I've tried the tactic on a few occasions. But I've never really mourned any of my breakups, so maybe I'm not the right person to ask." One of our classmates comes upon Kavya's feet and scowls. My best friend apologizes and tucks her legs back under her desk. "Come to think of it, rebounding's not really your style."

"What is?" I yank my binder out of my backpack. It's hard to have a breakup style when you've never had a breakup.

"Maybe you can eat chocolate?" she suggests.

I wrinkle my nose. "Gives me acne."

"Listen to sappy music?"

"Ari did make an *I'm Just Not That Into You* playlist. But is it cheating if I didn't pick the songs?"

"I know. You could watch the *Pride and Prejudice* miniseries. The Colin Firth one. You can keep replaying that scene when Mr. Darcy gets out of the lake, his wet shirt plastered to his chest."

I look at her like she's eaten too many rum balls. "What?"

She grins. "Your mom got me intrigued with all these old rom-coms. I found a list of classics, and I've been binge-watching them."

"You too?" I groan. "I hope I never watch a rom-com ever again."

"True." She smiles impishly. "You don't need to *watch* the movies, since you're living one."

I search my binder for something to throw at her and find a bunch of multicolored highlighters. I hold them up threateningly, and Kavya squeals, crossing her arms to ward off the attack. Mr. Kim, our trig teacher, clears his throat.

We dutifully face forward. As we begin graphing sines, cosines, and tangents, I realize that I haven't felt like crying for twenty whole minutes.

There's that, at least.

*T*he feeling doesn't last.

At lunch, I sit with Kavya at our usual table in the courtyard, unpacking my usual lunch—seaweed, sushi rice, and avocado. The ending of my middle-school friendship with Mat also seems to have ended my creativity in packed lunches. Either that, or I've just outgrown celery stalks with cream cheese and M&M's.

What's not usual, however, are the people sitting on the other side of the courtyard. Before last week, Mat never ate lunch out here. But there he is, thirty feet away, sharing a bench with Delilah Martin.

I try not to stare. But my eyes are drawn like magnets to the picture-perfect couple. Mat, with his long legs and his sculpted jaw; Delilah, with her glowing skin and her generous smile. Charisma rolls off them in waves. Their fans crowd around, and I can hardly blame them. I'd want some of that perfection to rub off on me, too.

I guess Mat wasted no time rebounding. Of course, that would imply that he had something to get over in the first place.

His face is solemn—neither a smile nor words crack his granite lips. Delilah sits to his left, her hip smashed against his hip. She runs her fingers along his arm, tracing his veins, maybe measuring his muscles.

No concerns about PDA with this couple.

Their lunches sit in paper bags on the table, unopened. They're either not hungry…or maybe they're hungry for something else.

Red-hot vines slither over my chest. If they're this open in public, how do they behave in private? Does he also wear down her defenses by making her laugh? Does he cradle her face in his hands before he kisses her?

She probably doesn't have overprotective parents she has to appease. She clearly isn't restricted to touching him once a week, on a pretend date.

As I watch, Mat turns his head and says something to her. She looks up at him, her eyes adoring, their lips inches apart.

My heart squeezes so tightly that the vines might as well have transformed into a vise. Despite the open air in the courtyard, I can't seem to get a full breath.

"Winnie. Look at me," Kavya commands. *"Look at me."*

I turn to my best friend, dazed. She gestures for me to pick up my temaki sushi, her eyes soft. "Taran's headed this way, so act natural."

Automatically, I swivel in my seat, searching for him. My best friend groans. No one's ever accused me of being smooth.

But it hardly matters, because a moment later, Taran plops onto the bench next to me.

I force myself to smile. "Hi. Joining us for lunch?"

"If you'll have me." As always, he's angelically handsome and devilishly debonair—a lethal combination, if you were inclined to fall.

I, unfortunately, am not.

"Of course," I say with as much enthusiasm as I can muster. After all, Taran's an innocent bystander in this mess. There's no reason to be rude to him.

Especially since he doesn't have to seek me out at school. That's never been one of Mama's requirements, but Taran seems to be going above and beyond his role of fake boyfriend. As did Mat.

At the thought of his name, my heart flinches, and I sneak another glance across the courtyard. Their paper bags are unpacked now, and Delilah is batting her eyelashes at Mat. He says something, and her peal of laughter can be heard all the way across the courtyard.

"Winnie," Kavya says between gritted teeth. "You were about to tell me what your mom has set up for you two this Saturday."

"I don't know how she's going to top the deli date," Taran says.

My smile feels like a pair of oversize plastic lips. "Papa asked me how many people I'd convinced to order my sandwich. I was forced to tell him zero, much to his disappointment."

"Did you tell him that you would moan louder next time?" my fake boyfriend asks.

"I said, maybe they should be more careful about choosing the movie they want us to reenact."

"Somehow, I don't think that will deter them in the slightest." He takes a bite of a deep-dish pizza from the school cafeteria, clearly not heeding my earlier warning. "What's in store for us this time?"

"Karaoke," I say mournfully.

He snickers. "Why am I not surprised?"

My parents are wild about karaoke. They even host karaoke parties that last into the wee hours of the morning, which always makes me realize, to my chagrin, that *their* social life is way better than mine. "There's this scene from this movie—"

"*My Best Friend's Wedding*," Kavya interjects. "I just watched it last week. Cameron Diaz sings hideously out of tune, and the hero just falls more in love with her for it."

"Why is that?" Taran muses. "In movies, main characters are always doing these cringe-worthy things, and it just makes them more lovable. I don't get it."

"It makes them more relatable," I say. "Think about it. You have these ridiculously good-looking actors. And somehow, you have to suspend reality enough to believe that they don't have whomever they want falling at their feet."

"*I* have movie-star good looks," he says playfully. "And I don't get any girl I want."

"Who would that be?" Kavya asks.

Instead of responding, he turns and looks directly at me, just as my eyes are about to wander off again.

I freeze, my thoughts stuttering. What kind of game is Taran playing? He's already said he's not interested in me. Has he changed his mind? Or is this part of some larger scheme I don't know about?

Flushed, I look away. And my gaze collides directly with Mat's. Guess I'm not the only one sneaking glances.

As soon as our eyes meet, however, Mat drops his head and brushes his hand against one of Delilah's dangling earrings. She smiles prettily.

I swallow, which is not as easy as it sounds, with a throat lined with spikes.

I don't hate Delilah. She might be a little gossipy, but overall, she's a nice girl with killer style. What's more, she's always been friendly to me, to everyone else, regardless of their social status.

But I don't think I'll wear dangling earrings ever again.

Chapter Thirty-Seven

I lie on my back in the middle of my bed, idly shooting foam bullets at the wall. My aim is off, either because I'm lying down or because the lights are dimmed. Or maybe it's because I don't have a particular target.

Normally, I can sketch Mat's face in five minutes flat. I've done it so often that I have his features memorized, from the straight eyebrows to the flared nose.

But I don't want to shoot a Nerf gun at Mat right now. I can no longer work out my feelings toward him with simulated violence—mostly because I don't have any anger left. Now I'm just sad.

I take aim at various parts of my room instead: the edge of my desk, a single blade of my ceiling fan, the top of my closet door. Any location where I don't risk the bullet bouncing back and taking out my eye.

When I run out of ammunition, I let the Zombie Sideswipe fall listlessly to my side.

I could do this all night, since it's Friday evening and I have nowhere else to be.

Correction: I turned down every invitation so that I *would* have nowhere to be. The moment I got home from school, I changed into pajama pants and a tank top. And then I did what I've been wanting to do all week. What I *would've* done, if Mama hadn't interfered.

I wallow.

My date with Taran is tomorrow. I suppose, when the time comes, I'll rally once more. I'll go through the motions that will make my parents happy. In the past, that was enough—being a good daughter, fulfilling their expectations. But now, the gesture feels empty…and inexplicably lonely.

I miss Mat. I miss not having him in my life, in one way or another, as a friend or an enemy or something else. Something more.

Looking back, I've finally figured out that you don't spend that much energy hating someone if they're not important to you. If they don't matter.

Mat has always been important to me. He probably always will be.

I miss his superiorly raised eyebrows. I miss his hilarious text messages. I even miss his casual confidence—because I understand, now, that it stems not from arrogance but a steady sense of self. He doesn't have to hide behind anyone else, because he's proud of who he is.

Unlike me.

I press my hands against my temples, not sure what to do. I don't know how to change the way things are. The person I am.

Downstairs, the doorbell rings. There's a commotion at the door, a few high-pitched shrieks, an excited shout or two. I don't move. Might be a package, possibly a visitor. Whatever or whomever it is, it can't possibly concern me.

The shrieks get louder, and footsteps pound up the stairs. I push up on my elbows. The voices are feminine, eerily familiar. It can't possibly be... But oy tai, what if it is...?

My bedroom door flies open, and Ari and Bunny rush inside.

I collapse on my mattress, shock turning my bones liquid. My sisters. But how? They weren't due for another visit home for months. They're so busy with studies, their friends, their new lives.

But they're here. I can't believe it, but they're *here*.

They jump on my bed, unconcerned by my lack of response. In an instant, we're tangled together, Bunny's perfume enveloping us, Ari's hair tickling my chin.

I burst into tears.

One of my sisters pats me. The other one smooths back my hair, tucking it behind my ear. I can't tell which hands belong to whom, but it doesn't much matter. Because I love them both, together and individually.

"Poor Winnie," Ari says, snuggling up to me.

"It will be okay." Bunny lies on her stomach, her chin in her hands. "We're home now."

I swipe at my cheeks. "But how? Why?"

My sisters exchange a glance. I may be out of practice interpreting their silent-speak, but I'm competent enough to figure out that they settle on the truth.

"Papa called us." Bunny flips onto her back, lifting first one leg and then the other. That's my sister for you. Never wastes an opportunity to fit in some exercise. "He was worried. He thought you didn't seem like yourself, and both you and Mama were giving him these short, one-word explanations."

Because we were trying, desperately, to hide my

betrayal from him. Silly of us to think that he wouldn't notice.

"We were free this weekend," Ari continues. "At least, there wasn't anything we couldn't move around. So we hopped on a train after our last class. And here we are."

I blink. "You came all this way to see me? But you're so busy."

Maybe I shouldn't be so surprised. I know they love me. But as unconditional as their love may be, our relationship has never been a two-way street. All the admiration and idolatry flow in one direction: from me to them. Rightly or wrongly, I've always felt that I got the time that was left over from their other pursuits.

"Winnie," Ari scolds. "Don't you know that you're our foundation? If you're not happy, then we're not happy."

"If someone's hurt you, then we need to kill him. I've sharpened my talons just for this occasion." Bunny wiggles her perfectly manicured nails in the air.

I laugh through my tears. "You remember when we went to Disney World and the sun came out, even though it was still raining? I thought it was pure magic. That's what you two are to me: magic."

As though planned, they drop their heads onto my shoulders in unison. Now *they're* the foundation propping *me* up.

"Spill it," Ari says. "Last week, everything was going so well. You had your first kiss, your first date with Mat. Now, all of a sudden, you're with Taran. What?"

I tell them everything, from Mat's kisses at Lowcountry to him walking in on Taran and me holding hands at the deli. From Taran wanting to date me to please his mother to Mat asking me to tell our parents the truth.

"Can you imagine? He wanted a real chance at dating

me. But that would never happen. Right?" I sit up, my sisters spilling off my shoulders. "I mean, our parents are completely unreasonable. They wouldn't even let you study with a guy. What are the chances they'd accept me with an actual boyfriend?"

I look at them pleadingly, begging them to back me up. To assure me that I was right for sending Mat away.

They exchange another look, but this one is too nuanced for me to decipher.

"A year ago, I would've said you had a better chance of getting a hole in your head," Bunny says slowly. "But the situation's changed. Our parents have college-age daughters now, ones who are not only allowed but also encouraged—no, *demanded*—to date. Maybe they've adjusted their thinking with regards to you, as well."

"What do you have to lose, Winnie?" Ari puts a hand on my leg to stop my bouncing knee. "It's not a slam dunk, but why not at least have the conversation?"

The bed is suddenly too crowded. I crawl off the mattress, onto the carpet, away from my sisters. My thoughts are too big for my head, my emotions too full for my body.

That's the million-baht question, as Mama likes to say. The one Mat couldn't understand, the one I refused to answer. *What do you have to lose, Winnie? What? What? What?*

"They might not love me anymore," I blurt.

Two sets of eyebrows raise. I might as well be holding a mirror between them. I watch as their eyes turn toward each other in slow motion and then face me once again.

"Why wouldn't they love you?" Bunny asks carefully.

My mind bangs up against a solid wall. Beyond that barrier are the essential truths of my identity. The ones that I've always known but have never said out loud.

"It's embarrassing," I mutter.

"Winnie, this is us!" Ari cries. "If you can't admit the reasons to your sisters, then whom can you tell?"

"Nobody," I shout. "That's the point. Nobody needs to know, ever."

"And then what?" Bunny rises to her knees, as though preparing for battle. "You continue to lie here, shooting foam bullets against your ceiling, forever?"

I pace in the tiny space between my desk and dresser. It's six feet, at the most. I'd kill for double digits. Think I'd died and been reincarnated for twenty feet. "You wouldn't understand, either of you. You've always been so perfect."

They both start to protest, and I hold up my hand, stopping them.

"For as long as I can remember, you two were…well, everything," I say. "Smart, outgoing, talented, pretty, poised, accomplished. That list could go on for paragraphs, if not pages. Our parents had ridiculously high standards for you because they knew you could meet them. I have so many reasons to love and admire you both. In addition to the above, Ari, you're so giving and selfless and kind. Bunny, you're bold and daring and original." I stop walking. My shoulders slump. "There aren't any adjectives left for me."

"It's not a zero-sum game." Bunny scoots to the edge of the bed. She lifts a hand, as though to touch me, but doesn't, in case I crumple. "A quality's not taken off the market just because we happen to have it."

"Try to see it from my perspective. At best, I would be a carbon copy of one of you. A flimsy facsimile. One that's similar to but not as good as the original. What would be the point?"

I don't wait for an answer, because there *is* no good answer. "I had one thing going for me. One thing that you two *weren't* amazing at. Listening. Being the good Thai girl. You're loud and smart and opinionated. You spoke up when you disagreed. You rebelled."

I take a breath. My sisters' eyes are as wide as lotus buds, but they don't contradict me.

"And so I figured out a long time ago that the only way for me to earn our parents' love is to be the girl who never rebelled. The one who obeyed. At all costs." I look down. I don't want to say the next part. Don't want to admit, even to my sisters, how pathetic I am.

But I'm already most of the way there. So I close my eyes, and I push out those final words. "If I give that up, what do I have left?"

Soft hands touch my elbows. I'm steered onto the bed so that I'm sitting between my sisters. Ari picks up one hand, intertwines it with her own, and Bunny picks up the other.

"Can I say something?" Ari asks.

I laugh without much amusement. "You can say whatever you want, whenever you want. You always do." I'm not bitter at the way things are. They simply are.

"We listened," Bunny reminds me. "Will you listen, too?"

"I'll try." I'm painfully aware that this was all that Mat asked of me: to try. I didn't do it then. But here, with my sisters, maybe I can now.

"We could tell you that none of what you described is true." Ari grips my hand. "That Bunny and I feel like the most pathetic freshmen to have ever attended Wash U."

"We could also tell you why we love you," Bunny chimes in, without missing a beat. They're so in sync that sometimes I wonder if they plan their speeches ahead of time. But how could they, this time, when they didn't know what I was going to say?

"We don't love you because you're copies of us, and it's certainly not because you obey," Bunny continues. "Which, frankly, I'm not so sure you're that great at anyway. Remember the time you took my strappy sandals and colored in the clear heel with a black Sharpie?"

"Not my fault," I protest. "That was during my *Frozen* stage, and you would *not* stop bragging about your icicle shoes. I wanted icicle shoes like Elsa, too."

"Girls," Ari warns. "Not the point."

"Right," Bunny says, her lips twitching. "Where was I? Oh yes. We love you because you're *you*, Winnie. People like being around you. You make people smile and laugh. You have this uncanny ability to make others feel like the best version of themselves. That's why people gravitate toward you. Our whole family, we all revolve around *you*. You're the glue. The very core."

"But that's not something we can *tell* you," Ari adds. "Or at least, we can, because we just did. But it's something that will sink in only when you believe it yourself. That's why I've always liked Mat, you know. With him, you always seem more confident. More you."

I pull my hands from their grasp. Not because I don't want their support but because our palms are getting sweaty. "That could take forever. The whole believing-in-myself bit."

"Well, yeah," Bunny says. "I mean, look at me. I know I seem like the ever-wise older sister—"

Ari nudges me and pretends to gag. I stifle a giggle.

"But don't forget, I'm only twenty months older than you and six minutes older than Ari. I'm a work in progress, too."

"Thank you for that, O humble one," Ari says with an exaggerated eye roll. She turns back to me. "The key is to surround ourselves with people who will help us become the person we want to be. That includes people who encourage us to take steps in the right direction."

I chew on the inside of my cheek, not convinced.

Bunny shoots to her feet. I recognize the brisk movement, the decisive action. This is the mannerism she adopts when she's about to take charge. "Do you love our parents, Winnie?"

"Of course I do."

"This is the same lecture I've been giving Ari all week," she says. "If you love them, you have to give them a little credit. Give them the chance to prove you wrong, to show that they've been growing and adapting right alongside us." She takes a deep breath. "Maybe this is both your and Ari's chance to clear the air."

"What do you mean?" I ask. "What does Ari have to come clean about?"

Bunny and I both look at Ari, who seems to be trying to fold in on herself. "Oh, um. You remember how Bunny was being totally outrageous at Family Breakfast, because she was trying to set the stage, in case I decided to confess?"

"When, Ari," my other sister interjects. "For *when* you decided to confess."

"I didn't actually make up my mind until this very moment." Ari straightens, her shoulders unfurling like the petals of a flower. That's when I remember that she met someone, too. Someone unexpected. "What do you think, Winnie? I can be brave if you can. Want to do this together?"

I'm still not sure what Ari's secret is. But I know one thing. Everything is easier—and better—with my sisters.

"Okay," I say reluctantly.

We come together in a group hug, and that's when I

realize that Mat was wrong about one thing, at least. My sisters may cast a long shadow, but it's not necessarily a bad thing for me to linger in their shade.

I don't have to hide there. Instead, I can seek refuge. I can admit my insecurities. I can bolster my true self so that when I finally emerge, into the light, I am that much closer to the person I want to be.

The Winnie I know I can be.

The girl who *can* stand on her own—but who understands that it's much more effective, heartening, and fun to stand with her sisters.

Chapter Thirty-Eight

The hallway is not wide enough for the three of us to walk abreast, so Bunny goes first, and Ari and I follow. Either because she's the big sister and she likes to lead or because Ari and I are mildly terrified and need someone else to pave the way.

"My knees are shaking," Ari whispers to me.

"Does that actually happen?"

"Mine are."

We look down, and sure enough, her knees are vibrating through her thick navy tights printed with little hedgehogs.

"Cute tights, though," I say.

"I thought you would like them," she says, brightening. "Bunny thought they were ridiculous, but I got them because they reminded me of you." She gasps, realizing what she just said. "I didn't mean —"

"It's okay. I'd rather be known for my supercute style than for, say, being clumsy."

"That was her second choice." Bunny looks over her shoulder, flashing pearly white teeth. "When she misses you, she goes to YouTube and watches videos of people falling down."

I suck in a breath. "Is that true, Ari?"

"Well…" She offers me a sheepish smile. "I only do it because I miss you. My baby sister. That should count for something, right?"

"I guess," I grumble, although inside, I'm smiling, too. The banter with my sisters manages what should've been impossible: taking my nerves down a notch.

When we round the corner, Mama's at the bottom of the stairs, craning her neck as though she's trying to hear one floor up. She jumps when she spots us, and by the time we descend to the main level, she's retreated to the kitchen and is sitting with Papa at the small dining table.

Papa's reading on a tablet and drinking chrysanthemum tea from a blue lace ceramic cup. The sink and counters are immaculate, as usual, and steam rises from the ever-present rice cooker.

Day or night, summer or winter, there is jasmine rice in our kitchen. Currently cooking, just finished cooking, or about to be cooked. Some people consider signs of the apocalypse to be empty city streets or flesh-eating zombies. I'll know that the world is falling apart if I come downstairs and there's no rice.

"Mother." Only Bunny can inject equal parts exasperation and amusement into that word. "Were you eavesdropping on us?"

"Next time, try a glass against the door," Ari says helpfully. "Or, you know, a baby monitor."

"Why would I eavesdrop on my own daughters?" Mama sniffs. "Don't you think I have better things to do? I was spending time with Papa. We were talking about—" She shoots him a frantic look.

"Thriving," he supplies. "Ways for us old folks to thrive, now that two-thirds of our offspring are at college."

"Ew." I cover my ears. "Not this again. Can you please go thrive on your own time?"

My sisters blink, mystified. I start to explain the article on thriving and public displays of affection when Mama interrupts.

"That's enough of that." Her face is the same color as Mat's when he sampled the Everythang sauce. "What was so important that you girls had to hole upstairs for more than an hour?"

"I thought you had more important matters than your daughters' affairs," Bunny teases.

"I do. Your father wants to know." She nudges his shoulder. "Don't you, Papa?"

"Hmm?" He glances up from his tablet. "Whatever your mother says, I completely agree." He makes a fist and pounds it on the table.

We all giggle, even Mama.

"Fine," she admits. "The truth is, I desperately want to know about all your lives. It's not easy being the outsider, only getting snippets of information here and there."

"Oh, Mother." Bunny swoops in and kisses her on the forehead. "You know we love you."

Mama pats her cheek. "You just don't tell me anything."

That's an opening if I've ever heard one. I nudge Ari. She pokes me back. I prod her once again, and we're in danger of disintegrating into a Nudge War when Bunny shoots us a warning glare.

"I have something to say." Ari puffs out a breath, dislodging her long bangs. We couldn't decide if our parents would react better to my news or hers. So we went with a coin toss—and she lost. "I've met someone. And it's serious."

Mama squeals so loudly that my eardrums vibrate. And then she's shaking Papa's shoulders. "I knew it wasn't too early to ask the fortune-teller about baby names. I knew it."

"It's not what you think," Ari says.

Her words are quiet, barely audible, but they cleave the air like a knife. Silencing Mama. Killing her excitement.

Her hand tightens on Papa's shoulders. *"Mai khwam wa arai?"* she asks in Thai, as though fear has chased away her English. *What do you mean?*

Ari's eyes bounce all over the room, wild, desperate, as though there's no safe place to land. And then they settle on her twin. Just like that, Ari's limbs still, and her features become smooth.

Oh, to have that twin wizardry.

"What I have to tell you," Ari begins, her voice the tensile strength of steel, "is that since I've gotten to college, I've realized that I'm bisexual. And the person I'm dating, the one I'm very serious about…is a woman."

No one speaks. Even the rice cooker has stopped hissing, even the faucet doesn't drip.

Papa clears his throat. "Well."

Mama rolls her shoulders like a batter coming up to home plate, focusing her eyes, emptying her thoughts. She opens her mouth—and I clutch Bunny's sleeve. I can't help it. There's no predicting where Mama will go. What she'll say. How she'll hurt.

"Is she very accomplished?" Mama asks.

I gape. I could be a meme for utter and total shock. Because that particular question? Didn't make the top one hundred responses that I expected.

"Very," Ari says, recovering first. "Her name's Sabrina. She's Black and a senior at Wash U. She's just been accepted to Harvard Medical School."

Ah, the magic word. No, scratch that. *Two* magic words. Using "Harvard" and "medicine" in the same sentence exponentially magnifies their power.

Tension leaks out of the air, and the whole room seems to take a breath.

"That's just wonderful." Papa holds up his teacup as though he's toasting us. "She'll be able to take care of you."

"Um, excuse me?" Ari arches a delicate eyebrow. "I can take care of myself."

"Of course you can," he says, as though she just stated that there was rebirth after death. "I raised all my girls to be independent. But this simply gives you an extra safety net—and me more peace of mind."

"When can we visit?" Mama pulls a calendar out of the island drawer and consults the dates. "She's Black, you say? We'll take her to a Thai restaurant. It's not home cooking, but at least we'll be able to gauge how she tolerates our spices."

"We'll order nam phrik kapi," Papa muses. "Notoriously stinky to falang. If she can eat that, she's in."

Bunny groans, pulling out a chair and dropping into it. "Seriously, Papa? Are you really going to evaluate all our suitors and suitresses with a taste test? That seems so wrong."

"Sabrina's cleared the other hurdles," he argues. "This is only one more."

I'm lost. It's like my family zipped over to another planet—and forgot to invite me.

"Wait a minute." I look from Mama to Papa. "You're not disappointed?"

Don't get me wrong. I'm thrilled that Ari's found someone who appreciates every last facet of her, from her eyelashes to her socks, from her strength to her loyalty. I believe love is love, and it is always beautiful.

But Mama and Papa come from a different generation. That's why we didn't know how they would react. That's why Ari was so nervous. Is it possible that she stressed for no reason at all?

Papa gestures for Ari and me to join them at the table, pouring tea into three more cups. I sit between my parents, and Ari joins Bunny at the other end.

"I think you've mistaken our rules for something they're not," Papa says. "They're meant to protect you. To guide you onto the most direct path to happiness. But how you girls get there is up to you."

"I worry, of course." Mama hands out the cups and waits for us to take a sip of the flower tea, sweetened by brown sugar. Always delicious, even during this whirlwind conversation.

"It's not easy to be in a same-sex relationship," she continues. "People can be unkind. We face enough discrimination, being Thai in this country. Ideally, I wouldn't want you to face any more. But Ari is who she is. And we will support her. Always."

Papa's eyes twinkle. "That is, so long as you give us, and especially your mothe—"

"Babies," she blurts. "I don't care which gender. Doesn't matter which race. Just so long as you give me grandbabies, to cuddle and love, before I die."

Ari beams. "Will do."

I've never seen any of us react so positively to Mama's grandbaby obsession, ever.

And now, I suppose, it's my turn.

I rotate the teacup in my palms, hoping to leach some confidence from its heat. Ari has done a beautiful job setting me up, even though that's not what any of us intended.

Please, pra Buddha cho, let my parents remember what they said about wanting us to be happy. About supporting us, for always.

"I have a confession as well," I say.

Papa extends his arm behind Mama's chair, touching her shoulder. She jumps, because she's not used to his newfound penchant for casual touches.

And neither am I. Let's hope this small change portends a larger shift in their attitudes.

"You don't know this, Papa, but I kissed Mat the other day," I begin.

He flinches so hard that I'm surprised his teacup doesn't crack. But although his face turns the color of a mangosteen, he must sense there's more, because he gestures for me to continue.

I look down at the pale-yellow liquid. A few chrysanthemum buds gather at the bottom of my cup, but try as I might, I can't read them like tea leaves.

"I told Mama the kiss didn't mean anything," I say. "That I was just trying it out, the way you experimented with cigarettes. But I was lying. The truth is, I really care about Mat. I might even love him. And not just as a friend."

I take a deep breath. This is it. The moment I put my love on the line…for love. My eyes find my sisters, sitting at the opposite end of the table. Bunny's fiddling with the pack of dried chrysanthemum buds, and she shoots one of the buds into her empty teacup. Ari flashes me a thumbs-up and mouths, *She scores!*

And I know, no matter how my parents react, that this is fitting. This is right.

I need to embrace my true self, and they can accept me or not.

Love me or not.

"I don't want to practice any more. I don't want to pretend any longer. With your permission, I'd like to date Mat for real."

The silence is expected. But oh, not the length. Not the depth and height. I count one hundred seconds. Bunny stops shooting chrysanthemum buds to cross her fingers, and Ari puts away her phone, where she's probably been texting Sabrina. My parents hold an epic eye conference that rivals my sisters'.

"Well. This is unprecedented," Papa says finally. "We've never let you girls date in high school before."

"Um, news flash," Bunny says, taking more chrysanthemum buds out of the package. She's worked through half of the bag already. "Mat and Winnie *have* been dating. That's how this whole thing started. Because of *your* rules."

Mama whisks away Bunny's teacup, filled with the dried buds. I think she's going to scold my sister for wasting them, but she simply swaps out the full cup with her own empty one. "Fake dates," she clarifies. "Why do you think I went to so much trouble to model them after the movies? To remind the kids—*and* us—that these dates are fictional and not real."

This conversation isn't proceeding the way that I wanted. They're not coming around as quickly as I hoped. Can a twenty-month age gap, the difference between college and high school, really matter so much?

Apparently so.

I need to tell them more. To explain more of what's in my heart.

"I've never asked you to reconsider your rules," I say. "Ari and Bunny are always forging new ground. They're constantly making you question your decisions and adapt. But not me. My rules were always handed down to me, and

I've never asked you to change them. Well, I'm asking you now. Not as the youngest of your three daughters. Not as an extension of the twins. But as *me*. Winnie."

I take a deep breath. "I know your rules are designed to make my life easier. I know you want to save me from heartache. And I was always happy to go along with your wishes because I wanted to please you. I wanted to be the good Thai girl." I lick my lips, but it doesn't do any good, since my tongue is furnace-dry. "I needed you to love me."

"Oh, Winnie," Mama says immediately. "You know our love for you is unconditional."

I shake my head. "I *don't* know that, though. That's part of the problem. But I'm realizing now, maybe that's my fault as much as anyone's. Because I never told you how I felt or what I needed. I thought…" I falter again. My sisters nod reassuringly, which gives me the strength to continue. "I thought that I always had to agree with you in order for you to love me."

"Not true," Mama says. "We love *you*, which means we also love your thoughts and your opinions. Even if they clash with what we think is best."

"And we always will love you. No matter what," Papa confirms. "Even if you girls are responsible for my ever-changing hairstyle. Pretty sure I got the white hair on my left side from worrying about Ari. And the white hair on my right from Bunny."

"Oh, Papa." Ari sighs. "Your hair is completely black."

His lips twitch. "That's because I dye it." He turns to me, his mouth sobering. "Just to be clear, you know what you're asking, right? You're asking me to increase my supply of hair dye."

I want to smile, but it's too soon. I haven't received their blessing yet. "Yes, Papa. Because you and Mama can't save me from my mistakes, from the inevitable heartache. From all the hurts that are just part of growing up. My life is going to happen, whether you like it or not, and you have to let me live it."

I pick up both my parents' hands. Never ones to be left out, Ari and Bunny join our circle.

"I'm not Ari or Bunny," I continue. "I'm not even *you*, Mama. You can't correct the pains of your past through us, and I'm begging you. Please let me forge my own path, whether it be with dating or school or my career."

With my newfound realizations, I'm now well and determined to pursue my art next year at Northwestern. But I can't push my parents too hard. That's a conversation for another time, another day.

My parents engage in another eye consult.

"You're right," Mama says finally. "It hasn't been easy to reconcile the way I was raised with the pace of life here in America. But I do love you, Winnie. Don't ever doubt that. I love you for who you are, not as a substitute for the twins. Not as a do-over for myself. If you're willing to meet us halfway…well, I think we can allow you to date Mat. At least, we can see how it goes."

My heart leaps. Am I hearing correctly? Or did my brain blank out during some vital phrases?

"I need to whiten that middle stripe, after all," Papa adds. "As it stands, my natural hair color resembles a reverse skunk."

Holy moly. I did hear correctly. My parents are letting this Tech girl date in high school. For real this time.

I collapse against my chair, dazed. I can't believe I've won this first battle. There's another battle to be fought, one whose outcome I'm not at all sure about. But I never truly thought I would get even this far, so I have to celebrate this hard-won victory for what it is. For what it means.

"Don't think you've seen the end of the composition book," Mama warns. "There will be rules."

"*Very* strict rules," Papa adds.

I gather enough energy to smile. "I wouldn't know what to do without them."

Chapter Thirty-Nine

For the fifth (and final) phase of my art project, I've outdone myself.

Across her grille, Mataline wears a plastic bib depicting a lobster. I've attached long pandan leaves—the kind you use to wrap Thai desserts—on each passenger door. A shopping bag hangs from one sideview mirror, and a particularly hideous yellow sweater is draped over the other.

In addition to these symbols of our fake dates, I've fastened mementos from our childhood all over the car windows: photographs of Mat and me making silly faces, foam bullets from our Nerf gun battles, even my lunch box from the seventh grade.

Essentially, I've turned Mat's Jeep into a collage of our entire relationship.

It's Monday afternoon, and my sisters spent the entire weekend helping me plan Mataline's new look before returning to Wash U on the Sunday night train. My art teacher, Mrs. Woods, excused me from seventh period so that I could put the whole ensemble together before school let out for the day. After I finished dressing Mat's car, I changed into a particularly cute burgundy skirt with cat heads printed all over it. Not because Mat likes this item of clothing but because we both do.

The timing was tight, but that's not why I wipe my sweaty palms along my skirt.

The truth is, getting my parents' permission to date Mat was only half the challenge. Because I'm really, absolutely *not* sure if Mat still wants to date me.

During our last conversation, he expressed his disappointment in me. He said that I wasn't the Winnie he thought I was. The brave girl he knew from childhood, the vulnerable one he's reconnected with these last weeks. By all outward appearances, he's moved on, to Delilah of the perfect skin. It may already be too late.

But still, I have to try. I *want* to fight for him.

Mataline's costume isn't enough. Words speak loudest when they're combined with actions, and I want to shout to him—to the rest of the world—that I care. That I'm not content to linger in the shadows anymore. That I'm willing to turn the spotlight on myself, in the most public way possible.

Matt's Jeep is parked in the third row of the school's front lot, and I'm hanging out by the headlights, again with their long, curly lashes (not technically representative of our relationship, but I couldn't resist).

The final bell rang a few minutes ago, and I squint at the front entrance of the school. Watching. Waiting. Students pour out of the building only to get snagged by the crowd that's forming around me. I can hardly blame them. I'm nothing short of a spectacle.

"Whatcha doing, Winnie?" Julia from trig asks.

"That's Mat's car," says Aziel, one of his friends. "*You* were the one behind the costumes? He never let on who it was."

"Are you and Mat together?" Lily, a particularly shrieky girl, shrieks. "Like, together-together?"

"Whatever is about to happen, I wouldn't miss it for the world," J.D. claims. "Don't care if Coach makes me run extra laps. Where's the popcorn?"

I tune them out as well as I can, rising onto my tiptoes to peer over the crowd. My eyes are trained on one spot and one spot alone: the front door. What if he left school early? Or took another exit? Chib-peng, what if he and Delilah found an empty classroom and are making out?

My stomach executes a front handspring. No. I can't think that way. I can't even allow that image to enter my mind or I'll tear into the streets, screaming.

Besides, I'm standing next to his car. He has to show up *sometime*. And I'm willing to wait. The crowd, however, may not. And I need them for my plan to achieve the full effect.

Just when I'm beginning to despair, the glass door swings open, and there he is. Tall, lanky. Black hair that falls into his eyes. A heart that may not be solid gold—but glittery enough to capture mine.

I push a button. Music streams out of the speakers I hooked up to Kavya's car, parked next to his. The karaoke machine throws lyrics on the screen, and I begin to sing.

Okay, to be fair, I screech more than sing. My pitch is only a tiny bit better than Cameron Diaz's in the iconic scene of *My Best Friend's Wedding*. I'm singing the same song. My voice warbles in a similar way. And I'm humiliating myself, just like her.

As if on cue, the crowd cheers. I don't know if they've

all seen the movie or if they just enjoy seeing someone make an epic fool of themselves.

Because I'm a fool, all right. My voice cracks on the high notes, and the crowd laughs, not necessarily with me. Adorable Cameron, I am not.

But that's a good thing. The only person I'm trying to be is me. Winnie Techavachara and no one else.

Still, I can't stop the doubts from sneaking in. Oy tai. What if this doesn't work? What if Mat doesn't forgive me and I've embarrassed myself for no reason?

I tighten my grip on the microphone. Stay positive. Even if I don't get the guy, I will have been true to myself. To my feelings. I have to hold on to that.

I mangle the song, keeping one eye on the lyrics and the other eye on Mat. Halfway across the lawn, he stops. He must've just caught sight of the crowd surrounding his Jeep. He looks around, as though he might bolt, but then—to my immense relief—he continues his approach.

Whispers zip through the onlookers, faster and more frantic with each of Mat's steps. And then the crowd parts to let him through.

When he's five feet away, I shut down the music, even though I am mid-lyric, and turn off the microphone. We stare at each other silently, and my mouth goes dry. How do we start? What do I say? How long will we stand here—?

"Hi," he says.

I laugh a little wildly. His greeting strikes me as hilarious, when I've clearly spent hours planning this scene. Or maybe it's not funny at all. Maybe my mind's just on the verge of revolting.

He studies the car, scrutinizing each piece of the decor, from the photos to the shopping bag to the bib.

"I was wondering about Mataline's final outfit," he says.

"Which emotion is this?"

I flush. I didn't expect to lead with this admission. But there's no hiding the answer, since photographs of each of Mataline's costumes will be on display in the art room.

"Love," I say simply.

His gaze darts sharply to me. As always, his eyes are deep, dark — and indecipherable.

"I told my parents," I say. "Everything. How I felt about you. My desire to date you for real."

He shifts the brown paper bag he's carrying from one hand to the other, not saying a word.

"I was supposed to go on a karaoke date with Taran on Saturday," I continue. "But I didn't. Because I realized that you're the only one I want to reenact ridiculous rom-com scenes with."

Out of the corner of my eye, I glimpse Taran in the crowd, standing next to Kavya. He was nothing but understanding when I explained the situation. He might not be my fake boyfriend anymore, but I hope I've gained a new friend.

Taran gives me a nod, and Kavya makes a fish face at me, one that never fails to make me smile. Bolstered, I face Mat once again.

"I'm not dating Taran anymore," I tell him. "In fact, my parents and I are done with this whole fake-dating business. I'm sorry it took me so long to figure out what I wanted." I fidget with my microphone. Would it help if I turned it on, if I shouted my feelings to the world?

I don't think so. In spite of the public scene that I've planned, all Mat ever asked is for me to be true to myself. "I'm done standing in the shadows. I'm ready to embrace the real Winnie. And, well, I want to be with you. This is me, fighting for you." My hands shake so badly that I almost drop the mike. "I hope you'll have me."

Gently, he takes the microphone from me and replaces it with the brown paper bag.

"I looked for you at lunch today," he says, his voice low and gravelly. "I couldn't find you."

"I, uh, spent the lunch period putting the final touches on Mataline's decor." *Do not babble. Please. Not now.*

"What's in the bag?" someone calls, saving me from asking the question.

"Bah mee moo dang," Mat says. Wavy yellow noodles and roast red pork. His eyes are on me, only me, as though we're the only two people in the parking lot. "Just like my mother used to make. Just like you used to love."

My breath makes it halfway up my windpipe — and gets stuck there.

"I don't know if it's edible," he continues, "but I wanted to make you lunch. I'm sorry that I pushed you away instead of giving you time to work through your feelings. Instead of trusting you. You were right. I got scared that you would leave me. Just like I was scared to talk to my mother. But I don't want to live my life that way." He takes a deep breath. "This weekend, I called my mother, and I asked her for the recipe. We didn't talk long, but it was a start."

He steps closer to me. "No relationship is perfect, Winnie. I know that. And *our* relationship might start and falter. But I hope that it never, ever ends. So yeah. I want to be with you."

My eyes are full, my heart fuller. Any moment now, the moisture that's gathering in my tear ducts will spill out. There's only one thing that I hate about this situation: that my gain must be someone else's loss.

"What about Delilah?" I ask.

Smiling, he picks up my hand, waves goodbye to the crowd, and helps me into his Jeep. We're not going anywhere, since my karaoke machine is still attached to Kavya's car, but at least we'll have more privacy.

"Delilah and I were never together," Mat says as he slides into the driver's seat, "but I told her on Thursday that I was interested in someone else. After I saw you at the picnic table with Taran, I knew I wanted to try and make us work."

He turns to me. His gaze is a warm caress over my face—my eyes, my nose, my lips. He's close, and one blink later, he's closer still. Now I understand why he wanted to retreat to the car. The crowd can still see us, but there's a thick windshield separating us from them.

He did this for me. Because of my discomfort with PDA. Because it's a compromise between our two positions, much like our relationship.

My heart swells. Pretty soon, it won't fit inside this car.

We kiss, and it is soft and chaste and perfect.

Outside, the crowd cheers, and our hugely public display doesn't bother me in the slightest.

I ease back a few inches. "I'm curious. How did you get the idea to make me lunch?"

He grins. "From your mother, actually. Last time we talked, she was raving about the ending of *Crazy Rich Asians*. And, well." He shrugs. "I don't have my mom's ring, so I decided to go with the next best thing. Her recipe for bah mee moo dang."

The laughter that bubbles out of me is full of joy. "I'd rather have this lunch over a ring any day of the week."

Epilogue

A *few months later…*

Me: Where are you today?

Mat: Kuala Lumpur. Wanna see?

A photo arrives of Mat in front of two silver skyscrapers, connected by a bridge. His right arm is out, as though it's draped around the air's shoulders.

Me: Good-looking girlfriend you've got there. So nice and…airy

Mat: I tried to explain to the locals that I was going to photoshop you in when I got home. They kept asking if you were fake

Me: And?

Mat: I said you used to be fake but now you're real, and that confused them even more

Me: Maybe you'd better stick with the invisible girlfriend. Easier to explain

Mat: Oh, her? She's great. Takes up no room and doesn't steal my food. She's not constantly knocking over water glasses, either

Me: You were the one who spilled the water at Lowcountry

Mat: That was once, Winnie. Once. You've done it how many times? Fifty?

Me: You wish you've had fifty dates with me

Mat: Isn't that a movie? Put it on the list. We'll watch it when I get back

Me: It's called *50 First Dates*. Drew Barrymore has anterograde amnesia and Adam Sandler has to convince her to fall in love with him every day

Mat: Easy-peasy. All I'd have to do is ply you with food. Works every time

Me: I resent that

Mat: Khanom krok. Bah mee moo dang. Nam phrik kapi. Are you drooling yet?

Me: Yes, but only because you sent me all those photos of the food stands in Bangkok. Also? I'd like to think I'm not that easy

Mat: Hey, you're not as easy as I am. All you had to do was smile and I was a goner

Me: Mat?

Mat: Yes?

Me: I miss you. Hurry home, okay?

Mat: Two more weeks. As much fun as I'm having, I'm counting down the seconds until I can see you

Me: What should we do first? Oh, I know. Let's have a marathon

Mat: A make-out marathon? *falls to knees, prays to the god who protects Wednesdays*

Me: I was going to say movie marathon, but we can probably slip in a kiss or two between shows

Mat: How about during the commercial breaks?

Me: They're movies, Mat. They don't have commercials

Mat: Let's get the kind WITH commercials

Me: Okay

Mat: O-KAY? That's it. I'm changing my plane ticket right now. In the meantime, tell me

Me: Tell you what?

Mat: Anything. Everything. What you did today, what art courses you've decided to take at Northwestern. So long as you're saying it, I want to hear it.

Smiling, I curl up on my bed, readying myself for another text session with the boy who's occupied a number of roles in my life. My childhood best friend. My sworn enemy. My fake date. Even my first boyfriend.

And maybe, just maybe, if we keep making each other this happy every day, he'll also turn out to be the love of my life.

Practice makes perfect, after all.

Acknowledgments

In these uncertain, harrowing times, I turn to stories to give me a little respite, a temporary escape, a few stolen moments of entertainment. It is my wish that Winnie (and her sisters—and her parents—and of course, Mat) will offer you these same bits of joy.

To my editor and publisher Liz Pelletier, who bought this book after a thirty-second pitch. From the beginning, you have been the biggest champion of this #ownvoices rom-com. Thank you, from the bottom of my heart, for bringing this story to life and for believing so thoroughly in my abilities to pivot to this new genre.

To THE Bree Archer (now that my nickname for you is in print, it will be memorialized forever), the cover. THE COVER. There is a girl who lives inside my heart, locked forever in her adolescence, who was made to believe that she was ugly because of her race. For her, and for all the other girls who might feel this same way, you have my everlasting gratitude.

Thank you to the wonderful team at Entangled,

especially Heather Riccio, Stacy Abrams, Curtis Svehlak, Jessica Turner, and Madison Pelletier. I am so grateful that *Dating Makes Perfect* is in such capable hands. Thank you, as well, to my publicist, Nicole Banholzer, for helping Winnie's story reach my readers, new and old.

My gratitude to my lovely agent, Kate Testerman. I so appreciate your support and enthusiasm for this story.

Thank you to the phenomenal authors who took the time out of their busy lives to read and blurb *Dating Makes Perfect*: Vanessa Barneveld, Kate Brauning, Piper J. Drake, Lydia Kang, Jodi Meadows, Farrah Rochon, Nisha Sharma, Christina Soontornvat, Becky Wallace, Abigail Hing Wen, Tracy Wolff, and Darcy Woods. Your kind words mean the world to me.

Every day, I am cognizant of my luck in the friend lottery. From high school to college to law school, from my author friends to my mom friends to my lawyer friends, I am so blessed to have each of you in my life. Special thanks to Vanessa Barneveld for your insights and to Brenda Drake for the sprints. Denny S. Bryce has the most gorgeous apartment for writing retreats, and Meg Kassel has the highest stamina for lengthy phone calls. To Darcy Woods: I *might* be able to do this publishing thing without you—but I'm not sure how. Thank you for being so solidly on my side.

A special shout-out to my best friends from high school, Anita Kishore and Sheila Pai (whom the jazz-hearted Kavya Pai, incidentally, was inspired by). This story made me think of a certain night at the end of a long driveway, where we swore that we would remain best friends for the rest of our lives. I am so happy, over two decades later, that we've kept that promise.

My family. Ah, my family. I'm not going to reveal *which*

parts of this book were inspired by *which* members of my family. But suffice it to say, all the warmth in this story stems directly from my personal experience. I love you all. I hope you can see from this novel exactly how much. Your support for me is immeasurable, and I appreciate all of you every single day.

I would be remiss, however, if I didn't give a special thanks to my dad for double-checking my Thai facts. To my sister, Lana: you are, without doubt, my biggest fan. It goes without saying that I am also yours.

A big thank you to Lowcountry. Yes, this restaurant is real, and yes, my brother Pan and my sister-in-law Dana are the owners. Yes, the Ridiculously Hot Everthang sauce will blow your mind, and yes, the food there is just as delicious as it sounds!

The four A's of my heart—Antoine, Aksara, Atikan, and Adisai. You are my breath, my joy. You are the center of my real life and every single one of my made-up worlds.

Last, but definitely not least, to my beautiful readers. Thank you for reading my books. You make this publishing ride worth every steep climb and stomach-dropping descent. And I don't even like roller coasters.

Turn the page for a sneak peek at the
charming romantic comedy

ADORKABLE

COOKIE O'GORMAN

Available now wherever books are sold!

CHAPTER ONE

My mother thought I was a lesbian. Terrific.

    After she'd set me up with her boss's nephew—who, by the way, chewed with his mouth open, tucked his napkin into his shirt bib-style, and stole the last dinner roll—I hadn't thought it could get much worse.

    Guess that's what I get for being an optimist. "Never again," Mom had said after the Bib Incident last summer. It hadn't ended well. "I'm never setting you up again."

    "Do you solemnly swear?" I'd asked.

    She'd nodded. "When it comes to you, Sally Sue Spitz, I am done. I'm hanging up my matchmaking gloves as of today." Too bad she'd handed those gloves down to someone even more meddlesome.

    Daisy Wilkins rang our doorbell at precisely 7:30 p.m. Mom let her in with a huge smile and introduced her as the daughter of Stella Wilkins, my mom's eccentric hairdresser, adding, "She's from New York." I didn't know everyone in our small town (though it felt like it sometimes), but I'd have known Daisy wasn't from Chariot just by looking at her. That Mohawk screamed big city.

"Nice hair," I said as we sat down for dinner. The pink tips were pure punk, but the bleach-blond roots were positively Malfoy-esque. Not just anyone could pull that off.

"Nice smile," she said back—which I thought was sweet. It wasn't every day you got a compliment like that, and from a complete stranger, too. Mom seemed pleased, and I'd assumed it was because she'd put an awful lot of money into my smile with the braces and headgear I'd worn for three years.

We were nearly done with dinner when things took a turn for the weird.

"So Daisy," Mom said, "do you have a date for prom? You know, Sally still doesn't have anyone to go with."

I did a mental eye roll. Thanks, Mom. Let's just advertise it, shall we: Sally Spitz, salutatorian of her senior class, President of the German Club, voted Most Likely To Be Terminally Boyfriend-less Until the End of Time.

"Not yet," Daisy said, picking at her mashed potatoes.

She didn't say so, but I suspected Daisy was a vegetarian. She hadn't touched her steak, and her purse had a bright pink patch with PETA on it. That plus the dirty looks she kept throwing the beef on her plate were pretty big clues.

"You hear that, Sally?" Mom raised her brows. "Daisy doesn't have a date, either."

"Hmm," I said, reaching for my water, glancing at the clock again.

When was Hooker's latest matchmaking disaster going to get here? My bestie, Lillian Hooker, had dreams of becoming a professional matchmaker—which unfortunately meant I was her special project. Boys would do anything for her. This included having dinner with her BFF and said BFF's mother on Sundays. Tonight's "date" was already an hour late. Not that I wanted to meet another guy in the long line of setups, but the Southern part of me revolted at the thought of his rudeness. The girly part of me was just ticked at being stood up.

"Maybe you two could go together?"

I choked, eyes watering. "*What?*"

Mom shot me a stern glare. "I said, maybe the two of you could go together. I mean, if Daisy's not going with anyone, and you're not going with anyone…" She trailed off, looking at me expectantly. When I just stared, she added, "Oh, come on, Sally. You both need dates, right? Why wouldn't you go together? I think you and Daisy would make a cute couple."

I simply blinked. At the time, I was incapable of anything else. She'd said "couple" like she meant…

"Very cute," Daisy agreed, and when I looked to her, she winked. Winked!

I swallowed. Good grief, that was *exactly* what she'd meant.

"Mom, can I see you in the kitchen?" I was out of my chair and steamrolling toward the door before she could answer.

When Mom came in behind me, she sounded put out. "That was very rude, Sally. Now Daisy's going to think we're in here talking about her. What's so imp—"

I rounded on her, voice incredulous. "Mom, you think I'm a *lesbian*?"

"Well, aren't you?" she said, confused.

"*No!*" I shot a quick glance at the door to make sure it was still shut. Seeing it was, I repeated, "No, I'm not. Not even a little bit. Mom, what…what would make you think something like that?"

"Lillian asked, and I couldn't rule it out." She shrugged,

looking down at her hands. "I don't know."

"It had to be something," I persisted. I needed to know. If Hooker and my own mother had gotten that impression, maybe other people had, too. Just how far did this misconception go?

"Well," Mom said finally. "First, there's the fact that you've never had a boyfriend."

"A lot of people don't have boyfriends."

"You're going to be eighteen."

"And?" I retorted. "What else?"

"There are those rainbow stickers you always carry around in your purse—"

"Those are for the kids at work!"

"—and then there's the whole Becks issue."

"What Becks issue?" I said.

"Sally, that boy is prime real estate to any female with eyes. You've been best friends with him since grade school, and never once have you said a word about how attractive he is."

"Becks is Becks," I said diplomatically. "And don't think I'm not going to tell him about the creepy comment you just made. Please, go on."

"You never go for anyone Lillian sets you up with," she huffed.

As soon as she said it, I knew this was the real reason.

"That's because they're either criminals or total idiots," I pointed out.

"That's not true," Mom argued. "There was Oliver Morgan—"

"Who constantly referred to himself in the third person."

"Devon Spurrs—"

"Currently in ISS for trying to steal Funyuns out of the

school vending machine."

"Andy Archer—"

"He couldn't remember my name, Mom. Kept calling me Sherry, even after I corrected him—eight times."

Mom would not be sidetracked. "Then there was Cromwell Bates."

"Well, there you go," I said, and she pursed her lips. "The name alone makes him sound like a serial killer. I mean, who knows? Maybe his parents know something we don't. Besides, he spit on me when we first met."

"He didn't do it intentionally." Mom lifted her hands in a helpless gesture. "Sally, the poor boy has a lisp."

I shrugged. The feel of Cromwell's spittle on my cheek still gave me nightmares. At the time, I'd been afraid of hurting his feelings, so I'd just let it stay there, forcing my hands not to wipe at my skin as I felt condensation settle into the pores. First thing I did when he left was wash my face—three times for good measure.

"You know…it wouldn't bother me if you were." Mom hesitated, tone shaky but sincere. "Gay, I mean."

"But I'm not," I said again. "Just because I haven't gone for any of the loser guys Hooker's sent my way doesn't mean I'm into girls."

Mom laughed suddenly. "No," she said, "no, I guess it doesn't." She took my hand and met my eyes. "I just worry about you, Sally."

I gave her hand a squeeze. Mom had been saying that since my fifth birthday, when I'd asked for a lightsaber instead of a Barbie doll.

"And don't be too hard on Lillian," she added. "She reminds me of me at that age, always trying to get people together."

"I wish she wouldn't," I muttered.

"Her heart's in the right place."

"I don't know why she feels responsible for my love life. Mom, I'm only seventeen. There's plenty of time for me to find the right guy…and it *will* be a guy," I reiterated just to be clear.

She shrugged. "One of these days, it could be The One, waiting right out there on our doorstep."

"Mom."

"I know, I know," she said, waving me off. "Occupational hazard, I guess. I'm a servant of true love; it's what I do, Sally."

I'd heard that one before. As a wedding planner, Mom really couldn't help herself. It was natural for her to want to put soul mates together. Her job was to give couples their happily ever after. She and Hooker were like two peas in a pink-heart-shaped, love-drunk pod. I just wished they'd use their talents for good instead of trying to match me up all the time.

"Don't go planning my wedding just yet, Mom."

"Oh, please. I've had your wedding planned since you were in the womb."

I couldn't hide my look of horror.

"Relax, I'm just kidding," she said with a laugh. "The truth is I don't want you to be alone." Her eyes went from sparkling to hollow. "Believe me, it gets old after a while."

It was moments like this that reminded me how much I despised my father.

"Better than being tied to a lying, cheating son of a b—"

"Sally," Mom said on a warning note.

I widened my eyes, all innocence. "What? I was going to say banker."

"Sure you were." Mom shook her head, looking toward the kitchen door. "Poor Daisy. I feel terrible about all of this.

I think she really liked you. She's going to be heartbroken when she finds out. What should we say?"

Daisy and I had gotten along fine, but I wasn't so sure about the whole heartbreaking thing.

I gave Mom's hand a pat. "I'll let her down gently," I said as we walked back into the dining room.

Daisy was typing something on her phone, texting someone. When we came in, she looked up and said, "Sorry, but I've gotta go." She stood, and I followed her to the door. "Mom just confirmed my flight. It looks like it's been moved up a few hours, so we're going to have to leave really early tomorrow. It was good meeting you, Sally."

"You, too," I said, noticing only now that Mom had somehow managed to disappear. Apparently, she was leaving this up to me. Well, I supposed there was only one way to say it. "So Daisy, there's kind of been a mistake. As much as I liked talking to you, I'm not—"

Daisy placed a hand on my shoulder, giving me a sympathetic look. "Listen, no offense, okay? You're cute and everything, but you're a little...dorky for my tastes." I opened my mouth, but she went on, "Oh, don't get me wrong. I'm not saying that as a bad thing. It's just not what I'm looking for right now. You understand, right?"

I swallowed, then said, "Of course."

She leaned in and gave me a peck on the cheek. "If you're ever up in New York, give me a call, okay?" As she opened the door, she glanced back over her shoulder. "We'll do lunch or something."

I stood there stunned, watching her taillights disappear around the corner, until Mom came up behind me a few minutes later. "So, how'd it go?"

"She said I'm not her type."

"Oh." Mom shrugged. "Well, that's too bad."

I was indignant. "She called me a dork. She just met me. How could she possibly make that call after only one dinner?"

Mom eyed my outfit critically and then said, "You do realize you're wearing your Gryffindor jersey, right?" I opened my mouth to tell her it was a collectible straight off the Harry Potter official clothing line, but she cut across me. "And you know that when Daisy walked in, you had your right hand up, fingers splayed in that strange *Star Trek* signal."

Yeah, I had, but that was just because I'd assumed it would be my date walking through the door—which, I guess, it actually had been—and I'd wanted to scare him off. In my experience, boys didn't look twice at girls who employed Trekkie references, let alone wore Potter memorabilia.

"It was the Vulcan salute," I muttered.

"Okay," Mom said, "but did you have to say 'Live long and prosper'?"

"I wasn't sure she knew what it meant." Daisy might've thought I was shooting her the bird in another language or something. I lifted my chin. "And you know what? I've gotten quite a few compliments on this shirt."

"From who, ten-year-olds?"

I flushed. "Becks said he liked it, too."

"Becks doesn't even care that you're a girl." It only took a second for Mom to realize what she'd said, but by then I was already heading up to my room. "Sally, I'm sorry."

"It's all right," I said, waving over my shoulder so she wouldn't see just how much she'd hurt me. "Night, Mom. Love you."

"Love you, Sally," came the solemn reply as I shut my

door. I could tell by her tone that she already regretted
it, felt sorry for speaking so bluntly. But how could I be
mad? She was just speaking the truth, and I knew that as
well as anybody. Still didn't take the sting out of it, though.

Plopping onto my bed, I dug into my nightstand
and pulled out my journal. Blogging wasn't really my
thing, and for the yearbook, my senior quote would read,
"Facebook steals your soul." Twitter wasn't my bag, either,
as I considered it one small step away from legalized
stalking, so for me, social networking was pretty much
out. But then, I'd always been a fan of the classics, anyway.

The first page was dedicated to Date #1, Bobby Sullivan.
Hooker had met Bobby at a wedding last spring, where
they'd gone to second base in the church. He'd agreed
to go out with me only after she promised not to tell his
grandma. Catholic guilt, still alive and well today. But the
worst was still Cromwell "The Spitter" Bates, Date #7. I
was officially scarred for life.

Flipping to my latest entry, I started up a new page. At
the top I wrote, Mystery Date #8, Daisy W. I followed it
up with a short summary of the night, starting with how
I'd been completely oblivious of the fact that she was my
date until the talk of prom, followed by Mom's reasons for
thinking I was gay, and ending with our little conversation
by the door. At the bottom, as I'd done in each of the
previous entries, I gave the night an overall success rating
of six—notably my highest rating so far. It didn't surprise
me that the date I'd rated highest had been with a girl
who'd called me a dork. The others were simply that bad.

My phone went off beside my bed. I swung up to sitting
and looked at the screen. There was a new text from Becks.

It read: **Scary Movie marathon you up for it?**

I sent my own back. **Not tonite.**

It took him less than a second to reply. **Bad date?**

I couldn't help but smile at that. Becks had always had the uncanny ability to read me, even through the phone. I thought it over, then sent, **Not too bad. Tell you about it later?**

Can't wait ;) Night, Sal.

"Smartass," I mumbled and sent him a **Night** in return. Hopefully, Becks wouldn't give me too much grief about the whole Daisy thing.

Chapter Two

Okay, so I knew there would be some grief. But seriously, was that grin really necessary? Becks was leaning against my locker, all six-foot-two of him relaxed, wavy black hair brushing the tips of his ears, watching me as I walked toward him down the hall. It wasn't like I could just turn tail and run. I had to get my books for first period, and he was in the way. His eyes, the ones I knew nearly as well as my own, were swimming with mirth, his expression expectant.

Determined to wipe the grin right off his face, I said, "Hey there, Baldwin. How's it going?"

He blanched. "Jeez, Sal. Not this early in the morning, okay?"

I smiled to myself. Baldwin Eugene Charles Kent, AKA Becks, had always hated his Christian name. With a name like that, even I wanted to hate him — and he was my best friend. Luckily, Becks had escaped that clumsy mouthful with a killer nickname. Born with the last name "Spitz," there'd been no hope for me. From the first grade on, my peers had refused to call me anything else.

"So, what happened?" he said, straightening as I reached past him. Becks ducked down, looking at me, but I avoided his gaze. "Oh please, it couldn't have been that bad. What, did this guy have webbed toes or something?"

I laughed despite myself. "How would I know?"

"You get another spitter?" I shook my head. He ran a hand through his thick hair, but, as usual, it fell right back into his eyes. "Honestly, Sal, I can't imagine what could be worse than that. What did he do? You know I'll keep asking every five seconds till you give it up."

I sighed. Might as well get it over with. No amount of stalling was going to change the facts, and Becks was stubborn enough to make good on that threat.

"*She* didn't do anything," I said. "It was the situation that was awkward."

"She?" Becks repeated and broke into a wide grin. "What's her name? Is she hot? Do I know her?"

Typical Becks, I thought. Only he would ask those questions, in that order, after hearing something like this.

Slamming my locker closed, I set out for my first class. With his long legs, Becks caught up in no time.

"Sal," he coaxed, nudging my shoulder. Left and right, people called his name, but, after acknowledging them, Becks turned back to me. "Don't be mad, Sal. I've always been overly curious. You can't hate me for that; I was born this way."

And that right there was why I couldn't stay mad at Becks for long. It was simply impossible.

"Her name," I said in answer to his first question, "was Daisy. And how should I know if she was hot or not? She had a pretty cool Mohawk, though. As to whether or not you know her, she's Stella's daughter."

"The hair lady?" I nodded, and Becks's look turned

thoughtful. "I think I might've seen her once or twice. Tall, decent figure, nose ring? Dang, Sal. What made Lillian think she was your type?" He laughed. "Do you have a secret bad-boy fetish I should know about?"

"Don't you mean bad girl?" I muttered.

Becks shook his head. "I don't get it. What's the big deal?"

"The big deal is Hooker set me up with a chick."

Becks shrugged. "Could be worse."

Frowning, I sent him a glare. "I'm serious."

"Me, too. Sal, these things happen."

Was he joking? "These things happen. That's the best you've got?"

"Well, it's true."

"*Wer*" — I threw up my hands — "*sag es mir, Becks, sag es mir sofort, denn ich will es wirklich wissen.*"

"English, please, Sal. I have no idea what you're saying."

And I had no idea I'd slipped into German; that only happened when I was upset. "Who exactly does this happen to?" I repeated.

He shrugged again. "To you, apparently." When I went to pinch him, he laughed and jumped back.

"This isn't funny."

"It's pretty funny, Sal. I, for one, think — "

Before he could complete that thought (and most likely earn himself another pinch), Roxy Culpepper and Eden Vice stepped into our path. The way they eyed Becks was enough to darken my day, but watching Roxy cock her hip, nearly popping the thing out of socket, was at least entertaining.

"Hey, Becks," Roxy said, giving him the head tilt and hair twirl. "Nice shirt."

"Yeah," Eden said eagerly. "The cut looks great on you.

And that's, like, my favorite color."

Becks and I both gave his white Hanes a dubious once-over.

But unlike me, Becks didn't roll his eyes. Oh no, that'd be too impolite. Smooth-talking, woman-loving charmer that he was, Becks simply tucked his hands into his pockets, flashed them a wink, and said, "Thanks, I've got four more just like it at home."

They laughed like a pair of hyenas, and Roxy reached out to run a hand over Becks's scruffy cheek.

"I see you're still keeping with tradition." As her fingertips lingered at his jaw, I had a real urge to smack her hand away—or stick gum in her hair, but I thought that sounded a little too grade school. Best stick with the smacking. It was considerably more adult. "Think we're going to win tomorrow?"

"You know it," Becks said.

"Oh, Becks, it's senior year. You have to win." Eden gave his other cheek the same treatment. "You just have to."

"I'll do my best."

"You'll win," Roxy said with certainty, hip out so far I was shocked to see it was still connected to her body. "Score a goal for me, okay?"

I glared as the two slinked away, but Becks couldn't have looked more satisfied with himself.

Watching him watch them was so not my idea of a good time.

Shifting around, I said, "Becks, how do you stand it? They come up to you and pat you like a dog. It's degrading."

"Is it?" Becks was still looking after Roxy and her amazing swaying hips. I swear that girl was born double-jointed.

"Yes," I said. "It is."

Becks's tone was dry. "I feel so used."

Rolling my eyes, I walked away just as another girl came up to fondle his face.

Due to a rumor started last year, it was now acceptable for people to come up and pet him out of the blue. When Becks had first told me about the ritual—how he'd stopped shaving three days before a game to avoid bad luck; he'd read it in some sports article—I'd written it off as superstition. But then again, last year was our first season going 23-0, so what did I know? Personally, I hated the five-o'clock shadow. Not because of the way it made Becks look—believe me, Becks was a stunner with or without the facial hair—but people thought it gave them the right to touch him. And everyone had, at some point or another.

Except me.

That was just not the kind of thing best friends did—and even if it was, I didn't have the cojones to do it, anyway.

"Wait up, Sal!"

I slowed. "Finally got away from all those adoring fans?"

"Don't be like that," Becks said, sidling up to me. "They're just excited about the game."

"Yeah, right."

"What's really bothering you? And don't tell me it's the fan thing. I know you too well."

He was both right and wrong.

"It's just…I can't understand what gave her that idea," I said, going with the least complicated of the two things bothering me. "My mom, I mean. What'd I do to make her and Hooker think…well, you know?"

"Parents," Becks said, as if it was some great mystery. "Who can say what makes them do what they do."

Stopping outside my first period, I tried to make my voice sound ultra-casual. "You never thought that, right?"

"Thought what?" Becks waved as someone called his name.

"That I was, you know"—I swallowed—"gay?" Becks gave me a half smile, looking completely unaware of how much his answer mattered—to me, at least.

"Sal," he said as I held my breath. "Gay or straight, we would've always been best friends."

I exhaled. Wasn't exactly the answer I was looking for, but I'd take it.

"I'll see you at practice?"

"Of course." I smiled. "Someone's got to write about the early years before you went pro. Might as well be me."

Shaking his head, Becks said, "See ya, Sal," and then kept going down the hall. As he walked, people—girls, mostly, but a fair share of the boys—greeted Becks with catcalls, pats on the back, and more cheek rubs. He took it all in stride, even when Trent Zuckerman gave him a chest bump that nearly sent him sprawling.

"So, Spitz, you coming tonight?"

I turned and came face-to-face with my self-appointed matchmaker. Lillian Hooker was the only person who had permission to call me that name and my closest bestie right after Becks. On paper, she and I looked a lot alike: same height, same pants size, same long hair. In reality? Hooker's hair was dark chocolate, mine sandy brown. Confidence and curves in all the right places set her apart. The perfectly tan complexion didn't hurt, either. She was unique while I was ordinary. In other words, Hooker was the Amidala to my Hermione.

"Don't know, Hooker." We'd bonded in the seventh grade over a great love of superhero movies and a deep hatred of unfortunate surnames. That first sleepover made our bestie status official. Hooker and I had been stuffing our faces with popcorn and watching TV when we flipped to a cheesy Western called *Tombstone*. Instant obsession. While other girls were dressing up like pretty princesses, we were Doc Holliday and Johnny Ringo for Halloween. "I'm still recovering from last night."

"I heard it went well."

I cocked a brow. "Should I even ask?"

She shrugged. "Martha texted me. She said you and Daisy really hit it off."

The fact that my mom and Hooker were texting buddies...well...I guess I should've seen that coming.

"Did she also tell you"—I lowered my voice—"that I'm not batting for the same team?"

Hooker laughed as we walked into our class.

"And by that, I mean I like boys."

"I knew it was a long shot. If you were gay, there's no way you could've resisted all *this*." She gestured to herself, and I couldn't stop my smile. "But you haven't responded to any of my guys. Stella's been doing my hair for years, and when I saw Daisy the other day, I figured why not?"

"Hmm, let's see...maybe because I'm. Not. Gay."

"Yeah, sorry about that," she said. "I'll make it up to you, promise. Anyway, you are coming tonight, right?"

"I've got some reading to catch up on, so I might have to pass."

"But you can't!"

I was immediately suspicious. "Why not?"

Once seated, she waved me off. "Oh, no reason," she said, her face completely guileless. "I was really hoping you'd come, though. It's going to be a lot of fun tonight. You just have to be there."

I narrowed my eyes. "Why?"

"Oh now, what kind of question is that?"

"A good one," I replied, watching her closely. "This isn't another setup, is it, Hooker? I told you I'm through with that. No more mystery dates."

Instead of answering, Hooker gave a long-suffering sigh and started chipping away at her nail polish. Today's color was a bright sea blue that perfectly matched the color of her eyes. The same eyes that, at the moment, wouldn't meet my own.

"I mean it," I insisted. "I told you before: I'll start dating when I want to."

"And when might that be?" Hooker was pushing back her cuticles with short, efficient jabs. "Before or after the day of reckoning?"

I crossed my arms, refusing to let it go.

"Okay, okay." She stopped the assault and looked me in the eye. "Opening night, new X-Men. You in or out, Spitz? I thought you'd like to go to the midnight show and see Storm kick some evil mutant ass. Excuse me if I was mistaken."

Letting out a breath, I finally relaxed. "Rogue has it all over Storm, and you know it."

"Puh-lease," she said, rolling her eyes, "Storm could cause a hurricane that'd knock Rogue back to last week."

"Yeah, and all Rogue would have to do is touch her, and Storm'd be out like a light, transferring her powers to Rogue in the process." Right as Ms. Vega was walking to the board, I asked once more, just to be sure, "So, no mystery men…or women?"

Hooker held out her palms. "Just Professor X and his crew."

"Then I'm in," I said back, and Hooker smiled.

Being so dateable herself, Hooker always seemed to have some guy on the side. For the past three months, it'd been Will Swift, a college boy fresh out of Chariot and attending UNC. Boys were just drawn to her. They'd been calling her up since middle school, and she couldn't understand why I wouldn't want her castoffs.

As my best girl friend and an aspiring professional matchmaker, she felt it her duty to "broaden my romantic horizons." She typically arranged meetings with guys who were hot and/or experienced—the bad part was she never actually told me beforehand. Sunday guess-who's-coming-to-dinner was just the start. I'd show up someplace (a restaurant, the mall, a football game) at a time we'd agreed to meet, and instead of Hooker I'd find Joe Piscotti, the second guy she'd set me up with, who, I admit, had been easy on the eyes—but who had also been twenty-six to my seventeen. Thankfully, Mom had never found out about that fiasco. Or Connor Boone, a nineteen-year-old self-proclaimed artist who'd offered to paint me in my birthday suit. I'd respectfully declined.

It wasn't that I thought I was better than them (except, well, maybe in the morality department). In fact, on the whole, it'd been the guys who'd ended the dates early. They hadn't been interested, simple as that. Honestly, I hadn't been, either, so it'd worked out great for everyone except Hooker, who'd taken it personally. I was now her mission.

Hooker had upped the amount of setups now that school had started, determined to have me matched by graduation.

"Senior year, Spitz," she'd said on our first day back. "I have to find you a guy."

"You really don't," was my response.

"Yes, I do." Her eyes were bright. "I want to be a matchmaker. What does it say if I can't even find my own bestie her man? Unacceptable."

"But—"

"No buts, Spitz. I'll find you a guy or die trying."

Too bad I couldn't tell her I'd already found one—*The One*, as a matter of fact.

But that was a secret I'd sooner take to the grave. Still, I'd asked Hooker countless times to stop fixing me up, but she never listened. She had to know it was a lost cause. Didn't she realize I was best buds with the Adonis of the school? The only girl in Chariot never once chatted up, picked up, or felt up by the town's best-loved playboy? There had to be something wrong with me. Not pretty enough, not girly enough, something. I'd accepted it a long time ago, so why couldn't she?

My classes went by quickly. After school, the German Club meeting ran a little long—which hardly ever happened, since there were only two other members—so I had to sprint out to the bleachers to catch the end of practice. I swiped a hand over my forehead, and the back came away damp. Apparently my glands had missed the memo about how girls aren't supposed to sweat, because I was definitely sporting more than a glisten.

My eyes wandered to the sidelines of the soccer field, catching Becks flirting with yet another legs-for-days cheerleader, his second of the day. Coach Crenshaw yelled his name, voice slicing through the air with all the finesse of a foghorn. Becks didn't even flinch. He was sweating like a fiend, but Miss Double Back Handspring didn't seem to mind.

Crenshaw called Becks's name again, turning red in the face, which was around the same time he noticed me. Still ignoring the coach, Becks jogged right over.

"Enjoying the show?" he asked, tugging the bottom of his shirt up to wipe his face.

A bout of girlish squeals erupted.

"Sure," I said, cocking my head, "but not nearly as much as they are."

"Ah, Sal, give me a break. I'm working my butt off out there. Are you going to write me a prize piece or what?"

"Oh yeah, definitely." I nodded, tapping my notebook. "Don't you worry. It'll be totally Pulitzer-worthy."

"Hey, listen." He cleared his throat as Crenshaw bellowed his name a third time. "If you can't stand the heat, get off the field." He paused, smiling wide. "So, what do you think?"

"About what?" I asked.

"I'm thinking that's going to be my quote for yearbook."

"Seriously?"

His face dropped. "Too obvious?"

"Yeah, just a little." Unable to stand that look, I added, "But for you, it kind of works."

"Really?" His face suddenly brightened. "Then I'll go with it."

"Take it off!" The shout brought on another round of feminine laughter.

Turning toward the giggling mass of girls, Becks grinned. "Only if you say pretty please."

"Pretty please," they replied in unison, and I nearly gagged. When he didn't immediately strip, the girls started up a chant of "Take it off! Take if off!" This was why they shouldn't let cheerleaders hold practice next to the soccer field. The words got louder and louder as they got bolder, an unruly mob of hormonal teenage girls with megaphones. It was a scary sight.

"You're not seriously going to listen to them," I said flatly.

"What else can I do?"

"Becks, beware of the dark side."

"What's that supposed to mean?"

"It's a Yoda-ism," I said, "and you know exactly what it means. Becks, have you no shame?"

"Nope," he said, lifting the jersey over his head in one swift pull, causing a mixture of applause, screaming, and appreciative sighs.

I shook my head, struggling to keep my eyes north of his jaw line.

"What can I say, Sal?" he said, backing away. "It's like that line from that show *Oklahoma*. I'm just a guy who can't say no." Flicking his jersey at one of the cheerleaders, he hotfooted it out to center field, grinning all the while. He gave a frowning Coach Crenshaw a swat to the backside, and then the team got down to business.

I wrote down Becks's quote, making a side note to include it in my next article, while the girl who'd caught Becks's jersey gripped the shirt to her heart and pretended to faint.

At least, I hoped it was pretend.

New York Times bestselling author Rachel Harris
delivers a passionate, emotional romance perfect for
fans of Sarah Dessen or Huntley Fitzpatrick

eyes on me

Look up the word "nerd" and you'll find Lily Bailey's picture.
She's got one goal: first stop valedictorian, next stop Harvard.
Until a stint in the hospital from too much stress lands her in the
last place a klutz like her ever expected to be: salsa dance lessons.

Look up the word "popular" and you'll find Stone Torres's picture.
His life seems perfect—star of the football team, small-town
hero, lots of friends. But his family is struggling to make ends
meet, so if pitching in at his mom's dance studio helps, he'll do it.

When Lily's dad offers Stone extra cash to volunteer as Lily's
permanent dance partner, he can't refuse. But with each dip and
turn, each moment her hand is in his, his side job starts to feel all
too real. Lily shows Stone he's more than his impressive football
stats, and he introduces her to a world outside of studying. But
with the lines blurred, can their relationship survive the secret
he's been hiding?

For every book nerd who's ever crushed on a guy from afar, this sweet contemporary romance will be sure to melt your heart.

The
BOOK
WORM
CRUSH

by LISA BROWN ROBERTS

Shy bookworm Amy McIntyre is about to compete for the chance to interview her favorite author, who hasn't spoken to the press in years. The only way to win is to step out of the shadows and into the spotlight, but that level of confidence has never come easy.

The solution? A competition coach. The problem? The best person for the job is the guy she's secretly crushing on...local surfer celebrity Toff Nichols.

He's a player. He's a heartthrob. He makes her forget basic things, like how to breathe. How can she feel any confidence around *him*?

To her surprise, Toff agrees to help. And he's an excellent teacher. Amy feels braver—maybe even brave enough to admit her feelings for him. When their late night practices become less about coaching and more about making out, Amy's newfound confidence wavers.

But does Toff really like her or is this just another lesson?

Let's be friends!

🐦 @EntangledTeen

📷 @EntangledTeen

f @EntangledTeen

📰 bit.ly/TeenNewsletter

entangled teen

an imprint of Entangled Publishing LLC